SOME

GIRLS

DO

ALSO BY JENNIFER DUGAN

Hot Dog Girl
Verona Comics

Some Girls Do

JENNIFER DUGAN

putnam

G. P. PUTNAM'S SONS

G. P. PUTNAM'S SONS

An imprint of Penguin Random House LLC, New York

Copyright © 2021 by Jennifer Dugan

G. P. Putnam's Sons is a registered trademark of Penguin Random House LLC.

Visit us online at penguinrandomhouse.com

Library of Congress Cataloging-in-Publication Data
Names: Dugan, Jennifer, author.
Title: Some girls do / Jennifer Dugan.
Description: New York: G. P. Putnam's Sons, [2021] | Summary:
"An openly gay track star falls for a closeted, bisexual teen beauty queen
with a penchant for fixing up old cars"—Provided by publisher.
Identifiers: LCCN 2020039410 (print) | LCCN 2020039411 (ebook) |
ISBN 9780593112533 (hardcover) | ISBN 9780593112540 (epub)
Subjects: CYAC: Dating (Social customs)—Fiction. | Bisexuality—Fiction. |
Lesbians—Fiction. | High schools—Fiction. | Schools—fiction.
Classification: LCC PZ7.1.D8343 So 2021 (print) |
LCC PZ7.1.D8343 (ebook) | DDC [Fic]—dc23
LC record available at https://lccn.loc.gov/2020039410
LC ebook record available at https://lccn.loc.gov/2020039411

Printed in the United States of America
ISBN 9780593112533
1 3 5 7 9 10 8 6 4 2

Design by Suki Boynton
Text set in Chronicle Deck

*To anyone
who's ever had their life
turned upside down
by love*

1

RUBY

There's an art to the extraction. First, I take Tyler's arm—heavy across my stomach—and slide my fingers beneath. I lift it slightly and move centimeter by centimeter to the right side of the bed. And when I'm mostly free, I grab one of his pillows—warmed by my own overthinking head—and slip it under his arm. If I'm lucky, he'll snuffle softly in the moonlight streaming into his messy bedroom, hug the pillow, and stay sleeping. If I'm unlucky, he'll wake up and ask me where I'm going: *Ruby, just stay. Ruby, please. Ruby, it won't kill you to cuddle.* I don't have the energy for that.

Tyler's messy brown hair falls into his face as he smiles in his sleep and hugs my pillow replacement a little tighter. I got lucky tonight—in every sense of the word. I grab my boots, leftovers from one of the ten million Western-themed pageants I've smiled my way through over the years, and creep out the front door barefoot, careful not to let the screen door slam and wake his parents.

The motion-sensor light clicks on as I shove my feet into my boots and make a beeline for my car, my soul, my lifeline: my baby-blue 1970 Ford Torino. Yes, it's old as hell, but it's the one thing in this world that's truly mine. *I* bought it, rusted and rotten, off my great-aunt Maeve's estate for three hundred bucks. *I* painstakingly put it back together, scavenging pieces from junkyards and flea markets. *I* restored it to its current state of splendor. Me. I did that.

Okay, so maybe I had a little help from Billy Jackson, the town's least-crooked mechanic, but still.

I climb inside and shift it into neutral, taking off the emergency brake and letting the car coast backward down Tyler's long hill of a driveway and into the street, where I finally flick the ignition. It rumbles to life, the sound closer to a growl than a purr. I resist the urge to rev the engine—god, I love that sound—and point my car toward home, feeling loose and boneless, relaxed and happy, content in the way one only can during that tiny glint of freedom between chores and obligations.

Not that Tyler is an obligation—or a chore, for that matter. He's nice enough, our time together fun and consensual. In another universe, we'd probably be dating. But we live in this one, and in this universe, I love exactly two things: sleep and my car.

Tyler is a great stress reliever, an itch to scratch, a good time had by all. Nothing else. We have an arrangement, a friends-with-benefits sort of thing. No strings. If he called me tomorrow and said he wanted to ask a girl out, I'd say *Go for it as long as it isn't me*—and I'd mean it. I hope he'd say the same. Which is why I'm driving home from his house two hours after getting a text that simply said: **big game tomorrow, you around?**

Be still my heart.

But then, a couple weeks ago, I texted him: **pageant in the AM, come distract me?** And he was crawling through my window within minutes.

See, it's not an all-the-time thing; it's an as-needed thing. Some people get high; Tyler and I get twenty minutes of consensual, safe sex—always use a condom, people—and a subsequent awkward exchange about how my leaving right after makes him feel weird. Thus, the sneaking out once he falls asleep: the ideal compromise, at least on my end.

I pull into the dirt-patch driveway in front of my trailer. It might not seem like much to some, but it's ours and it's home. Just me and my mom. Well, some of the time, anyway. The better times.

But the lights are still on in the kitchen, the TV flickering in the living room, and my heart sinks. Mom works the overnight shift cleaning offices, and her car's not here, which means this will not be one of those "better times." Literally nothing could drag me down from a good mood faster than having to be around her boyfriend, Chuck Rathbone.

Chuck and my mom have been together off and on for the past few years—and unfortunately for me, lately they've been more on than off. "Getting more serious," I heard her say to a friend. Which is why he has unrestricted house privileges. Along with *eating our food and wasting our electricity even though we can't afford it* privileges.

I get why Chuck can't help chasing my mom around—my mom is the kind of beautiful that even hard jobs and tough luck can't dull, a beauty queen and Miss Teen USA hopeful right up until that second line showed up on her pregnancy test eighteen years ago. (Sorry, Mom.)

But I don't really understand why my mom always takes him back. Chuck is, objectively, the worst.

I'd crash at my best friend Everly's house if I wasn't so sure Chuck had heard my car—my engine is less than stealthy, and normally I like it that way. But if I leave now, he'll definitely tell Mom, and that's one guilt trip I don't need. On a scale of "needs an oil change" to "engine's seized," being rude to my mom's boyfriend rates somewhere around "blown head gasket"—not a fatal blow, but like most things when it comes to my mother, expensive and difficult to fix.

I turn off my car, listening to the tick of the engine as it cools down in the spring air. The curtains in the living room move, no doubt Chuck stumbling around, trying to see what I'm doing and why I'm not inside. I reach into the back seat to grab the bag of stage makeup Mom made me pick up earlier and get out.

Our door creaks as I yank it open and ignore the siding falling off next to it, then step over a particularly suspicious stain on the carpet. Five yapping Jack Russell terriers come tearing down the hallway. Mom's other pride and joy. Please, god, do not have let them in my room; they're barely house-trained—and by "barely," I mean not at all.

"Shut those mutts up!" Chuck yells from the kitchen as he pulls open the fridge, as if I have any control over them. As if anyone has control over them. Mom likes them a little wild; she says it's more natural that way. I'd personally prefer if their "wildness" could be limited to the rooms with vinyl flooring.

I crouch down and pet as many of them as I can, as fast as I can, while being tackled by the others. Tiny paws dig into my sides and legs as they fight for attention. "Shh, shh, shh," I coax, calming them as much as it's possible to calm five under-exercised terriers that rarely see the outside of our home.

"Goddamn dogs," Chuck says, carrying two cans of beer over to the recliner in front of the blaring TV. Fox News. As usual. He drops into the recliner, drips of beer falling onto his faded black T-shirt, which reads DON'T TREAD ON ME. He looks like he hasn't shaved in days, flecks of gray poking through his brown stubble. "You're home late."

"Yeah, sorry. I was studying with a friend," I say, standing up once the dogs decide that sniffing one another is more interesting than tackling me. I wonder if they can smell Tyler's cat.

Chuck raises his eyebrows, the last wisps of hair on his head flopping comically. "Your mom might fall for that garbage, but I know what girls like you do at night, and it's not studying."

"What would you know about studying?" I say, hating that he's right but determined not to give him the satisfaction.

"I know you don't get hickeys from math homework." He laughs, and his eyes flick to the talking head on the TV.

Goddammit, Tyler, no marks means no marks. My hand reaches up to my neck as my cheeks flame.

"Hey, hey, it's all right, I won't tell your ma."

I look at him, waiting for the catch.

"Come here, darlin'," he says, but I stay where I am, poised for a quick escape. He leans forward, a conspiratorial look on his face. "So, what did you really get up to tonight?"

"What time is Mom coming home?" I change the subject with a smile that shows too many teeth.

He frowns slightly. "I don't know. It's slow this week, she said. They lost another client."

"So anytime, then?" I ask, and he looks back at the TV. "I'm gonna head to bed. Night."

"You sure you don't want one?" he asks, gesturing toward the beer can beside his on the tray. And did he, what, think I'd get wasted and spend the night watching conservative shitheads spout lies on cable TV with him? No, thanks.

"It's a school night."

"Does that really matter to you?" On the TV behind me the host blabs on and on. I stare at the wall, taking a deep breath.

I won't take the bait.

"This shit'll rot your brain, Chuck," I say, grabbing the remote and clicking it off.

Because I will not be intimidated in my own home. I will not take crap from any stupid man sitting on the recliner that I got Mom with my Little Miss Sun Bonnet winnings years ago. I will not be scared of the Chuck Rathbones of the world.

"Fuck off." He laughs, chugging his beer and turning the TV back on.

I scamper to my room and lock the door behind me, praying to any god that will listen: *Please don't let this be my future too.*

2

MORGAN

"Do you have everything?"

"Yes!"

"Do you have lunch money?"

"Yes, I have lunch money."

"Your track schedule? Practice goes until at least five thirty most days, they said."

"Yes, and then I'm gonna jog or walk to the apartment after."

"Okay, I'm usually at the shop until about six thirty, so if you beat me home, don't worry."

"Oh my god, I'm not worried. I can handle being home alone."

"I just want this to be good for you. You deserve it after—"

"Can we not talk about that? Fresh start and all?"

"Okay, well, what would Mom say?"

"I don't know. 'I love you'? 'Have a good day'?"

Dylan smiles, a serious look in his eyes. "I love you. Have a good day."

"Holy crap, Dyl, (a) your impression of Mom needs work, and (b) you're taking this 'in loco parentis' thing a little too seriously."

"I just don't want to screw anything up," he says. "Mom and Dad will kill me if I break you or lose you or whatever you do with kids."

"Dude, I'm seventeen." I groan, pulling my long brown hair up into a ponytail.

The car behind us beeps, and someone shouts, "The drop-off lane is for drop-offs. Get out or get moving."

"Yikes," Dylan says, looking into the rearview mirror.

"Yeah, hell hath no fury like a suburban mom late for her latte," I say. "But don't worry, I'm going to be fine. And you need to go." I give him a quick one-armed hug and then dart out of the car before he can stop me.

But despite what I told Dylan, I have no clue what I'm doing. A bunch of kids bustle past me, laughing with their friends, completely oblivious to the fact that I'm new. I shift my backpack higher on my shoulders—or at least I try to, which is exactly when I realize it's missing. Crap.

"Dyl!" I call, but of course he can't hear me on the other side of the parking lot with his windows up. So I do what I do best: I run, fast. I fly through the parking lot, weaving between rows, hoping to cut him off as he moves slowly through the traffic jam that's formed in front of the school entrance. I'm just about there, one more row to go, when a loud horn and the screech of brakes makes me freeze in my tracks.

And there, a foot away from my hip, is the bumper of a very shiny blue car. Seriously? I look back to Dylan's car just in time to see it pull out and disappear down the road.

"Dammit!" If it weren't for this stupid car, I would have made it. I wouldn't be standing in the middle of the parking lot of a new school without my schedule, a notebook, or even a friggin' pencil. "What is wrong with you?!" I spin around, slapping my hands on the hood of the car. "Watch where you're going!"

I look up to glare at the no doubt macho asshole driving this stupid muscle car and am struck with the brightest pair of blue eyes I've ever seen—which promptly narrow and glare back at me.

"You're the one running through the middle of a parking lot," she says, hopping out of her car and shoving me out of the way to inspect her car hood. "If you so much as put a scratch in this—"

"You could have killed me!"

"It would have been your fault if I did," she says, straightening up so we're nearly nose to nose. "Where were you even going? School's the other way, if you haven't noticed."

And, oh no. Oh. No. She's . . . very . . . cute. And before I know it, my brain is unhelpfully making a list of everything I should *not* be wondering about. Like how her perfectly tanned hand might look linked with my lighter, peachier one. And whether there are tan lines underneath her fitted gray hoodie and obscenely tight jeans. And, oh god, I am a creep.

It would be so much easier to stay angry with her if she really were some asshole dude, but this is a complication. One that will require a full system reboot if I want to get out of this without embarrassing myself. Step one: close my mouth, which is currently hanging open like I'm witnessing a miracle. Step two: pull it together with a quickness.

Like, the objective part of my brain recognizes that she still technically sucks. But the nonobjective part of my brain still really wants her name and number and to know if she's single and how she would feel about dating a marginally disgraced track star of the female persuasion.

"Hello! I asked you a question." She waves her hands in front of my face. And, yes, that was helpful. Please keep being an asshole, car girl.

"I forgot my backpack in the car," I answer the second my brain comes back online. "I was trying to catch him before he left."

"Why didn't you just call him?" She looks pointedly at the phone sticking out of my pocket. And, okay, good question.

"Instinct?" I say. "I'm a runner. I run. It's what I do."

"Yeah, well, don't run here. This is a parking lot. For parking. It's what it's for," she says, mocking my tone.

"It was an emergency situation."

The girl huffs and pulls her hair—long dirty-blond strands that look like they've been highlighted to within an inch of their life—into a messy bun on top of her head. "You're lucky there are no scratches from you punching my—"

"I didn't punch your car. I lightly pressed my hands against it in frustration."

"Sure. Well, the good news is all it's going to cost you is a car wash to get your grubby prints off the hood." She smiles in a mean kind of way that should *not* make my stomach flip down to my toes but absolutely does. And seriously? Seriously?! Can I just for once not be attracted to someone who looks like they could eat me for dinner without batting an eye?

"I am *not* paying for you to wash your car just because I touched it."

She shrugs and walks back to her still-open door. "It was worth a shot. She's due for one anyway."

And now when my mouth pops open, it's with annoyance instead of awe. "Worth a shot? Are you—You almost killed me! You almost killed me, *and then* you tried to scam me into paying for a car wash you're already getting? What kind of a monster are you?"

"The kind that didn't forget her backpack *and* isn't going to be late for homeroom," she says before sliding into her car and reversing down the row.

"Asshole!" I yell, flipping her off for good measure, but she just rolls her eyes and laughs.

I have the good sense to wait until she's out of sight before admitting defeat and pulling out my phone. Dylan answers on the first ring, sounding totally panicked. Once I reassure him that, yes, I'm fine, the world has not ended, nothing irrevocably bad has happened in the five minutes or so since he dropped me off—barring almost being run over by the rudest girl in rude town, which I definitely do *not* mention—he calms down enough to promise to bring me my backpack.

I find a bench near the track with a good view of the parking lot and wait. So much for coming early to find my classes. There are a couple girls running on the track, no doubt members of the school team, and I wonder if they're making up a practice or if they're running penalty laps. My old coach at St. Mary's was big on those. Coming in early was good for the soul, she used to say, although my body wholeheartedly disagreed.

I recognize one of the girls as she runs by: Allie Marcetti—we've run against each other a few times, and I kind of know her. She's fast, but not as fast as me, and definitely not for as long. No one is. Well, no one around here at least. I heard a rumor she was switching to sprinting for her final season anyway.

They rush past me, their matching ponytails streaming behind them, and I bounce my leg, wishing I were running too. I can't wait until later, when it's finally my feet slapping the track, pushing myself until my muscles burn and my stomach shakes and . . . I stop, reminding myself I'm technically not an official member of the team yet, not until my waiver comes through.

If it comes through. But with my past ranking, Coach had no qualms about letting me practice with them for the last couple months of school. I even signed an early letter of intent to run for my dream school—although at the moment it's "on pause" while they "evaluate the incident."

I've spent a lot of time convincing myself this is all fine and none of it hurts. That going from star athlete to high school scandal is a totally normal progression that I am both equipped for and totally saw coming. But, yeah, I look away as the girls cross the finish line, trying really hard not to think about how that should be me, at my old school, with my old friends.

My mom keeps saying it's just a matter of time before I'm cleared to compete again and everything is sorted with my college. Apparently, being given the choice to withdraw or be formally expelled from your old school—a school your parents are currently suing for a myriad of reasons including but not limited to discrimination and harassment—makes it seem a lot less likely that your new school is poaching elite athletes. Let's just hope the High School Athletic Association agrees when they finally rule on my case.

Coach didn't poach anyone. We both just got lucky that my brother has an apartment in a school district with a decent running program in the same conference, *and* the school happens to have a spot for a distance runner. If it were up to me, I'd still be racing with my old crew at St. Mary's, but it's not.

That's what happens when you lose it on a teacher who tells you that being queer is against the code of conduct at your stupid private school . . . and then decides to make your life a living hell because of it.

We tried the homeschooling route when everything first went down. We naively thought we could just remove that one part of my life and everything else would still be the same. But then the local news picked up the story, and I started to feel like everyone was watching me or something. Maybe it was in my head at first, but then my friends stopped calling, and their parents stopped texting my parents. And then I just had to get out of there.

Whatever. No wallowing. Fresh start. New me. Out and proud. Taking a stand. So fun! This waiver just better come through before states, or they'll have to chain me to the bench to keep me from competing. I will not miss the final track season of my high school career, so help me god.

The first bell rings, and everybody rushes inside, the parking lot and school grounds becoming a ghost town in seconds. And I stay sitting, waiting for Dylan. Late for my fresh start already.

3

RUBY

I laugh when she flips me off, because me? *I'm* the asshole? She's the one darting between rows of parked cars like a squirrel on speed. If anybody is wrong here, it's her. Definitely. So what if I did try to scam a car wash out of it? The girl slapped her hands on my baby. She's lucky I didn't cut them off.

I pull into a parking space, far enough away that I don't think she can see me, but where I can still sorta see her and her very angry big brown eyes. There was a second there, when the sun hit just right, that they almost looked amber. Not that I'm really interested in her or her kinda amber, mostly brown eyes. More mildly curious. It's a pretty small school, and I've known most of these kids since I was little.

It's not often we get new kids, especially not this late in the year—there's got to be a story there.

A tap on my side window pulls my attention, and I turn to see Everly—literally the only person on earth cleared to touch my car besides me—giving me a funny look. I pop my door open and she steps back, running her fingers through her twists. One of the boys from the lacrosse team whistles as he walks by with his teammates, flashing her a grin and tacking on a "Looking good, ladies" to round things out.

Everly clucks her tongue. "Wish I could say the same for you, Marcus."

Marcus grabs his heart dramatically, walking backward as the rest of the team falls into a chorus of "ooooh" and "ouch."

Everly gets that a lot. I mean, when you're Harrington Falls's answer to Amandla Stenberg, it'd be hard not to, but still. I'll take "Looking good, ladies" any day over what people say to me when she's not around. I guess that's what you get when pretty much everybody considers you a trashy time bomb. Like it's only a matter of time before I start spitting out kids and ruining lives or something.

I push my seat forward, shoving a pair of heels, my tap shoes, and some garment bags out of the way to grab my backpack. "You know he's into you."

"I do." She smiles.

"But?"

"But nothing. He hasn't asked me out, and I'm not about to ask him."

"Wow," I say as we start to walk toward the building

entrance. "Way to set back women's rights about ten billion years. If you like him, you should go for it."

"Says the girl who sneaks around with Tyler Portman every time he texts her for a hookup."

"Hey." I hold up a finger. "There's nothing wrong with owning your sexuality. I text him as often as he texts me. And it's a mutual understanding. No pining, no feelings—"

"The boy likes you."

"He does not!"

"That hickey on your neck says otherwise."

I snap my hand up to cover it. "I put makeup on it!"

"Yeah, well, not enough." She laughs. "Credit to Tyler, though—it's amazing you can even see it with all that spray tan you got on."

"That was my mom's doing," I say, holding out my arms and frowning when I notice a small streak.

"Yeah, well, tell your mom if she makes your white ass go full Kardashian, I'm gonna stop shooting you on principle until you turn back to the shade of skin god gave you."

I huff; I don't even remember what shade that is anymore. My skin and nails and hair have been tanned and painted and bleached since I was a little girl. Sometimes—all the time?—I wish I could peel it all off, just to see who I am underneath.

"You think I'm playing?" Everly smirks. "Maybe your mom will leave you alone if she has to start paying for those Instagram pics."

Everly is obsessed with photography, and it shows in her work. She's fantastic. She's been doing my headshots for the last couple of years and providing content for the Instagram account my mom manages for me. Mom thinks it will lead to modeling gigs or something, but all it's led to so far is creepy dudes in my DMs.

But forget posed pictures and promoted posts. Everly is the queen of candids. She's always got her Nikon around her neck, shooting when we least expect it. Her entire senior art project is based on the idea that candids can show you who a person really is, without their guard up.

I wouldn't know; my guard is never down.

I pull my hair out of its messy bun and fluff it around my shoulders, covering my neck as best as I can. "Better?"

She flicks her eyes over to where Tyler has joined Marcus and the rest of the lacrosse team. "I guess that depends on who you're asking."

"Oh my god, Everly. A hickey is a sign of an overzealous night, not a lasting declaration of love!"

"Uh-huh, well, what about when you combine it with his whole *Please don't leave me, Ruby, why can't you stay the night?*" She claps her hands together like she's begging.

"Never happening." I give her a shove, but I'm laughing.

"Uh-oh." She gasps.

"What?" I look around, trying to figure out what just freaked her out, but the only thing remotely out of the ordinary I see is the new girl pouting alone on a bench.

"Oh, nothing. Just your daddy issues showing."

"Screw you," I say, but I don't really mean it. If there's one person on this earth that can and does call me on all my bullshit on the regular, it's Everly. "It's not daddy issues. It's *I don't want to be tied down to a dumb boy in high school and end up like my mom* issues."

Everly opens her mouth to say something else, but I can't hear it over the sound of the bell signaling that we all better drag ourselves inside before we get marked as absent.

"Saved by the bell," Everly says as we catch up to Marcus and the rest of the guys. He slings his arm around her and whispers something in her ear that makes her giggle.

Tyler stands on the other side of him, watching. He hangs back from the crowd a little, slowing to match my pace. He's a catch by most standards—six foot one, all lean lacrosse muscle, with floppy hair and a kind face that lights up when he smiles.

I'd run, honestly—anything to avoid this awkward morning-after dance . . . except he's in my first period.

"You left again," he says when the others are out of earshot.

"I leave every time." I still don't understand why he's so surprised by that. "And *you* left a mark," I add, shifting my hair just enough for him to see. I don't miss the hint of a smirk on his face before he pulls his features back into place. "Did you do it on purpose?" I ask, loud enough that Everly turns her head to look at me.

"Relax, it was nothing. I just got a little overexcited."

"Well, if you could not get a little overexcited on my body, that would be great."

He leans in. "Doesn't that defeat the purpose of our whole arrangement, then?"

I shove him away with my shoulder. "Just don't do it again. Okay?"

"It was an accident, Ruby," he says, his tone becoming less playful. "You're not gonna make me feel like an asshole because you came over to get some and I delivered."

"Jesus, Tyler. Don't be a dick."

"I'm not the one being a dick."

"What does that mean?" I drop my bag onto my desk. And, okay, I guess this is going to be the theme for the day. First I'm the asshole, and now, apparently, I'm also the dick. Perfect.

"You know exactly what I mean," he says, and crosses the room to his seat.

Except I don't. I really don't.

Unless he means the leaving thing, which, no.

I glance out the window, a headache already forming behind my eyes. I watch the new girl get off the bench and walk over to a shitty Honda Civic—gray, with little spots of rust on the bumper. I catch a glimpse of the driver as he leans over to pass her a book bag. Definitely not her dad—way too young—but the way he ruffles her hair when she takes the bag means not a boyfriend either. A teeny-tiny piece of me relaxes at that realization. I try not to think too hard about what that means.

I search my backpack for a pencil, anything to tear my eyes off the girl outside, grateful when my phone vibrates in my pocket. I pull it out to find about a dozen texts from Mom, reminding me that I have tap class tonight at six thirty, and to wear the good shoes, and to smile, and to be sure to post-date the check a week, and . . . and . . . and . . . There are always more instructions. Mom likes to say, "The only thing better than being a pageant queen is being a pageant queen's mama," except I find that really hard to believe.

But there are some things you can't say out loud: like how her dream isn't my dream anymore, hasn't been for a while, no matter how hard I try to force it. Like how I wish that post-dated check were for bills and groceries and not tap lessons I hate and spray tans that won't do anybody any good. Like how I've been faking my smile for so long, I'm scared I don't know what the real one feels like anymore.

4

MORGAN

I'd like to say the rest of the morning went better, that after forgetting my book bag and almost getting hit by a car, it was all smooth sailing. But it wasn't. The hall monitor gave me the third degree for being late and then sent me to the office, seemingly not convinced that I was a new student, because "new students don't start at the end of the year." Which, fair, but I am, and I did.

After that was straightened out, I went to my locker, where the combination definitely did not work, and by then homeroom was over and first period had started. I think the hall monitor felt more pity than annoyance as she walked me back to the office, where the principal said, "Miss us already?" One late pass and new combination later, I was on my way. Sort of.

Because I was also late to third period. Silly me, I thought all the 200 rooms would be on the second floor, but it turns out that room 215 is actually in the new wing of the first floor. And why not?

Miraculously, I make it to my fourth-period class, Government—the last before lunch—early. The teacher introduces herself as Mrs. Morrison, hands me a textbook, and tells me to sit anywhere. Which is when I realize the desks are lined up in a semicircle around the room instead of in rows, like all the rooms had been at my old school. Clearly, order means nothing here.

"You don't have assigned seats?" I ask, looking around as all the students filter in.

"No, Ms. Matthews, not in my classroom. You're free to pick any desk."

I scan the room, selecting a seat to the right and toward the back, one with a good view of the teacher and everyone else. Not that there's much choice; with the way things are set up, everyone is visible at all times. Clever. It's going to be next to impossible to text or zone out without her seeing it.

Allie comes in, giving me an encouraging smile as she walks a few steps into the room. She takes an empty seat next to someone I can only assume is her friend by the way they instantly start chatting. It's fine. Or it will be, after school, when I can meet the team, which will hopefully be more accepting than my old team—they dropped me like a hot potato after I came out. Or maybe it was after I called the coach a misogynistic homophobe. Either way.

I duck my head and flip through the book, scanning the

pages and wishing I could be anywhere but here, until someone kicks my chair. I look up and find myself face-to-face with
the girl from the car. The messy bun is gone, her hair cascading back down around her face, which I have absolutely been
staring at for too long.

She clears her throat. "You're in my seat," she says, not
exactly rudely, more like extremely firmly . . . with no room
for discussion.

"I thought there weren't assigned seats," I say, even though
my instinct is to grab my stuff and run. But I'm done backing
down. This is the new me.

She grits her teeth. "It's implied."

"How?"

"Look, I appreciate you're new and all, but this is my seat
and has been since September, so if you could go run over to
someone else's—"

"Funny you should say 'run over.' " I smile. "That's kind of
your thing, right? Running things over?"

I swear to god her nostrils flare. It would be cute, if she
weren't so damn annoying. Scratch that, it's definitely still
cute, but I'm trying to ignore it. Unless angry nostril flaring
counts as flirting, in which case—

"*You* almost hit *my car*, not the other way around."

"Is there a problem, ladies?" Mrs. Morrison asks, turning
from the whiteboard and raising an eyebrow.

I open my mouth to say yes, there is a problem, a very big
problem, actually, not the least of which is my level of attrac-
tion to this person, who is clearly the queen of all assholes
ever, but I'm cut off by another voice across the room.

"Morgan, right?" Allie says, and I snap my head toward her. "Sit with us." She taps her pencil on the empty desk beside her.

I flick my eyes to the girl hovering over me, hesitant to let her win, but she looks more bored than annoyed now, so it doesn't seem like it's worth taking a stand. At least not today. I grab my books and slide out of the chair.

"Tough first day?" Allie asks when I drop into the seat beside her. She's changed out of her running clothes and into a soft-looking sweater, the sleeves pulled down over her hands. Her bright red nails peek out, in stark contrast to the whiteness of her skin.

"Something like that," I answer as Mrs. Morrison announces she left a handout in the office and will be right back. She tells us to open to page 106 and then disappears out the door.

"So, this is Lydia. She's also on the track team." Allie points to the girl beside her.

"Hey, Coach is amped you're here," Lydia says, pushing back the black hair that falls in loose waves around her face. She's cut off the neck of her too-large sweatshirt and slid one side down her shoulder, exposing even more of her light brown skin. The teachers at my old school would have a heart attack.

"Yeah? How does everybody else feel?" Just because Coach is "amped" doesn't mean the rest of the team is. I'm a bit of a controversial recruit.

Allie and Lydia share a look that tells me all I need to know.

"That great, eh?"

Lydia twirls a little bit of her hair. "For the most part it's cool. And the rest you don't have to worry about. You clear your waiver and get us to states, and people will look the other way about everything else."

Right. Everything else. Like the whole super-gay thing, and the whole transfer-or-be-expelled thing, and the whole "getting one of my D-I offers revoked and the other put 'on pause' for going to the news about it" thing. But, hey, any college that doesn't accept me—all of me—isn't a school I'd want to be at anyway, right? At least that's what I tell myself when I wake up every morning.

"They just don't want to get involved," Allie cuts in. "Like, we don't care that you're gay or anything." She whispers the word "gay" like it's some kind of horrible secret. Which, no.

"Cool, well, I actually *do* care about that," I say, which makes an awkward silence stretch between us, but I figure it's better to get that out in the open now rather than let myself be shoved into the closet.

Allie looks mortified. "Oh my god, that came out so wrong. Of course you do. Of course I do! It's cool! It's—"

"Allie, shut up." Lydia smiles, leaning farther forward to face me. "Look, since we all made this weird already, I'll just come right out and tell you that, one, Allie puts her foot in her mouth a lot, and two, I'm pan, so you're not the only queer girl on the team. When I said people will look the other way about everything else, I meant, like, the being-kicked-out-of-your-school stuff. Nobody on the team cares who you, me, Allie, or anybody else is hooking up with, as long as it stays off the track. At this point, we're all just looking to nail our meets and survive these last couple of months. And I think it's pretty cool that you fought your old school on this. It was bullshit what they tried to do to you."

I hadn't realized how big of a weight I had felt in my chest, until just now, when it all lifted. I smile for the first time all day as the teacher returns, waving around a bunch of papers.

"Who's ready to learn about amendments?" she asks in a singsong voice.

"So what's her deal?" I ask later that afternoon, after sports study hall, when we're walking on the track for warm-ups.

Allie turns her head in the direction I'm looking, where the girl from this morning is sitting surrounded by a group of other kids on the bleachers. "Who?"

I shrug. "I don't know. The girl from class, the one who said I took her seat."

"Yeah, that's Ruby Thompson. I'd recommend staying away from her."

"Why."

"Because she's trouble?" Allie says at the same time Lydia says, "Because she's a mess."

I glance toward Ruby one more time. "What do you mean?"

"Um, where should I start?" Allie says. "Besides her, like, general air of *I will kill you if you look at me wrong*? Let's see, she's obnoxious, she's always in detention, she kind of sleeps around, she barely talks to anyone except for, like, Everly

Jones, and I swear to god she has Tyler under some sort of a spell. He's, like, in love with her—"

"Wait, who's Tyler?" I ask.

Lydia shakes her head. "Tyler Portman. He's a lacrosse boy and Allie's crush since sixth grade."

I tilt my head. "So is this like a mean-girl thing? You two don't like her because of who she's hooking up with?"

"No," Lydia says. "Ignore that part. Her reputation for being trouble long precedes her and Tyler, trust me."

"Seriously," Allie says, taking my hand and pulling me closer to the track. "Avoid, avoid, avoid. And definitely do not do anything else to get on her bad side."

"She almost hit me with her car this morning." I wince. "And then I may have sort of slammed my hands on the hood, so I'm pretty sure I'm already on her bad side."

Lydia's eyes go wide. "You touched her car?"

"She almost hit me!"

"Yeah, I would have just let her," Lydia says.

Allie nods. "At least it'd be over faster."

Before I can respond, Coach blows her whistle.

Practice has begun.

5

RUBY

I catch the new girl, along with Lydia Ramírez and Allie friggin' Marcetti, staring at me as they start to warm up. I'm sure
they think they're being subtle, but they're not. I wonder
what they're telling her—probably something along the lines
of *Ruby's trash, stay away,* which is fine. I'm not a stranger to
people talking about me; I just wish they were being a little
less obvious about it.

"Hey, Ruby," Marcus says. He gives my shoulder a light
shove as he drops onto the bleachers beside me, running his
hands over his fade before pulling out his AirPods. "You think
you could take a look at my mom's car this weekend? It's making a rattling sound that's got her stressing out."

"Yeah, no problem," I say as the varsity girls start running slow laps around the turf below us. "You know the deal, though."

Marcus nods solemnly. "She's already got the ingredients on the list."

I grin. I've known Marcus Williams since we were kids. He and his mom live on the other side of the trailer park from me. His mom used to babysit me sometimes when I was little and my mom was working double shifts. I don't remember a ton about those years—it's kind of a blur of pageants and random sitters—but I remember Mrs. Williams makes the best mac and cheese I've ever tasted in my life.

One time, I worked up the nerve to ask her if it was Velveeta, because it sure as hell wasn't the store-brand powdered cheese and pasta that I was used to. At $3.99 a box, Velveeta always felt like this glorious, unobtainable thing. Mrs. Williams just laughed, though, and said, "No, baby, I made this from scratch."

I don't think I'd ever really had a meal made from scratch before that. Not that Mom didn't try. I mean, she can twirl a mean baton and smile like a model and talk about wanting world peace, but her pageant training didn't really cover skills like "how to raise a baby at sixteen when your mom kicks you out and your boyfriend ditches you" or "your toddler and you: how to make nutritious, homecooked meals on a two-dollar budget after working a double shift under the table when you're barely old enough to vote."

And even now, the only time I really have a good meal is when Mrs. Williams needs me to fix her car up. She and

Marcus say I can come over anytime to eat, but I never take them up on it. Eating other people's food doesn't seem right, but trading for it seems fair enough.

Everly comes up beside us, giving Marcus a good-natured shove before dropping down next to me. He stares at her with big puppy-dog eyes as she pulls out her camera and tries to keep from smiling. They've been dancing around being together for a few months now, and as much as it kills me to say it, I think they'd be perfect together. We're joined a second later by a few lacrosse girlfriends and some stragglers.

The lacrosse team has a "friendly" scrimmage with another school today, and normally Marcus would be down there on the field, but he's "not progressing fast enough" through the concussion protocol, so he has to sit it out. Technically, it's a friendly match, but I know Tyler's still going to go all out. He would even if the guy who pegged Marcus in the head with a ball—costing them their best defender—weren't on the opposing team.

And maybe it blurs the lines a little bit for me to be here to cheer him on, along with the rest of our crew and the slew of lacrosse girlfriends, but I've got nothing better to do this afternoon, and god knows I don't feel like going home now that Chuck has taken up permanent residence in our living room.

"We miss anything?" one of the girls behind me asks, and I roll my eyes because clearly the guys are just walking onto the field now.

"Just the runners starting their drills," Everly says, sounding bored. She raises her camera and starts snapping pics as the lacrosse team pours out of the locker room and onto the field. Tyler is in the center of the herd, grin on his face, helmet in his hand, while the rest of the team ping-pongs around him like giant, sweaty versions of my mother's dogs. I don't know how he stands it.

I flick my eyes to the track just in time to see the new girl finish first. Lydia, who's been the fastest in the school since track-and-field day in fourth grade, finishes several full seconds later. Huh, I guess the new girl's actually good. She folds her hands up over her head as she walks, her cheeks flushed from the effort, her chest heaving, and then she looks right at me. I swear to god the whole universe falls away, and all I can think of is *wanting*.

Click.

I snap my head toward the sound. Everly lowers her camera and studies its screen. "Wow, this is beautiful. I didn't think I'd ever get a candid of you, what with that stick you keep up your ass all the time."

"Delete it, please," I beg, and she frowns.

"Why? Look at it." She holds the camera toward me, but I look away. I don't want to see it. I don't want to know what I looked like in the single solitary moment I let myself get caught up in her. *Lock it down, Ruby,* I tell myself, shoving thoughts of the new girl, sweaty and breathing hard, into the biggest lockbox in my head with a hard *nope.*

"Wow, she's pretty fast," one of the lacrosse girlfriends says. I don't bother learning their names; the guys never keep them around long enough . . . and yet somehow I'm the one with the reputation.

"I think her name's Morgan," Marcus says.

Everly turns back to him. "It's weird that she transferred in so late in the year."

"I heard she came from some rich-bitch private school in Connecticut," another girl says.

"I heard it was a Catholic school, and she punched a nun or something," the first girl says.

Marcus shakes his head. "Nah, I heard Allie talking about her last week in precalc. She's some big-deal track star or something. She's just here to finish out the season and take us to states. Allie made it sound like she might go D-I."

"What does that mean?" I ask, because the only D1 I know of is the make and model number of the spark plugs I had to custom order for one of Billy's clients the other day.

Everly grips my shoulder and scrunches up her face in disbelief. "How can you watch your boy toy play this much lacrosse and not even know what a Division I school is?"

"He's not my boy toy." I push her hand away. She knows better than to do this, especially in front of his friend. And excuse me for not knowing, but I guarantee if I asked her to explain the difference between a cupcake dress and an A-line gown, she'd be just as lost as I am right now.

"You hook up with him, don't you?" Marcus asks, pulling me from my thoughts. "And you *are* here to watch him play. Can't blame anybody for getting ideas."

I look at Everly, pleading—but instead of finding solace in my best friend's face, she just taps her camera screen. "I mean, he has a point. Candids don't lie."

And, *Oh, shit,* I think, looking at the picture. I look like I'm ready to jump the fence and propose.

"Delete that," I say, to which Everly replies, "Nuh-uh," clearly thinking this is some kind of joke.

But it's not a joke; it's not. Even if Everly thinks I was looking at Tyler when she snapped that, I know the truth. And I don't need it staring me in the face like this.

Suddenly, I feel claustrophobic, the bleachers filling up with parents coming to watch the scrimmage, and I . . . I can't be here. I grab my bag off the step beside me and tromp down the stairs, fighting against eager moms with babies strapped to their chests, and nearly tripping over a diaper bag in the process.

"Ruby, wait!" Everly says, bouncing after me. "I was just messing with you. Everybody knows you're just hooking up."

"Oh my god." I groan, because shouting that doesn't make things any better. "Can we drop it?"

Everly scrunches her face up into her patented *did I go too far? please don't be mad* look. "Postgame meet up at the diner? Or do you have to work tonight?"

"No, but I have a tap lesson at six thirty."

"After that, then?" And I don't miss the hopeful lilt in her voice.

"We'll see," I say. I flip her off as I walk backward, slapping on what my mom calls my "realistic" smile. Not to be confused with my *please, judges, look how much time I spent bleaching my teeth* smile or my *who, me?* smile, which I reserve for the pervier judges who prefer their contestants coy.

Everly laughs and responds in kind, reassured that we're still cool. But she doesn't see how my face falls when I turn around or the way my eyes well up when I get to my car, google "division one," and realize that it's just another thing out of my reach, like Velveeta mac and cheese or a mom who actually listens.

Billy's garage is only about a ten-minute drive from school. It's a rusted-out old building with two bays housing creaky lifts and glass on the doors so dirty you couldn't see through it if you tried. Out back are a bunch of old junk cars we scavenge for parts, and out front are two ten-year-old pickup trucks he's trying to sell and a couple classic cars he wouldn't part with even on his deathbed. I swear to god, he's gonna ask to be buried in one. If I get a say in it, he will be.

Billy's basically my dad. Well, stepdad. Ex-stepdad, technically. My actual dad is more of a sperm donor than a father, so Billy's the closest thing I got. He and Mom were married for almost six years before the arguing got too much for him and they split up. I don't blame him; my mom is a hard person to live with. He gave it a good run.

Billy's the one who taught me how to work on cars, and he lets me hide out here whenever I need to. If Mom knew how much time I spent here, she'd probably try to burn the place down. She never really got over Billy—I think she thought he was going to be the one to stick. And he has, sort of, just not for her. Add it to the list of things I feel guilty about.

I pull into my usual spot outside the office, feeling the

weight of the day—and Marcus's comments—slide off me. Sure, this place is a shithole, but I can get my hands dirty and feel like I'm doing something with my time. Fixing something broken just feels good.

I shut my car door as Billy steps out, wiping the sweat off his face with a greasy rag and spitting into an empty bottle of Gatorade. Billy doesn't smoke—he says his shop is too flammable—but he does dip, which is just as gross. He's fit for a guy in his forties, and unlike me comes by his tanned skin naturally. It's not unusual for him to pick up odd jobs—landscaping, roofing, whatever—when the shop is slow. Billy and I are alike in that way. We both prefer cars, but neither of us really cares what we're doing as long as we're working with our hands.

My mom, on the other hand, spends her time trying to keep me still and yelling about my manicures.

"Ruby," he says, a smile on his lips. "I didn't expect to see you here today!"

"Yeah, well, she's pulling a little to the right," I lie. "Thought maybe you could take a look with me."

He looks me up and down, narrowing his eyes before nodding. We both know I've done enough alignments to fix this with my eyes closed if needed. "Let's get her up on the lift, then," he says, not prying or pressing the issue. He always gets it—just because a person doesn't want to be alone doesn't mean they want to talk about it.

6

MORGAN

"Hey." Allie bounds up behind me, flicking my shoulder. I'm studying the list of clubs tacked to the bulletin board in the main lobby of the school. The final bell just rang, and while most kids are heading to their buses, we're supposed to be on our way to sports study hall before practice.

We've fallen into an easy routine, even just in the week I've been here. I thought some of my teammates would be pissed that I showed up out of nowhere, but they've been mostly really nice. I low-key wonder if the lawsuit my parents have going against my old school has something to do with that, but I try not to think about it too hard.

"Hey yourself," I say, pulling a Pride Club flyer down and shoving the pin back into the corkboard.

"You coming to study hall?"

"I kind of want to check this out," I say, because aside from Lydia, I haven't really met anyone else that's queer like me. Not that it's exactly easy when you're the new kid; you can't just walk up to someone and be like, *Hi, I'm super gay. Are you?* despite what my mother seemed to think when we Face-Timed last night.

"Ohh, very on brand," Allie says, eyeing the flyer.

"You want to come?"

Her face falls, just for a second. Just long enough for me to catch it. "That's not really my kind of thing," she says, her discomfort cutting me like a knife.

"It says 'allies welcome,' " I press. "Which you are, so—"

"I know, and it's cool and all. I don't have a problem with anyone who goes. It's just not my scene."

"Does Lydia go?"

Allie shakes her head. "Uh, no, her parents are very much 'look the other way and pretend it's not happening' when it comes to who she's dating, and she's pretty quiet about it at school. Plus, I don't know how the team would react if she *really* put it out there." She says it sort of offhandedly, like she's talking to someone else—not someone queer and on the team.

"What does that mean?"

"Oh!" she says, her eyes getting wide. "I didn't mean you. Nobody feels weird about you or anything! I swear! It's just Lydia is . . . Lydia. We grew up with her. It's different."

"Okay." I'm not really sure how it's different, but also I don't want to lose 50 percent of the friends I've made since moving here over this either.

"We're proud that you're proud, but I'm not proud."

I narrow my eyes.

"I mean, I'm proud of you! Obviously! But I don't have, you know, *pride*." She whispers the last word, and, ah, okay, I get it.

"I know that you're straight. That's why I pointed out the whole 'allies welcome' thing."

She seems relieved, like maybe she thought I was going to hit on her or try to convert her or something. And even though I'm smiling, inside my stomach hurts. Because why does this always have to be this huge, awkward thing? Just because I like girls doesn't mean I like *every* girl.

I sigh and spin around to repin the flyer when—like the cherry on top of my solid crap sundae—Ruby Thompson pushes through the throngs of kids around us, and I smack her spectacularly with my track bag.

"Jesus, Matthews, watch what you're doing," she says as she stomps past. I watch her go, trying to stay annoyed and not care at all that she knows my name. Well, my last name at least. Don't care. Not one bit. Who cares? Not me.

Dammit. Why does she have to be so cute?

"Sorry about that," Allie calls after her, like she can actually apologize for someone else.

I shove the pin in a little harder, wishing I could stick a pin in my whole stupid crush. "Is it just me, or is Ruby perpetually pissed?"

"We tried to warn you." Allie takes my arm. "Avoid, avoid, avoid."

"It would be nice if she didn't hate me for no reason, though."

"You did touch her car." Allie laughs. "But seriously, don't take it personally. The only things that Ruby doesn't blatantly hate are that car and Tyler Portman's dick, so."

I'm so caught off guard that I literally choke on my spit.

"What did you do now?" Lydia asks, walking up and fake glaring at Allie.

"Nothing, I swear." She holds up her hands in surrender. "I think her body just full-on rejects any mention of dick."

Lydia smacks Allie's arm.

"What? It's true! All I said was Ruby liked Tyler Portman's—"

"Anywaaaaay," I say, desperate to change the subject.

Lydia holds up her Government book, throwing me a bone. "You ready?"

"Um, actually," I say, slouching a little, "I think I'm going to go to the Pride Club meeting instead, but I'll meet you at the track for warm-ups . . . unless you want to come?" I focus on Lydia, trying to telepathically beg.

She hesitates for half a second, flicking her eyes to Allie before shaking her head. "No, I have a ton of homework. So I'll see you at practice, then?"

"Yeah." I watch them walk away. "See you at practice."

I have no idea what to expect when I walk into the Pride Club meeting. We didn't have anything like this at my old school. Just the thought of a club like this existing anywhere probably keeps the headmaster up at night in a cold sweat.

My mouth goes dry as I step into the room. I'm desperate for the springy feel of tartan track under my feet or asphalt under my sneakers or literally anything comfortable and expected. Running—running I get, but this . . . I don't know what this even is. What does one do in a pride club? Is it a hangout? Or is it like group therapy? Should I even be here?

At my old school, pride was not something I was allowed to have—even acceptance was apparently pushing the envelope. I take a deep breath and then another. *This is your fresh start,* I remind myself. *You promised yourself this.* No more hiding. No more blending in. No more running away from the tough conversations.

But that doesn't mean I'm ready to sit front and center for them either.

I head straight to the back of the room and slide into a seat in the very last row, trying to remain inconspicuous while I feel things out. There are about a dozen kids sitting up at the front, some cross-legged on top of desks, some eating snacks, but other than a few curious glances, they mostly ignore me. I don't know what I was expecting—not a group hug or a giant welcome banner, but maybe, like, at least a lone "hey" or "hi."

I pull out my phone and start checking my texts, not that I have any good ones. Most of my old friends cut me off, either by choice or because their parents made them. It was like they thought they could catch the gay—or the expulsion—from me. At least there are like a thousand texts in the group chat between me, my parents, and Dylan to catch up on. I jump in just long enough to say *Hi, I'm alive, yes, I'm having a good day, and no, I don't need anyone to drive out and check up on me just because I took too long to respond today.* I'll see them at our regular family dinner in a few days—one of my parents' conditions for my moving here.

My parents are admittedly kind of freaking out with me gone. Which I get. I had to move; they didn't—or couldn't really, not with their jobs. But with college looming anyway, this is practically a trial run of a semester away . . . at least that's how I'm trying to think about it. And, hey, people lose their friends back home and make new ones in college all the time. It's normal. This is normal. I stare down at my now-empty text alerts. What happened at St. Mary's was just an acceleration of the inevitable, that's all. Friends move on after high school.

"Oh! We have a new face today!" the teacher says as she walks in. It's Ms. Ming, my English teacher. I was not expecting that. "Happy to see you here, Morgan. I was hoping you'd turn up."

"Thanks," I say.

"Why don't you come up here and join us."

I hesitate for a second, because this feels important. This feels big. Like a first step I can only barely understand and—

"We don't bite," one of the girls says with a friendly smile. She has one perfect dimple and deep bronze skin that pops against the bright white of her Harry Styles hoodie. I think I recognize her from my second-period class. Anika, maybe?

"Speak for yourself," another kid says, lobbing a candy wrapper at her and gnashing his teeth. He's East Asian, I think, and when he turns toward me with a wink, I realize he's wearing a *Hamilton* shirt. I like him already.

"Enough, Drew," Ms. Ming says with an impatient smile as I take a seat near the front. "Brennan, will you lead us off today?"

The boy sitting beside me—Brennan, I'm guessing—flashes me an easy smile beneath a mountain of bright red hair and freckles and then grabs a notebook off his desk to join Ms. Ming up front.

He starts to run through what he calls "old business." Apparently, he's reviewing the club's expenditures and remaining budget after a recent field trip to see *The Prom* on tour. The words wash over me; I'm only half listening as I look around the room, taking in the idea that all of these kids from across the entire high school social scene are here working toward the common goal of acceptance and unity. It's everything I ever wanted, maybe even *needed*.

But I can't help but feel that something's not quite right. Something's missing, and it takes me a minute to figure it out. Every group in the school seems to be here, represented in this room, except one. Except mine. I wait for them to wrap up the updates, and then raise my hand, not really sure what the protocol is but wanting to get Ms. Ming's attention.

"You don't need to raise your hand, Morgan. This isn't a class; it's a club."

"Sorry," I say, lowering my arm. "I was just wondering, um, if any school athletes come to these meetings?"

A girl turns and glares at me. "What, are we not good enough for you?"

"No, that's not why I asked."

"Uh-huh," she says, and turns back around.

"Sports and Pride Club don't always mix at this school," a boy says, almost apologetically.

"Well, I do sports. Sport, really. I run. Well, sports plural if you count track and cross-country as two different things," I mumble. "But yeah, I do sports and I'd like to mix." A couple kids laugh, and I blush.

"Let her talk!" Drew says, shutting them up.

"We didn't have anything like this at my old school. And I'm still trying to figure out where I fit at this new one. But if you're saying sports and Pride Club don't mix, then . . ." My words trail off, my face burning as I struggle to work out what to say next.

A short white boy with dyed black hair and the darkest green eyes I've ever seen stands up and moves to the empty seat on the other side of me. "Hi, I'm Aaron," he says, holding out his hand. "Gay, trans, he/him, and I may not be a sports kid, but I can definitely kick your ass at kickball."

I shake his hand for way too long, utterly caught off guard. And then the girl in the white hoodie raises her hand with a little wave. "Hi, I'm Anika, queer, she/her, and I hate most sports, but I can do a mean doggy paddle. And you mix with us. You do."

I stare at her for a second, just kind of floored by the niceness, before she adds, "Now, are you ever going to tell us who *you* are?"

And who am I? It's such a loaded question. One I've been running from just as hard as I've been holding on to it. But in this moment, it feels right. In this moment, I want to claim it. Loudly. And hopefully never stop.

In this moment, I feel proud.

"Hi, I'm Morgan." My voice breaks as I swallow back some tears, because for the first time, maybe I'm exactly where I need to be, exactly where I fit. "I'm a lesbian. She/her. And I like to run."

7

RUBY

"Shit, shit, shit." I slam my car door and squeal into reverse. I'm so late. Mom is probably already waiting backstage at the pageant, having rushed there straight from her night shift to make sure I don't screw anything up. And I already have. I need to get there. I need to—

I glance at the clock. It's eight forty-five a.m., because I overslept because my phone died because it couldn't charge last night because my mom didn't pay the electric bill— again—and since we're out of the coldest months, the electric company can legally cut us off now. Which is just fabulous.

I knew I shouldn't have picked up that new dance leotard she'd put on layaway. I knew the electric was due—but how do you say that to your mom? How do you even begin to suggest that maybe you know better than she does where to allocate the few bucks you have to your name? How do you tell her that this Miss America pipe dream she has is delusional at best, considering you haven't made it farther than third runner-up in a pageant since you were ten?

Simple: you don't.

You swallow it down. Even if you choke on every word. You lend her *your* body to chase *her* dreams. And you act grateful for it, because if you don't she'll remind you of what she gave up for you every chance she gets.

I plug my phone into the USB charger I installed in my cigarette lighter and hope it boots up fast. There's a good song on the radio and I turn it up, trying not to notice the clock has ticked over to 8:46. I take a sharp left onto Main Street, my tires squealing a little in the cool morning air. Check-in ends at 9:15, and Parkside Hall—home of the Parkside Beauty Pageant—is a half hour away even in the best traffic conditions. If I miss check-in, I'll be disqualified despite the fact that we're already registered and paid.

Okay, breathe. I can make up time on the highway.

I take another hard turn and flick my eyes to the dress rocking precariously on its hanger in the back, praying it doesn't fall. I don't have time to stop the car and pick it up, and god knows the wrinkles from spending thirty minutes crumpled on the floor would be enough to lose me the competition.

I'm slowing to a roll at a stop sign when the hanger finally loses its grip on the tiny hook. The dress slides down, and I'm reaching behind me, a futile attempt at averting disaster, when I catch movement out of the corner of my eye.

I slam on my brakes, dramatic even at three miles per hour, and feel a small thump against my bumper. My eyes go wide. I overshot the stop sign. Oh, shit, shit, shit. There's something on the ground in front of my car. Please don't let it be a dog. Please just let it be one of those lawn bags of leaves or a garbage can or something that just . . . happened to be in the middle of the road. For no reason. Shit.

I shove open my car door and run around the front just as a very pissed-off-looking Morgan Matthews pushes herself off the ground.

"Oh, thank god!" I yelp. "I thought you were a dog."

"What the hell, Ruby!" A small trickle of blood drips down the side of her leg. Which is when it hits me, like really hits me, the gravity of what just happened. I just hit a person with my car. Morgan Matthews, to be exact.

"Are you okay?" I take a step forward, but she moves back with a wince.

"Get away from me." She limps to the sidewalk and drops to the grass. I swear to god she looks like she's going to cry, and, oh god. Oh, shit. I can't deal with this.

"I didn't see you. I swear."

"I was in the crosswalk! How did you 'not see me'?" she says, her fingers flying up to make air quotes.

"My gown was falling!" Okay, that's probably not the best excuse. She glares at me and rubs her hip.

I look at my car and then at her. I really, really, really have to go, but I can't leave her like this.

"Oh, don't let me hold you up just because you mowed me down with your stupid car."

My annoyance at the word "stupid" flares up, but I let it go. *Not the time, lizard brain.*

"Hang on." I run and grab a handful of napkins out of the glove compartment and then carry them over to her. "You're bleeding."

"Thanks, I noticed." She snatches them from my hands and dabs at the road rash running up the length of her right thigh.

"Are you okay?" I ask again, only to be met with yet another glare. Yeah, I probably deserve that.

"Just go." Her voice breaks, and yikes, I've never been good with emotions. It's too uncomfortable; it's too much. I'm tempted to leave. In fact, every instinct is telling me to do just that; *she's* even telling me to do that. Plus, there's still a chance I can make it to the pageant, small and fleeting as it may be.

But then she sniffles, and it's like my whole heart clenches up for a second. I drop onto the grass next to her, feeling a little bit like I'm going to throw up. "Look, I'm really fucking sorry, Matthews. Are you . . . Can I take you to the hospital or something?"

"Excuse me if I don't trust your driving," she snaps, dabbing at her leg a little more. And I did that to her. It's my fault. This totally nice new girl is sitting here bleeding because of me, because I screw everything up. And now I'm going to miss my pageant, and my mom's gonna lose it and . . .

And now it's me who feels like crying, which absolutely 100 percent cannot happen. I bury my forehead in my hands and take a deep, shaky breath, waiting for the stinging behind my eyes to stop.

"Hey," Morgan says, her hand on my arm, "I won't, like, sue you or call the cops or whatever if that's what you're freaking out about."

I scoff and look at her—just the fact that she thinks my family has anything worth coming after proves how little she knows me. But then I remember the rumors, that she's suing her old school, her old coach. Maybe that's just what she does. Once, a credit card company sued Mom and took half her paycheck. Half of not much still felt like a lot of everything.

I lower my head between my legs and feel like I'm going to pass out because *I won't sue you* sounds a lot like what someone says when they *are* going to sue you. I have to find a way to fix this.

"I'm sorry," I say, looking up at her with as much sincerity as I can muster. Because I am sorry. *I am.* "But you should know if you sue us, you won't get very far."

Morgan raises an eyebrow, like it was a dare or a threat, and I can tell she misunderstood.

"I don't have anything for you to get. That's all I meant. We don't even have electricity right now." I don't know why I just told her that, and shit, here come the waterworks. I rub at my eyes, and she's polite enough to pretend she doesn't notice.

"It's going to be okay." She squeezes my shoulder, and I'm not sure if I should lean into it or pull away, but everything I locked in that little box in my brain labeled MORGAN MATTHEWS is suddenly trying to claw its way out.

Morgan lets her arm drop, and I settle my hand in the grass as close to hers as I dare. I try to force out a perfect Miss Congeniality smile, but it falters on my face when our eyes meet.

She's looking at me like she actually cares. Like she actually wants to make it better somehow.

"It's really not. I'm supposed to be at a pageant in like ten minutes. My mom is gonna kill me, and we *really* needed to pay some bills with the money she spent on the entry fee. Even if I pick up extra shifts at my pageant coach's studio, it's still not going to be enough, and . . . Jesus, fuck, why am I telling you this?" I suck back some snot. "I don't even tell people I *like* this."

She huffs out a laugh. "I'll pretend you didn't just say that."

"I didn't mean . . . I just don't really know you. You know?" *And you confuse the hell out of me,* I almost add. I take a deep breath, pulling myself together as much as I can. "Look, are you sure you don't you want to call the cops or something? Jail might be better than facing my mom."

"Do you . . . Can I hug you?"

"What?"

"You're freaking out. And when I'm freaking out, I always want a h—"

Morgan's cut off when a police cruiser pulls up next to my car, turning on its flashers and letting out a little *whoop whoop* of the siren as the driver puts it in park. And of course, it's Deputy Davis. My elementary school D.A.R.E. officer . . . and also the guy who's been called to our house on more than one occasion for domestics between my mom and Chuck. Sometimes he takes her; sometimes he takes him. I guess today it's finally my turn.

"How did I know it was you, Ruby?" he asks as he walks over, puffing out his chest. "We got a call about an accident involving a pedestrian and an 'old blue sports car.'"

"It's not a sports car; it's a—"

"Miss," he says, cutting me off and turning to Morgan. "Can I get your name? I'll get some medics on the way for you, and then we can figure out if this is going to be a ticket or a charge for our friend here."

Oh, god. I was kidding about the whole jail thing. I don't . . . I can't . . . I grab Morgan's hand without thinking, squeezing it a little as I try to tamp down the fear. She freezes beside me but then gently squeezes back.

"I'm sorry, Officer, I think you have the wrong idea," Morgan says, her voice slicing through my panic. "I was running, and I stepped off the curb wrong—Ruby stopped to help me. I'm just lucky she came along. Please don't call an ambulance. It's just a scrape, I swear, and you'll get my parents worried for nothing."

Deputy Davis looks from her to me, suspicion still clear in his eyes. "Are you sure you don't want to at least get checked out?"

"Only if you cover my copay," she says with a friendly smile. "I really appreciate your help, sir, but this just calls for some Neosporin and a Band-Aid."

"Do you need a ride home?" he asks, and my jaw almost hits the ground. I knew, theoretically, that some people actually got the "serve" part of "protect and serve." I've just never seen it before.

"I'm giving her one," I say, feeling suddenly protective. "I know her; we have a class together."

He takes one long look at both of us and then nods, heading back to his car. I don't dare breathe until he pulls away.

"You didn't have to do that," I say quietly. "But thank you."

She shrugs, like it's no big deal. Except it is a big deal. It's a very big deal. Now I owe her. And we're . . . still holding hands.

I pull my hand away, watching her face. "Why did you?"

"I don't know," she says, her cheeks getting a little red, and then we're both quiet.

"Come on, let's get you home." I stand up and hold out my hand.

She hesitates, but then lets me help her up. "It's fine. I can walk. If you hurry, can you still make the pageant?"

"Nah, I'll give you a ride. I'll figure out the pageant thing later," I say, even though there's nothing to figure out. It's too late to make it on time, the money spent now doubly wasted. My stomach churns at the thought of asking Billy for another loan, but I push it down. That's a problem for future Ruby. Present Ruby needs to get Morgan home.

I pull open the side door, not missing how she winces when she sits down as I cross over to my side of the car.

"I'm in Melbourne Apartments," she says, and I nod. That's a really decent apartment complex, right in the center of town. Figures she would live there. She shifts in her seat, clearly uncomfortable.

"You sure you don't want to at least go to an urgent care?" I hand her another napkin for her leg. "Is the copay really that bad?"

"I can't risk my brother finding out and telling my parents."

"Your brother?"

"Yeah, he's been trying to act like super dad or something since I moved in with him. If I end up in urgent care, he'll flip, and then my parents will flip, and probably my new coach too. And if a doc says I can't run . . . I can't risk that. Not this close to the end of the season. Not when we're still fighting for the waiver."

"What waiver?"

She frowns. "Long story."

"But you can barely walk . . ."

Morgan tilts her head. "Doesn't mean I can't run."

"Yeah, it sorta does."

"I've run through worse," she mumbles, reaching for the stereo, probably to signify the conversation is over. Normally, I would lose it on someone daring to touch my stereo, but for some reason I let her. I tell myself it's penance for almost killing her.

When we finally get to Melbourne, she directs me to her apartment. It's more of a town house, really—it even has a garage. I can't imagine. If I had garage space to mess with my car at home, I don't think I'd ever leave.

"This is really nice."

"Thanks," Morgan says in a casual way that tells me her parents' house is probably even nicer. "You want to come in? My brother's at work."

Definitely not, I think, but the box of feelings inside my brain rattles. I bite my lip before answering, "Yeah, sure," and turning off my car. She gets out with a tiny grunt, shifting a little extra weight onto the car door. I hate that I caused this, but I also weirdly respect the fact that she's determined to pretend nothing happened.

Her house is sparsely decorated but clean. You can tell a

dude put it together, but also that the dude isn't a total scumbag. Like there's a beer bottle on the end table, but it's on a coaster. There's a leather sofa to one side, and a huge TV with a couple gaming systems on the other next to a giant autographed picture of Gigi Hadid. I fight the urge to ask her if the picture belongs to her or her brother. There are rumors about her at school, but it's really none of my business. God knows half the rumors about me aren't true.

Morgan kicks off her shoes by the door and limps into the room, slumping on the couch with a sigh. I stand awkwardly by the entryway, not sure exactly what to do now that I'm here. I want to be helpful, but . . .

"Want me to get you some ice?" I ask, and she smiles, like I wasn't the one who just hit her with my goddamn car.

"That'd be great. It's in the freezer."

I let out a little laugh. "I figured."

She drops her head. "Right, yeah."

I slide off my shoes and head into the kitchen. It's bigger and nicer than mine, with a sparkling silver faucet and not a single stray crumb on the counter. The fridge is one of those with double doors and a giant slide-out freezer underneath. I open it, just to take a peek, and am met with more fresh produce then I've ever seen in my entire life. There's like a month's worth of groceries in here.

"Everything okay?" she calls from the living room, and I hear her turn on the TV.

"Yeah, yeah, great." I slide open the freezer and grab a bag of NOW TOTALLY ORGANIC! flash-frozen peas off the top and then a LaCroix from the fridge door for good measure. A little thrill runs through me as I walk back into the room, because for once, I am not screwing up.

Morgan arches an eyebrow when I sit on the coffee table and hand her the peas.

"For your hip," I say, like it should be obvious. I'm not sure why it's not.

She takes it from me and angles herself to rest it across her side. "Thanks."

I crack open the seltzer and pass it to her. "I figured you might be thirsty after your run."

She smiles a little wider and reaches for it, which makes the bag of peas slip. I grab them quick and tuck them around her. My hand accidentally catches on the edge of her shirt, my fingertips grazing her soft, warm skin. I linger without realizing it until the sound of her breath catching snaps me out of it.

"Sorry, I just—sorry."

Morgan clears her throat as I tuck my hands into my pockets. "There's a new rom-com that just dropped on Netflix. Want to watch? I guess it's about this girl who—"

I glance at the TV. "I know what it's about," I say, grateful for the subject change. "Everly's obsessed. She has this massive crush on Noah Centineo."

"Valid choice, but I have to say Madelaine Petsch is more my style."

Her eyes meet mine when she says that, but I look away, because as much as I want to stay in this strange little bubble where accidentally hitting her with my car leads to us both smiling and watching Netflix, I don't want to lead her on. I know I can't have this. Whatever this even is.

Even though I escaped Deputy Davis, I definitely haven't escaped my mom.

"I have to go," I say, sounding sadder than I mean to. "Can I get you anything else first, though?"

"You sure you can't stay?"

"Some other time," I lie.

"I'm going to hold you to that."

You can try.

8

MORGAN

I'm on my third Netflix rom-com—and still trying to decide whether Ruby hitting me with her car and handing me a bag of frozen peas this morning constitutes a meet-cute or not—when my parents get here. Dylan isn't home yet—he had to pick up the pizzas for tonight's family dinner—so I get the honor of flinging the door open and getting smothered by their hugs first.

Mom's wearing her wool coat even though it's almost spring, and I inhale hard, trying to catch the scent of home.

"We missed you, kiddo," Dad says, dropping his one-armed hug and carrying a bag over to the counter. "It's been too quiet."

I untangle myself from my mom and follow him. "What's in the bag?"

He pulls it open to show me a massive container of his famous homemade peanut butter cookies. Dad peels up a corner of the lid with a smile. "Fresh from the oven! Still warm. Or rather, they were an hour and a half ago, when we got on the highway."

I don't even care. I've missed my dad's cooking so much I can't stand it. Dylan is practically useless, which means I've been surviving mostly on takeout and frozen food since I got here. I reach my hand out, practically drooling, but Dad snaps the lid shut and pushes the container behind him.

"Not until you've had dinner," he says, pointing his finger at me sternly.

He makes it about two seconds before we both dissolve into laughter.

"Wow, Dad, so convincing."

"It's not his fault, honey. He's out of practice."

"Yeah, there's no one at home to sneak cookies but your mother," he says, kissing her on the cheek.

Dylan walks in right then, a large pizza box with several takeout containers balanced in his hands and a two-liter of orange soda wedged precariously underneath his arm.

"Little help?" he calls, and we all rush over as he kicks the door shut with his foot.

Dad and I take the food into the kitchen and start setting up the table while Mom and Dylan share a long hug.

It doesn't take long once we're all sitting around the table for the conversation to turn from day-to-day catching up to the real elephant in the room. Mainly because I can't help but bring it up. It's been two weeks since I moved in with Dylan, and updates on the lawsuit have been almost nonexistent. Dylan says they're probably just trying to shield me from it, but I don't want shielding; I want to be a part of it.

"Soooo . . ." I drag the word out until everyone looks up. "Any updates from Brian?"

Brian Masterson, partner at Masterson & Wilcox Attorneys at Law, is the lead on our case. He's the one who sends me questions and requests for statements and stuff—well, his assistant, anyway. But any true updates are filtered through my parents first, like I'm an afterthought to him, even though this case is for and about me.

"Nothing important," Mom says cheerfully, grabbing another garlic knot.

"How about the unimportant stuff?" I ask.

Dad sighs. "These things take time, Morgan. You can't expect results overnight."

"I don't expect results overnight, but I'd like to be kept in the loop the way I was when I was still home. I—"

"The whole purpose of you coming here was to give you a fresh start," Mom cuts in. "If you're just going to be worrying about it all the time, then you might as well have kept homeschooling with us." She squeezes my hand. "We're only a couple months in, and Brian said these things move incredibly slow. I want you to enjoy what's left of your senior year."

"I'm good. I told you. I'm settling in. I'm making friends. I'm doing as much normal kid stuff as possible when you're a runner banned from running and your college decision is up in the air. I know what you're trying to do, but not knowing what's going on is just freaking me out more."

I glance at dad. His elbows are on the table, his hands clasped in front of his mouth the way he does whenever he's thinking hard about something.

"Dad?"

He clears his throat and sits up straighter. "St. Mary's offered us a deal last week."

I can tell by how hard Mom exhales that he wasn't supposed to mention this.

"A deal?" Dylan asks, his eyes shifting from Dad to me and back again. "What kind of a deal?"

"They'll support the waiver going through and give a 'positive reference' to any or all of your offering colleges."

"In exchange for . . . ?" I trail off, my knee starting to bounce.

"Dropping all civil actions."

I let out a nervous laugh and rub my hand over my forehead. "You said no, right?"

"We're still considering all of our options, but—"

"What does Brian say?"

"Brian thinks it's a fair offer," Dad says. "You'd get back everything they tried to take from you. You'd be in good standing again. You could run—"

"A fair offer? After what I went through?"

"Maybe you should consider it," Dylan pipes up, but I shoot him a look that has him instantly diving into the pizza box to avoid my gaze.

"I want this to mean something. I *need* something good to come out of it, not just 'Morgan gets to run again.' What they did to me, how they made me feel . . . nobody should have to go through that. And there are other queer kids at that school . . ."

"I know, baby," Mom says, and my eyes start to well up.

"Does Brian think we have to take the deal? Do we have to give up?" I ask, my voice wavering.

And, god, here I really thought getting hit by a car was going to be the worst thing to happen to me today.

"No, no," Mom says, rubbing my arm reassuringly. "We're not giving up."

"Beth," my dad says.

"We are *not* giving up," my mom says again, looking him in the eye. "There are just a few hiccups we have to deal with."

"Like?"

"For one, Brian says the harassment claim isn't going to go anywhere because you *gave* as much as you got at first, and we need to make you look as sympathetic as possible—"

"That's hardly the biggest issue," Dad interrupts.

I look between them. "Then what is?"

Dad purses his lips, like he's deciding how much to say. "Because St. Mary's is a private school, all the typical freedom of speech and discrimination laws don't apply."

"Are you serious?" Anger wells up inside of me. "So this was all for nothing?"

"No," Dad says. "No. The publicity from this lawsuit put tremendous pressure on them. They're willing to back off on the waiver stuff now, and before they wouldn't even consider it! I call that a win. You'd get your life back."

"That's it?" I shout. "They just get away with it, then?"

Dad sighs. "Morgan—"

"There *is* precedent in California," Mom cuts him off. "The state ruled that private-school students don't lose their constitutional rights at the door. We can try to run it up the ladder here and see what happens. Brian says it's a slim chance, but possible."

"Okay." I take a deep breath and try to calm down. "Okay, then we keep fighting, right? A slim chance is better than none."

"We can try, honey bun," Mom says with a soft smile.

Dad gets up and clangs his dishes loudly in the sink. He stands there for a moment, head hung, fingers clenching the counter, but when he turns around, a familiar smile is fixed on his face. "Is there a game on, Dyl?"

"Um, yeah," my brother says, carrying his own plate to the sink and then pulling a couple beers out of the fridge. "Yankees versus Red Sox started about fifteen minutes ago."

Dad cracks open a beer and gulps down half of it in one solid swig. "Go, Yankees."

9

RUBY

My mother spends all day Saturday crying.

I sit in the dark with her and apologize over and over for missing the pageant. I promise to get the money to cover both the registration fee and the electric bill until she finally falls into a fitful sleep. Tonight is her night off from work. She only allows herself one a week, and now I've gone and screwed up her sleep schedule with all my drama.

At least Chuck isn't here. He told Mom he was going on some hunting trip with buddies. She believed him, even though I don't think it's hunting season for anything in this state. Whatever. Not my problem.

I tuck her in and go to my room, too embarrassed to call Everly and tell her the electricity's out again, and not wanting to risk wasting my phone battery anyway. It's too dark to read now, and there's nothing else to do and nowhere to go, so I lie down in my bed drowning in my thoughts as the moonlight glints off all the trophies I won when I was little.

Mom keeps them on display on a shelf in my room. She won't let me take them down, despite the fact that the last one I earned was nearly six years ago. I don't know why she likes them so much. Maybe because it's proof we were happy once. We were good. We were winners. Or maybe she just likes to look at shiny things.

The biggest trophy looms over all of them, tall and imposing in a way that's supposed to invoke pride but really strikes fear. Except I don't hate it the way I hate the others. Because that one . . . that one was from when it was still fun to put on tap shoes and smile for the judges. I was only eight, and when Mom told me I was going to be Miss America someday, I still believed it. I still wanted it.

When they put that crown on my head and handed me that trophy, all I cared about was how big my mom grinned and how rare of a sight that was. But it didn't stop there. There were ribbon cuttings and fundraisers, and once I even threw the first pitch at a minor league game. I was so proud. Mom was so proud.

It didn't matter that we lived on ramen and pancakes. I hadn't yet caught on that some people always had hot water and phones that worked and TVs with too many channels to count. I hadn't yet figured out that we were less than, not equal to.

But then things changed.

Not right away, or all at once, but in quiet, subtle ways that were somehow just as jarring. It was like my winning Little Miss Holloran set something on fire in my mother. At first, it was extra pageants at the malls, the meaningless ones—"Only for practice, my sweet girl," she would say. And then came the pageant coaches and dance instructors who thought tough love was the only love.

And then I grew taller and older, and makeup wasn't enough. It was tanning and bleaching and waxing. It was fake eyelashes and hair extensions and shoes that pinched and hurt. It was dance lessons until my legs burned, and interview prep until I memorized the answer to every question from "What sets you apart from the other contestants?" to "What's the biggest issue facing our education system in this country?"

And all the time the fire raged inside my mom until it burned both of us down. Gone was *Sweet girl* and in its place were *Stop complaining* and *Do you know how much that cost me?*

Even when the trophies stopped, the pageants kept coming. And now I'm eighteen, older than my mom was when she had me, and I'm still trying to make it up to her. Deep down, I'm scared I never will. That every breath I take for the rest of my life will belong to her. That I'll never be anything more than a brain stuck inside a body more my mother's than my own. Forced to live out the life I stole from her forever.

I wake up early and go to Billy's. He isn't in yet, so I sit on the stoop and wait. I'm not even supposed to be here today. I'm due at the studio soon to help my pageant coach with her classes—a futile attempt to work off my own ever-accruing bill—so he knows something's wrong when he sees me. And even though I try to get around it, asking for extra hours or to pawn some parts from my car, he figures me out, sending me home with the breakfast sandwich he picked up on his way in and enough cash to cover all the expenses.

He calls it an advance on future pay, but we both know it isn't.

I drive real slow the whole way home, looking both ways, going under the speed limit. I come to the same stop sign where I collided with Morgan and can't help but think of the way her lips curved up when I handed her a drink. The way she squeezed my hand back when I was scared.

But then when I pull into my driveway, I hear my mom and Chuck arguing, and I remember all ten thousand reasons why I shouldn't ever talk to her again.

10

MORGAN

Ruby Thompson is avoiding me.

At first, I thought I was reading too much into it. But after nearly a week of her skipping out on eye contact and me trying not to get caught staring at her in class with puppy-dog eyes, there is no mistaking it. It's deliberate.

God, why do I always go for girls like this?

I should have learned my lesson at my old school. I *did* learn my lesson at my old school. But here I am anyway, sneaking glances at the bleachers as I run laps around the track with Lydia, hoping she shows up again. Which she hasn't, not once all week, even though her friends have been here and that guy Tyler is always practicing in the center of the field.

Real talk, Ruby could be straight. I mean, I know logically that's a possibility. A strong possibility. The strongest of possibilities ever, if we account for the captain of the lacrosse team. Maybe I'm reading too much into everything that happened. Maybe she just felt guilty for almost running me over and was trying to be polite . . . but then again, maybe I'm reading things exactly right, and that's the problem. Maybe she's scared.

I glance at the Ruby-less bleachers again, just as Lydia laughs and pulls ahead at the last second. We both cross the line and bend over, hands on our hips as we try to catch our breath.

"You're eleven seconds late, Matthews," Coach barks as she walks over. I rub my hip without thinking about it, and she raises her eyebrows. "You still sore?"

"No, Coach," I lie, straightening up. "I'm good."

She scribbles something down on the pages of her clipboard. "I want you to rest it. Take the weekend off."

"I don't need to."

"I'm not asking; I'm telling." Coach looks me in the eye before turning her attention to Lydia. "Good work today, Ramírez."

"Ugh," Lydia groans after Coach walks away. "Running without you this weekend is going to be so boring. Allie can never keep up."

"At least you get to go." I sigh. Missing even our unofficial runs makes me want to crawl out of my skin.

"Hey, a day or two off from running isn't the end of the

world. We all see how hard you're trying not to limp in front of us."

"Am not."

Lydia arches an eyebrow. "I'm still not buying that whole 'stepped off a curb weird' excuse you gave Coach."

I shrug because this is like the fifth time she's tried and failed to sniff out the truth. "Guess I just bruise easy?" I say as I sneak another glance at the bleachers.

"Who are you looking for?" Allie asks, trotting over to join us. "Is your brother coming?" She flashes a hopeful smile. She's been semi-crushing on Dylan since coming over after practice a few days ago to hang out. It would probably be disturbing if Dylan actually noticed. Fortunately, he's completely oblivious. And I'm pretty sure he's super into this woman who brings her three-year-old into his shop for haircuts—even if he won't admit it yet.

"Sorry to disappoint, but he's working until seven today."

"Then who?" she asks, a puzzled expression on her face as she follows my line of sight.

"I don't know what you're talking about. I was just zoning out." Crap. I didn't think I was being that obvious.

"Maybe she's looking for the reason she gained eleven seconds on the eight hundred today," Lydia says.

"No, she's definitely looking for *someone*." Allie taps her chin. "If it's not your dashing big brother . . . Ohh! Is it someone from Pride Club?" She studies my face. "Oh my god, you *did* meet somebody, didn't you? Were they supposed to come watch today?"

"I didn't." I shake my head. "Well, technically, I did, but not the way you mean. Trust me, I'm not seeing anybody. And nobody came here to see me."

"Well, obviously, or I wouldn't have epically beaten you," Lydia says. "I've seen you show off before, and that wasn't it."

"I was holding back! It was just a training run."

"Wait, you seriously beat Morgan?" Allie's full-on transitioned to sprinter now, which means she practices on the other side of the track. Guess she missed Lydia's *just barely passed me as we crossed the line at the same time,* supposedly "epic" win.

"I did and it was awesome," Lydia says.

I throw up my hands. "I was holding back!"

"Uh-huh. Fine, keep your secrets for now, but I'll find out. I know, like, every out girl in the school. Oooh, but what if she's not out?" Allie whispers to Lydia conspiratorially, "What if she's like you? Most people don't even know about you."

Lydia rolls her eyes. "Just because I'm not *out* out, doesn't mean I'm not *not* out."

Allie and I just blink at her.

"You know what I mean." Lydia groans.

"I'm just saying, maybe Morgan's mystery girl is 'not *out* out' but 'not *not* out' too."

"There's no mystery girl," I insist, my cheeks getting hot, because not only is Ruby Thompson not *out* out, by all accounts and indications she may not even have anything to come out about. But the way her hand slipped against my skin . . .

"Uh-huh." Allie laughs.

"Look, just drop it, okay?"

They seem to sense my shift in mood, and Allie immediately goes back to complaining about how it must somehow be a violation of her constitutional rights for Coach to force sprinters to do weekly distance runs. She's five minutes into rambling about the difference in stride lengths when my phone goes off.

It's a text from Aaron telling me that he and a few other kids are meeting up at the diner later and offering to pick me up if I want to come. I text back that I totally do, but I'd rather just ride my bike there. It's not like this town is that big, and as crappy as it probably is to say, I want an out if things get awkward. Other than a few random texts this week, I've barely talked to him, and if there's one thing I learned after the St. Mary's debacle, it is to always have an exit plan. Better to bring a bike and wish I hadn't than to sit through two awkward car rides with a stranger.

Lydia leans over my shoulder, reading my texts. "Oh, fun, I love that diner. And Aaron is really nice. I think you'll get along for sure."

I glance up at her. "You and Allie want to come with? I mean, I know it's just kids from Pride Club, but I don't think they'd care. And it's not like you wouldn't fit right in."

Her face falls. "No, I can't tonight. But thanks?"

"Okay," I say, more than a little disappointed. "I guess I'll just see you tomorrow, then."

"No, you won't," Lydia teases. "Because you're banned from running, and I expect you to spend the entire weekend on the couch resting."

"Don't remind me."

. . .

Aaron and Anika beat me to the diner, along with two other kids I recognize from Pride Club but haven't really gotten a chance to talk to. Anika is in one of my classes, but I deleted all my socials when I moved, and we've yet to exchange numbers. The others I've really only seen in the halls.

They scoot over to make room for me as Aaron gestures toward us with his french fry, like a conductor leading a band. "Morgan, you remember Brennan and Drew, right?"

"Yeah, hey, guys," I say, and I'm met with warm smiles and half waves as I slide into my seat.

"How's life?" Aaron asks.

"Fine, I guess," I say as the waitress brings out plates of chicken fingers and quesadillas to go with our apparently bottomless fries. I spin around to ask her for ketchup, which is when I notice Ruby sitting with a few of her friends at the counter. We make eye contact and I smile, but she just slowly turns her stool away.

"We usually split apps," Drew says, saving me from spending any more time staring at the side of Ruby's head. "But if that freaks you out, feel free to order or skip."

I grab a chicken tender and tear a piece off, calculating what my share of the bill will be and praying I brought enough cash. Mom and Dad have been sending money to Dylan for taking care of me, and he's been giving some to me, but I feel bad spending it knowing how much they're paying the lawyers. I feel like I should be paying *them*, honestly.

Aaron is still looking at me, though, and I realize belatedly he probably wants more than a "Fine, I guess" answer to his "How's life?" question.

"I miss my old friends and school and life." I sigh. "But I really like the track team here, Allie and Lydia especially. I tried to get them to come here tonight, but . . ." I don't miss the look shared between Aaron and Anika. "What?"

"Nothing."

"No, really. What did I miss?" Everyone at the table suddenly becomes extremely interested in their food and phones.

"Nothing important," Anika says.

I shift in my seat, clearly uncomfortable.

Anika looks at Brennan, who just shrugs. "It's just you were right at the meeting. School athletes don't really hang out with us. So I wouldn't take it personally that they don't come. You're more the exception than the rule."

I roll my eyes. "They're not like that. Allie and Lydia are, like, the furthest thing from being stuck-up I've ever seen, and I dealt with that a lot at my old school."

"Wait, who said anything about being stuck-up?" Aaron asks, scrunching his face up.

My ears get hot because I just assumed . . . "I thought you meant they wouldn't come because of some snotty sports popularity thing?"

Brennan puts his hand on my arm. "I don't know what the social hierarchy was like at your old school, but the teams aren't necessarily at the top of the food chain here."

"Oh, okay. Sorry," I mumble into my glass of water.

"You *are* half-right, though," Drew says.

"I don't—"

"They're not like that. But they're also not like you," he continues. "Allie's sweet, but this is so not her scene. And Lydia, well, she's the queen of *I can neither confirm nor deny—* so don't expect her to be hitting up Pride Club meetings and hanging out after school wearing a pin that says *ANGRY LESBIAN.*"

I reach for the lapel of my denim jacket, touching my pin with a laugh. "Yeah, I guess I'm not super subtle." Not anymore, at least. In fact, this pin graduated from desk drawer to favorite jacket right after my parents left last weekend.

"You came here already out too," Drew says. "Of course they're going to give you more latitude or whatever. But just because most of the student population is cool with a new student being out doesn't mean they're going to be cool with it when it's someone they've been sharing crayons with since kindergarten. Trust me, I know."

"I had people change their lockers in gym after I came out because they thought they were, like, god's gift to queer girls or something and I wouldn't be able to resist staring at them." Anika huffs. "And that's just losers from gym class. It's probably twenty times worse when it's a teammate."

"But your school—*our* school," I correct myself, "has an active Pride Club! It's even openly advertised! There's so much more support here than at St. Mary's. I thought it was different here."

Drew nods, swirling his quesadilla through a dollop of

sour cream. "Well, it is, probably, for you at least. But the reality is that this place is kind of a dead zone when it comes to liberal ideals. Like the town puts on a good show, but it's still pretty conservative underneath the rainbow flag stickers they slapped on some of the businesses. A lot of the adults here are still stuck in the stone age, and that kind of trickles down to their kids. If your parents are shitheads, you're going to feel a lot freer to be a shithead yourself. And if your parents are shitheads and you happen to be gay, I promise you're going to be a hell of a lot less loud about it."

"Well, that's garbage," I say, maybe a little too loud as I shred my chicken finger to bits. I did not come out at my old school just to be shoved back in the closet at this one. "Is it really so radical to think people should be able to date who they want without having to hide or transfer or sue somebody?"

"Hey, hey, you're preaching to the choir here," Anika says.

I sneak a peek behind me just to see if maybe Ruby heard me and was going to, I don't know, jump out of her chair agreeing. I look away quickly when I'm met with a glare.

"You should come down to the center," Aaron says.

"The center?"

"Yeah, there's an LGBTQ+ resource center outside of town, near the college. One of the things we do there is peer counseling, and there are a couple athletes who would probably really benefit from your story. You should talk to Ms. Ming—she's the one that coordinates volunteers. It counts for Honor Society hours too, if you need them."

"See, the town isn't all garbage," Anika pipes up, slurping the last of her soda through a straw. "It's just *mostly* garbage."

"The center sounds cool," I say. "I'd love to feel like I'm doing *something* to help. Right now, it's like my parents and their lawyers are doing everything and I'm just along for the ride."

"Awesome," Aaron says. "I think you'd be a super-good fit. I'm going to be there Sunday if you want to come."

"Yeah, sounds great." I smile and grab another fry, letting the conversation drift on to other things. I'm just scraping the last bit of ketchup up when Ruby walks by, heading toward the bathroom.

I get up to follow her without thinking. I mean, I *should* wash my hands after touching all that greasy food, right? Right.

"Are you stalking me now?" Ruby asks, narrowing her eyes in the mirror when I step inside the ladies' room. She's fixing her makeup, sliding an inky black line across her eyelid with near-surgical precision.

"No." *Kind of.*

"Right." She doesn't look convinced.

I rush into one of the stalls and bolt the door behind me. I really didn't think past coming in here. I guess I just wanted to see if she would look at me the way she did at my house the other day—as if I was someone she kind of liked instead of someone she couldn't stand.

Except she didn't look at me like that at all, and now we're surrounded by automatic flushing toilets and the scent of wet paper towels and bad air freshener. This is not how I imagined it going. Maybe the fact that I imagined it going anywhere at all was a major error on my part.

"You know I can see your shoes by the door, right?" she asks. "I know you're just standing there. If you came in here to say something, just say it. Otherwise quit being creepy."

"Oh," I say, because that's not embarrassing at all. Why is this so hard?

Maybe because when I finally put my heart on the line for Sonia Delecourte—after our third date, mind you—she told me kissing me was just an experiment, just to see if she liked it, which she didn't.

And then the next day she ran and told the headmaster that I came on to her.

And then I was called up for a conduct meeting.

It's been a long, painful series of "and thens" ever since, which somehow led me to this moment, standing in a toilet stall, possibly making the same mistake all over again.

"Look, if you're gearing up to sue me or whatever for hitting you, just tell me. I don't have time to stress over this anymore." I hear her zip up her purse. "I have the Miss Tulip event tomorrow, and missing that last pageant seriously screwed stuff up. I have to focus on that, and not *Why is Matthews lurking in a bathroom stall?*"

Wait, does she seriously still think I might sue her? Is *that* why she's avoiding me? Not because she's weirded out but because she's worried? Hope surges up into my throat as I slam the lock back and practically fall out of the stall.

"I'm not going to sue you. I just want to—"

But I've missed my chance. The door clicks shut behind her as the smile slips off my face.

Then I see it: her eyeliner pen, forgotten beside the sink. And a blooming, wild sense of hope surges, because tomorrow's a new day, a day I have off . . . a day that I know right where she'll be.

And I have some eyeliner to return.

11

RUBY

The last thing I expect to see as I step forward to be crowned second runner-up in the Miss Tulip event is Morgan friggin' Matthews sitting in the third row of this rapidly overheating pop-up tent thing the town dug up from somewhere. She gives me a little smile and wave, and I nearly stumble as I collect my roses and sash, because what the hell, Morgan?

It was weird enough that she followed me into the bathroom last night, but this is next level. What is she doing? Is this some kind of revenge for last weekend? Is she gonna serve me papers in front of this whole audience? I mean, I googled her. I know her parents are willing to sue anything that moves.

Shit, I thought it was bad enough she's been hanging out with my neighbor Aaron, which means I'm inevitably going to run into her going next door someday. I never thought I'd have to worry about her popping up here too.

My fake smile falters for half a second, and I fight the urge to lick the Vaseline off my teeth. I flick my eyes to Mom instead, trying to ground myself in her presence. She's standing up now, her fingers stuck into the corners of her mouth, pulling her lips up like an extra-deranged version of the Joker. I smile bigger, letting my perfectly bleached teeth have their moment in the spotlight, my red lipstick pulled tight as I clutch my roses.

The host keeps going, deeming Lily Carter first runner-up and crowning Melanie Cho the new Miss Tulip, and I stay frozen, staring blankly at the back of the tent, making my mother proud. Beside me Lily takes my hand and squeezes. Pageant speak for *help me not lose it.*

I let myself, for one second, remember when it was Morgan's hand in mine, and then I stuff it back down. She's not here for any *good* reason. There won't be any more hand-holding. There *can't* be.

"Dammit," Lily says, the second we leave the stage. "I thought I had this one."

Lily and I have been doing pageants together since we were babies. In another life, one where my mom wasn't inherently suspicious of everything and everyone, we'd probably be best friends.

As it stands now, we're more like very polite coworkers.

"Sorry, Lil," I say as we head to the dressing area. "I thought you had it too."

She shrugs and disappears into a blur of taffeta and crying

girls, and I head straight for the corner where I stashed my stuff earlier. If I can get out of the changing room and into my car as soon as possible, I'll minimize the risk of both my mother coming backstage and melting down (a frequent and embarrassing occurrence) *and* having to find out whatever horrible reason Morgan has for being here. (Which has to be bad. Because, why else?)

I get changed as quickly as possible and grab my kit, pushing past a dozen or so girls. I give Melanie a quick congratulatory hug, wiping her obligatory happy tears off my cheek, and yank open the curtain separating us from the rest of the tent. Then I lift an emergency flap and duck out the back.

"Hey," Morgan says the second I'm outside. And shit, we're alone here. Behind the tent. Where no one goes. How did she . . . ?

"Just get it over with," I say, holding out my hand. I've never actually been served with papers before, but I imagine alone behind a tent works just as well as standing in my driveway.

Morgan scrunches up her face. "Okay."

She slaps something into my hand, but it's definitely not paper. It's my lucky eyeliner, the only real splurge that's just mine. They don't even sell it at Walmart; I have to order it straight from Sephora. I was freaking out all morning looking for it.

"Where'd you find this?"

"You left it at the diner yesterday."

"And you came all the way here just to give it back?" I tilt my head. "Why?"

Morgan looks at the ground, toeing a patch of dead grass. "I wanted to thank you for the other day. For taking care of me when I was hurt. I know you missed a pageant, and they seem really important to you. I was hoping this would make us even?"

And that is so misguidedly sweet that my stomach does a little flip.

"Thanks," I say, turning to go. "For my eyeliner and for not suing me."

"Still with the suing? Why would I?"

I look back at her, eyebrows up. "I hit you with my car."

"I fell, remember?" she says with a little smile. "You just happened to be there."

I shake my head. "What's your deal, Matthews?"

"No deal."

"Did you *really* drive all the way out here just to give me this?" I ask, holding up the eyeliner pen.

She shrugs. "Maybe I also wanted to see who the new Flower Princess was going to be. Seems like crucial information to have now that I live here."

I smile; I can't help it. "Miss Tulip," I correct her. "And it's Melanie Cho."

Her eyes crinkle a little as she leans forward, close enough that I can feel the heat of her skin against my cheek. Her breath against my ear. My heart thudding so hard I swear the whole world can hear it.

"You should have won," she says.

I swallow hard. "I—"

"Ruby, I have been standing out there waiting for you.

What are you doing?" I jerk back to find my mother walking up beside us, her face pinched.

I nearly drop my dress. "Nothing!"

"Who's your friend?"

"Just someone from school." I shift slightly between them.

"I'm Morgan," she says, holding out her hand around me and clearly missing the point.

My mom shakes it, a skeptical look on her face. "Ruby's never invited any school friends to her pageants before."

"Oh, well, I wasn't invited, per se. I—"

"We're just about done," I say, cutting Morgan off. "I'll meet you by the car, Mom?"

My mother stares at me for a second before pulling the dress out of my hands and turning toward the parking lot. "Don't be long."

"Your mom seems nice," Morgan says as soon as she's out of earshot.

And, shit, that fake politeness—that attempt to pretend my mother was anything but rude—is mortifying. I drop my chin. "Why are you really here, Matthews?"

"I just wanted to return your—"

"Well, you did. So I guess that's it, then?" I try to make my voice sound hard.

The surprise—and hurt—on Morgan's face makes my head buzz. I hate this. So much.

But not as much as I hate the talk I know I'll be getting from my mom on the way home.

"Yeah, I guess it is." She looks pissed. And, oh god, I deserve that.

"Who was that you were you talking to?" my mom asks when we're halfway home. "You two seemed friendly." I don't miss the accusation in her voice.

"Just someone from school, like I said," I mumble, because if there's one thing I definitely don't want to talk about with her, it's Morgan Matthews.

"What was she doing there?"

I sigh. "She was just returning something I forgot at the diner last night. My eyeliner."

"You two were standing awfully close."

"I couldn't hear what she was saying. It was really noisy back there."

Mom hums a little to herself and looks out the window. "I just don't want anyone to get ideas about you, Ruby. I know how you get."

How I get.

I squeeze my hands a little tighter on the steering wheel, remembering when I was thirteen and my mother decided I was getting a little too close to Katie Seawell, a frequent flier on the pageant scene just like me. Katie was different from the other girls, at least to me. Her smiles looked real, and she laughed loud and often. I couldn't decide if I wanted to be her best friend or if I just wanted to be *her*. I'd find excuses to make sure we always got ready together. We'd fix each other's makeup and make fun of the judges, and it was . . . nice.

After a particularly tough loss, my mom came backstage

and caught her wiping my tears and telling me over and over again that I was beautiful and that it would all be okay. And maybe it would have been if my mom had gotten enough sleep, or if Billy hadn't just left, or if I hadn't let my latest celebrity "girl crush" slip over breakfast. But she didn't, and he did, and I hadn't yet learned the importance of keeping my mouth all the way shut.

That's when it was decided that I was no longer allowed to get ready with the other girls. Or ever talk to Katie again. After that I just kind of shut myself off, and all the other pageant girls learned to stay away.

Mom taps her nail against the armrest and then fixes her gaze on me. "Enough about that, though. Would've loved to see you get a win today."

"Sorry." I keep my eyes steady on the road, clenching my jaw ever so slightly.

"You hesitated during your interview."

"I didn't hesitate; I was being thoughtful."

"It looked more like you didn't know what to say."

I bite my tongue until it hurts and then force out a smile. "I did know, though. I paused, Mom. I didn't hesitate."

"You need more sessions with Charlene if we're going to take this to the next level," she says. "And you were sloppy during talent too. Maybe we can get some private tap lessons, because those group classes don't seem to be working."

I shake my head, swallowing down the truth that it's not the tap lessons, it's me. I can barely stand to practice anymore. Every clap of my shoe against the floor makes me feel like one of those marionette puppets, with my mother holding all the strings.

"I never did like group lessons," Mom continues. "If you want to excel—"

"We can't afford private lessons right now, and besides, they told me last time that they won't take any more post-dated checks." I sigh. "Maybe there isn't a next level for me."

"I'm not throwing away your future just because we're broke. I'll pick up extra shifts if I have to. We both know I'm sitting next to the future Miss America right now."

I rub my hand over my forehead and let it drop. Because every time she says "throwing away your future," the *like I had to when I had you* is implied. Nothing like spending another Saturday afternoon feeling guilty for being born.

"Hey," she says, messing with the strap of her purse, "I just want more for you."

"There's no way I'll make it to—"

"You deserve to have what I didn't."

And what she didn't have was a lucrative career as a beauty queen, apparently. Mom was winning every pageant she entered the year she got pregnant with me, and she had her sights set on Miss Teen USA. She was somehow even more beautiful then, before her mom kicked her out and cut her off, before my dad left her six months pregnant and alone, before the weight of the world fought with Father Time to press creases into her skin.

Maybe I do owe her my future for stealing hers, no matter

how much I wish I could get lost inside of an old muscle car and never look back.

"What if I'm not supposed to be Miss America?" I ask, like a prisoner begging for a key. "I haven't won anything in ages. Not even the mall pageants, which don't count. I don't even think I'd *qualify* for a state competition."

"Oh, Ruby," she says, patting my leg. "Don't ever doubt yourself, baby."

"I . . ." I trail off, letting the misunderstanding ride. There's never any use talking to her about this. But how does she not see it? How?

"I know we don't have as much as some of the other girls, but you've got a mom that loves you and will do anything to get you where you need to be," she says, tucking some of my hair behind my ear. "And that's half the battle."

I nod and turn up the radio, hoping a little music will drown out all the chaos in my head. I'll be working off this debt as long as I live.

"Speaking of, I've got good news!" she says, twisting in her seat so fast I almost slam on my brakes.

"What good news?"

"I was able to register you for the county pageant after all."

"You what?" The deadline was yesterday, and I know we can't afford it. It's one of the more expensive ones.

"There was money left over from last week."

"That was for the electric bill." I groan. "How'd you get them to turn us back on, then?"

"Chuck put it in his name, said he's subletting the place. I put a little toward our closed account and the rest toward the registration fee."

"That money could have brought us current!"

"That's not for you to worry about," she says, like it's that simple. "You want something that will qualify you for state. Well, here it is."

"That's not what I meant," I say through gritted teeth.

"This could open up a lot of doors for us, Ruby. A lot. You're already the right age for Miss America, baby. Now we just gotta get you those titles, and this is a great first step."

"This one doesn't actually seem so bad," Everly says, sliding the laptop across her bed. She's got the county pageant website pulled up.

"It doesn't matter, Ev."

"But this one has a prize that your mom can't ruin for you." Shame heats my belly. No matter how much I try to keep her out of it, Everly always sees through the bullshit straight to how bad things are.

"Doubtful," I say.

"Well, if she did, that would be really impressive, because it's a scholarship to Hudson Community College for the top six finishers, *and* it includes a stipend for the dorms. It could get you out of your mom's house for good." She taps the screen. "This could be your way out."

"I can't leave my mom."

"She'd be fine, Ruby."

"Okay, in that case, let me just get right on crushing her dreams and abandoning her like everyone else has because Everly Jones said she'd be fine." I'm being dramatic, but I can't help it.

"What about your dreams?"

"I don't have any of those." I smirk, clicking her laptop shut.

She rolls her eyes and flops down beside me, looking at me out of the corner of her eye. "You're such a liar."

"Come on, I'm about as likely to go to college as I am to win Miss America. You and I are not the same."

"Ruby, I love you, but cut it out. I take pictures of people when they're not looking. You restore cars and keep them running. If one of us is more equipped to have a career, it's not me."

"You really think so?" I ask because I never really thought of it that way.

She crosses her arms and stares at me until I reluctantly agree that she *maybe* has a point, and then I reopen her laptop to distract her with Netflix movies.

But later, after Marcus comes over with a pizza and everyone but me is asleep, I click back over to read about the scholarship. Because my guidance counselor did mention once that Hudson had a killer automotive tech program. And if I *did* have a dream, it would probably be that.

I always figured I would end up working at a gas station or something, scrapping parts for Billy in between pageants with Mom. It didn't seem like "more" was really an option. But Everly is right; the prize covers tuition plus room and board in the new student housing building they put up last year. Finishing even top six could be tough in a county-wide pageant, but it might be doable if I *really* try. I click through to the website, trying to find the loophole or fine print, but it all looks legit.

It even says I can apply for grants to cover my textbooks and meals, but I don't need all that. Books maybe, but I've been living on ramen and vitamins for as long as I can remember anyway. I'm sure I could get enough side work at Billy's to at least cover that. And I'd be close enough to keep an eye on my mom. Maybe we could compromise even, like I still do some local pageants or whatever. Maybe this *could* be the first step, just not in the way she meant.

Everly snuffles and rolls over, and I power down her laptop, powering down my dreams right along with it. It was stupid to even think about. I've got responsibilities. I've got a duty. I've got . . . too much energy right now and no place to put it.

I pull out my phone and type out a text. Tyler replies right away.

12

MORGAN

Aaron's standing near a white woman who looks to be about thirty, by what appears to be a hastily arranged bookshelf, when I walk into the center.

Dylan enthusiastically dropped me off on his way to work, calling me "quite the joiner" and telling me he was "proud of me" and to "get in there and change lives" until it got embarrassing. I essentially had to shoo him out of the parking lot just now. If I'm being honest, though, I maybe didn't totally mind it. I think I needed some positive reinforcement after the way Ruby played Ping-Pong with my emotions yesterday.

"Morgan!" Aaron's face lights up. He sets down a pile of books and comes over to give me a welcoming hug. "You made it!"

"Wouldn't have missed it," I say. "Thanks for inviting me."

"For sure! Um, this is Izzie." He points to the woman, who looks slightly exasperated when a few books fall over beside her. "And, Izzie, this is Morgan."

"Hi, Morgan. Sorry, for the mess. We got a pile of new donations this month, and I'm trying to get everything organized." She blows some of her dark brown hair out of her eyes. "It's so nice to finally meet you. Aaron really talked you up."

"I'd love to help out here however I can." I eye one book in particular that has a boy and a dog on the front covered in what appear to be . . . Post-its? "All these books were donated? That's awesome."

"Yes, we have some very generous patrons. Each book features a main character that falls under the LGBTQ+ umbrella. You're always welcome to borrow the books yourself, if something catches your eye."

"Cool," I say, picking it up. "I definitely will."

"Perfect. I know the end of the year can be stressful on students; it's always good to sneak in some self-care," she says. "The library is available any time we're open, and it's an honor system, so no need to sign them out or anything. We trust you." She leans closer. "And honestly, if some of them don't make it back, we don't mind—as long as they find a good home."

I grin because that's ridiculously cool. I'm the type of person that would 200 percent return every book I borrowed—I don't even crack spines or dog-ear pages—but I'm kind of obsessed with the idea that if a kid really fell in love with one, it would be okay if they kept it forever.

"So, what exactly *do* you guys do here?" I ask.

"What don't we do?" Aaron says.

"He's right; we handle a little bit of everything." Izzie shrugs. "Counseling, support, school visits. We help with the establishment of Pride Clubs and Gay Straight Alliances in places that don't have them—Aaron and I actually set up the one at your school with Ms. Ming. We help put teens in touch with the resources they need if they're in an unsafe living situation. But we also handle Pride Proms and other fun events—"

"It's kind of your one-stop shop when it comes to the gay." Aaron throws up some finger guns, and I try not to laugh. "Come on, we'll show you around."

I look in each room dutifully as they point out the director's office, the lounge, the kitchen area, the main rooms, the peer counseling space, and the playground in the backyard, like they're trying to convince me how great it is or something. But I already knew before I got here that I was definitely in.

"So what exactly would I be doing as a peer counselor?"

"Peer counselors are students who volunteer here, either for National Honor Society hours, or simply because they want to," Izzie says. "We match them with other teens that we feel would benefit from their experiences—and often it turns into a mutually beneficial match. Our counselors tend to get as much out of it as they give.

"If you're interested, we'd have you study our online handbook, and we'd run a background check, of course. We'll have you sit in on a few sessions with Aaron or myself until you feel comfortable. Aaron is our senior peer counselor, so he's always here to help answer your questions or partner with you for a difficult session."

"So we just . . . talk?"

"Sort of," Aaron says. "Sometimes people come in and just want someone to listen to them. Other times, they want advice. You'll get the feel for it as you go."

Izzie tilts her head. "I actually already have someone in mind I'd like to pair you with. I think it would be an excellent match given both of your histories."

"The football player?" Aaron asks.

She nods. "We have a boy that comes here every so often, an athlete like yourself."

"He gives us a fake name every time but doesn't seem to remember it, so it's never the same," Aaron says. "Definitely doesn't go to our school, so who knows how far he travels. Some people come a long way to get here—less of a risk of someone you know seeing you walk in."

"I get it. I hate it, but I get it," I say.

"I think you would be in a unique position to give him advice."

"Yeah," I say. "I really want to find a way to work with student athletes. It's messed up. People don't understand the challenges we face if they haven't lived them."

"Well, I think you'll find working at the center a great first step in your advocacy. You'll be able to get your feet wet helping people one-on-one."

"That sounds great."

"Welcome aboard, then," she says. "Aaron can get you set up with an online log-in to review all the material. He has an appointment later this afternoon too, if you have time to stay."

"I do," I say, wanting to get going on this stuff as soon as possible, to feel like I'm doing something that matters for once, instead of hiding behind my parents and lawyers.

Later on, after sitting in on an appointment with Aaron and this girl Caroline, filling out copious amounts of paperwork, and taking a couple online quizzes, I am officially a peer counselor. I still have to sit in on a few more sessions while we wait for my background check to clear, and Izzie is going to be dropping in on me once I start counseling on my own, but it feels like a big step.

At the end of the day, when my brother gets home with celebratory cake, he gives me the biggest hug.

"What's that for?" I ask when he finally lets me go.

"Nothing," he says. "I'm just glad you're my sister."

13

RUBY

Charlene smiles when I walk into the studio that she shares with her twin sister, June. She's tall, nearly five eleven, with gleaming white teeth and dark hair dyed to hide the gray. Over thirty years removed from her Miss USA title, and a bit older and softer than she used to be, she's still a force to be reckoned with on the pageant circuit.

"Hello, Ruby," she says. "You're a little early."

"I know." I duck my head. "I was hoping we could talk."

"Of course. Why don't we talk in my office before your students get here?" She sets the papers she's holding down at reception desk and heads toward the back.

Charlene isn't just my pageant coach; she's also sort of my boss. She and her sister run a small but respected business—Charlene runs the pageant coaching side, and June offers ballet and modern dance. There was so much overlap in their clients it just made sense to open up shop together.

I follow Charlene into the smaller of the two offices—she says it's her curse for being three minutes younger—and take a seat across from her.

"What can I do for you today, love?"

"I want to win the county pageant." The words slice out of me, feeling more like an admission of guilt than a declaration of intent. "I was wondering if you'd be willing to do some extra lessons with me if I pick up more classes to work it off. I know I'm barely covering what we already owe you, but I *need* this."

"May I ask why?"

"I need it to be eligible for state, and I need to win state to get to Miss America." I hate lying to Charlene, but I can't risk her telling my mother the truth—that while she sees this as an important first step, I see it as an escape hatch on an otherwise sinking ship.

Charlene shifts forward in her seat, studying my face. I fight the urge to shrink down, conjuring my best pageant posture instead. "You can't bullshit a bullshitter," she says, steepling her hands.

"I'm not," I force out. "I need your help." At least that part's true.

"We both know that's your mom's dream, not yours."

"Please." I can feel it slipping away. The door slamming in my face. No automotive program. No way out. It'll be third-rate mall pageants and county fairs for the rest of my life.

Charlene sighs. "June's assistant is out on maternity leave. I was going to bring on a sub, but if you can be a second set of eyes on the Struts & Strides classes, along with teaching your usual makeup lessons, we can call it even. One private lesson a week plus homework, but you have to mean it, Ruby. You've been phoning it in for years. If your mother hadn't been one of my best students, I would've dropped you already. I know what you're capable of. I know what's in your DNA. It could all be yours if you wanted it bad enough."

"Yeah." I look down, rubbing at a spot of grease staining the edge of my thumb. How come everybody seems to know what's in my DNA but me?

"Now go get ready. The girls are going to be here soon for your class, and we've got the six-to-eight-year-olds coming in for Struts & Strides after. You stay for both, and we can start your extra lessons next week."

"Deal," I say, shaking her hand. I was planning to go to Billy's after, but I'll shoot him a text letting him know I can't. A short-term loss for a long-term gain.

14

MORGAN

I'm flopped over a bright red barber chair in my brother's shop, watching him sweep the black-and-white checkerboard floor. He just finished cutting all my hair off—well, he left a little on the top, enough to say it's a pixie cut or whatever when Mom calls later. The fact that he also dyed it pink is something I may need to . . . ease my parents into. God knows it would never have been allowed at my old school. Even Dylan was hesitant at first, but when I said I'd just do it at home with some bleach and Kool-Aid, his little hair-loving heart got on board real quick.

I could tell by his smile when he dusted off all the stray hairs and spun me around to face the mirror that he loves it just as much as I do.

But still, even though cutting off my hair and dyeing it a color I could only daydream about before *feels* exciting, like a real, actual change, deep down I know it's not. Or at least, it's not enough of one.

I toe my chair around in lazy circles. Next to me, Dylan's best friend, Owen, is shaving a hard part into a twelve-year-old's hair while the kid's mom and sister watch from a row of subway seats along the wall. Owen and Dylan met in barber school and became "accelerated best friends" as Dylan says. They may not have known each other forever, but apparently the intensity of barber school creates a bond. They went their separate ways right after, but the second they could afford to open a shop together, they did.

I spin the chair around a few more times with a sigh. Dylan cocks an eyebrow and shoves my foot out of the way as he slides the broom under my chair. "You know, if you're so bored, you can sweep up your own hair."

"I'm not that bored."

"Then what?" Owen asks, pulling the smock off the boy and brushing the hair from his neck. "Because your sighing is scaring the customers."

The boy looks at Owen when he says that, and the mom laughs and hands him some cash before disappearing out the door.

"See, look how fast they ran out of here," Dylan says, resting his arm and chin on his broom. "Okay, I'll bite. What's up?"

"Don't get all fatherly on me." I snort.

"First of all, when has Dad ever said *What's up?* Second of all, I'm not getting fatherly, I'm getting brotherly, which became my right when you filled my spare room with all your stuff."

"Oh, like you don't love having me here," I tease.

"I didn't say that. I said having you here gives me the right to pry."

"It's true," Owen adds. "It's in the brotherly bylaws."

"Hmm," I say, "I haven't seen any bylaws."

"Well, you wouldn't have, because you're a sister."

I suck in my lips and let them out with a *pop*. "You know, sometimes I feel like I could search the entire world and still never find two bigger dorks than the ones standing right in front of me."

"Morgan," my brother says, "enough deflecting. What's got you sighing and throwing yourself over my chairs like a Disney princess?"

I don't want to say it, really. I kind of just want to let this moment of levity sink into my bones until I don't care anymore. But it's Dylan, and I tell him everything—regardless of the "brotherly bylaws."

"Honestly?"

"Honestly," he says.

"It turns out a lot of the kids here don't feel any safer about coming out than they did at St. Mary's. Especially the ones who play sports. I guess once I finish my training, I'm getting partnered with some football player who drives, like, forever to get to the center. And then there's Lydia, who won't even come to a Pride Club meeting even though there are straight allies there. She's stuck in this half-in/half-out gray area, and it sucks."

Owen tilts his head. "Did she tell you it sucks?"

"Well, no," I say, spinning toward him. "But I've been there before, and I know it does."

Dylan narrows his eyes. "If she doesn't seem bothered by it, then I would worry less about her and more about the kids who want to come out but feel like they can't."

"And I'll find them all how?"

"It sounds like you've already found one through the center, and you've barely even started."

I sigh. It's a fair point, but . . . "It doesn't seem like enough, though. I made this big stand at my old school, and now I'm here and it feels like nothing's really different. It's the same stuff, just a different setting."

"Well, it's changing for St. Mary's, thanks to your lawsuit."

"Maybe. And again, that's *one* school."

"It could help a lot of kids in the future, maybe set a precedent statewide."

"Something tells me even if they put out an official *we tolerate gay kids* policy at St. Mary's, no one's going to feel super comfortable coming out at an ultraconservative private Catholic school. I want to do more than just change things on paper."

"I know," Dylan says. "And that's why I think helping out at the center is going to be really good for you."

"Yeah. Probably."

"Wait," Owen says. "That doesn't sound convincing."

Dylan scrunches up his forehead. "It really doesn't."

"I think we have to double Dad her until she smiles." Owen stalks toward me.

"Oh my god, stop." I laugh.

Dylan moves beside him, and they both bring their hands to their chins in matching fake-thoughtful faces.

I roll my eyes. "I'm fine. I promise."

"I'm sorry, Morgie. That's just not good enough."

"Yeah," Owen says. "We're here for you. You got a problem, your brother dads will solve it."

I blink at them. "Nope, not doing this." But they keep staring at me with expectant faces like two golden retriever puppies who somehow manifested themselves into people right before my eyes. "You honestly think I'm gonna vomit my feelings about school and the waiver and Ruby and stuff just because you keep looking at me like that?"

"Ruby?" Dylan looks at Owen. "Wait, who's Ruby?"

"Yeah, we've definitely never heard of Ruby."

Ugh. I can't believe I let that slip. "She's no one. Just a girl from school."

Owen groans. "How do you have a girlfriend already? I've been here two years and don't have one."

"That's because you're annoying, Owen," Dylan says, clamping his hand on his shoulder. I laugh; I can't help it. "*Do you have a girlfriend, Morgan?*"

"Yeah, no. I have a person who can't decide if she likes me or hates me, but she also could be straight or so far in the closet she hasn't realized she's not yet."

"Oooooh, someone has a crush," Owen sings, clutching his heart. I resist the urge to smack him. Having one nosy brother was bad enough. How did I end up with two?

"Morgan," Dylan says, his voice getting serious. "Promise me you won't settle, okay? Find someone who respects your feelings and your time."

The *unlike the last girl you were into* is implied, but I hear it loud and clear.

I swallow hard. "Don't you both have hair to sweep?"

Because no matter how big of a crush I'm fighting, I know he's right. I won't make that mistake again. Ever. I deserve to be wooed. I deserve to know that the person I'm falling for is falling for me right back. I deserve grand gestures and romance and all that other good stuff.

If Ruby Thompson—or anyone else, for that matter—is interested in anything with me, then they're going to have to make the first move, and it's going to have to be big.

15

RUBY

I don't mean to overhear.

I wouldn't even be walking by right now, under these ominous clouds threatening to rain on me any second, if I didn't have detention for coming in late. At least it was for a good reason—Mom's car wouldn't start after her overnight shift and I had to go get her. I couldn't just leave her sitting there all day. God knows Chuck would never spend the gas.

By the time I remembered I needed an excuse, I was already late and halfway to school. Going back would have made me even later, and I would have had to wake Mom up to write it. I couldn't bear that. I know she really needs the sleep.

So I was late. Again. Automatic detention. Nothing like sitting in a little room and writing an essay about the impact of tardiness on the student body as a whole to get the blood pumping.

Then I had to meet Mrs. Morrison right after to talk about my grades. I'm not failing, thank god, but I'm not too far off. It's just that Government puts me to sleep. So does English and, okay, most classes, to be honest, except for, like, shop. I'm pretty good at lunch and gym too, to be fair. I just need to be moving, doing things with my hands. I can't concentrate when I'm sitting still.

But that doesn't matter anymore. I have to take things seriously. I have to nail *every* assignment. I have to graduate on time, not opt for summer school instead. Because I'm holding on to Everly's question like a life raft now: *What about your dreams?* And if I manage to place high enough in the pageant to win that scholarship, I don't want to lose out because of some little technicality like not actually graduating high school.

In another life, I would already be at Billy's shop troubleshooting the problem with Mom's car, or hanging out with Everly and Marcus, or doing *anything* other than walking up on Morgan Matthews and a couple of assholes from the lacrosse team, Chad and Clayton Miller. I wouldn't have heard them call her names, or seen her and that new haircut that makes her cheekbones look like cut glass in the very best way.

But I'm not that lucky. So I stop and wait to see what happens next, ducking near the field entrance just barely out of their line of sight.

I hope she walks away, because then I can too. I can just

head straight for my car like nothing ever happened. But that's not her style. That's not Morgan Matthews at all. I didn't even need Google to tell me that.

"What did you just say to me?" she asks, her hands already balled into fists.

"Isn't that what you are?" Chad asks, puffing out his chest.

"Maybe," Clayton says. "Or maybe she just needs a little dick in her life."

I roll my eyes. The twins both suck, but I've always hated Clayton a little extra. At least now I don't have to feel bad about it.

She takes a step forward, and *no, no, Morgan, go*. These are not people you talk back to. These are people you don't leave your friends alone with at parties.

"Well, you definitely are a dick," Morgan says, trying to move past them, "but I'm not interested."

"Fuck you." Clayton shoves her.

"Don't touch me!" She shoves him right back. He barely moves, a small runner no match for the oversized midfielder.

"Clayton!" I shout, jogging up to them before it can get any worse. "What the hell are you doing?"

"What do you care, Ruby? She got you on the rainbow ride now too?"

I grit my teeth and, for a half second, panic that he's actually figured out what I'm trying so hard to ignore. The thing I've worked really fucking hard to hide.

But this is Clayton. He's not clever; he's just an asshole.

"Nice," I say. "No. But if she reports you and you get suspended for this, then I have to listen to Tyler bitching for the rest of the season about losing two of his best players." I shoot him a glare that I hope looks convincing. "Now get out of here before I pop your alternator and give you something to really complain about."

"You don't always have to be such a bitch, you know?" He bumps into my shoulder as he walks by with Chad in tow. I follow them with my eyes, first to make sure they're really leaving, but mostly to give Morgan a chance to compose herself. When I finally look back at her, a small smile of relief on my face, I'm met with five feet, three inches of pure rage.

"I didn't need your help," she practically growls.

"Clearly," I say, annoyance roiling up in my head at the realization that she thinks I screwed up *again*. "You were two seconds from getting in a fistfight with a lacrosse midfielder. You definitely had things under control. Sure."

"I did." She bends down to furiously retie her shoe. "I've dealt with way worse than him."

"Yeah, not without lawyers, though."

She looks up at me, eyes flashing. "What?"

And, damn, that was kind of a low blow. I backpedal a little, rubbing my neck. "I was just trying to find your Instagram. It's not my fault a bunch of news reports popped up instead."

"Great," she says. "Does everybody know, then?"

"I mean, probably. I doubt I'm the only person who decided to google the new girl."

She opens her mouth to say something—which is the exact moment the dark clouds above us finally open, rain cascading down in sheets. Fucking perfect. We're drenched in a heartbeat, darting under the old snack bar awning to escape the worst of the downpour.

"Great." She groans, wiping the water off her face. I pull my hoodie a little tighter, doing everything I can to ignore the way the rain dips and pools over her skin. Too much skin. God, doesn't this school have a dress code? How is this tiny track uniform even allowed?

Morgan clears her throat, and, shit, who knows how long I've been staring at her legs, her neck, her arms, her . . .

"You want a ride home?" I blurt out, even though I know it's a bad idea, a colossally bad idea, an even epically worse idea now that the cold is making her—

"No, thanks," she says, and jogs out into the rain. I stand there for a second, stunned by her quick exit, before I snap to my senses.

Fine. Let her run home. See if I care. Because I don't. *I don't.*

I head to my car, slamming the door when I get in and not even caring that I'm getting the seat wet. I slide the key into the ignition, and it rumbles to life as she cuts out of the entrance to the school.

It's fine. Morgan Matthews is not my problem. She's nothing to me. Not even that new haircut can change that. She's just the newest distraction in a long line of distractions that definitely don't matter. I don't even care.

I pull out of the parking lot, trying not to think about how hard it is to see or how Morgan has a habit of running into traffic.

"Dammit," I say, tapping the brakes.

I should keep going. If she wants to run all the way home in this stupid rainstorm, I should leave her to it. So why am I stopping the car, then? Why am I popping the passenger door right as she runs by?

"I don't need your pity," Morgan calls, pausing just long enough to shout through my open door.

"It's not pity."

"Then what is it?" Her eyes meet mine, and it feels for a second like she can see right through me.

"It's . . ." I hesitate because I don't fucking know, and I can't think straight with her staring at me, soaked and shivering. How does she still look hot? This isn't fair.

"It's . . ." she says, waving her hands around like *hurry up*.

"My civic duty?"

One side of her mouth quirks up. "Your civic duty," she deadpans.

"I—"

But she's already sliding into the seat beside me, buckling up. "Seems legit."

I wait for her to shut her door, and then I hit the gas, my car bucking forward when I slam the pedal down too quickly.

"So was stalking my Instagram your civic duty too?" she asks.

Shit.

"I was . . . curious?" I flick my eyes over to gauge her reaction, but she's just staring at the road, indifferent.

"I deleted it before I moved here."

"Clearly, or else I wouldn't have had to click through to the horror that is page three of Google results."

She laughs, and it's small, and I probably shouldn't feel good about it, but I do. I grip the steering wheel a little tighter, trying to focus on the road, on the sound of my windshield wipers, on anything else that isn't the girl sitting next to me and the way all the tiny hairs on her arm are standing—

"What were you so curious about?" she asks, which feels too loaded to answer truthfully.

"Just stuff," I say finally.

She hums and looks out the window, and I feel like I failed a test.

"I was curious what you were like at your old school," I blurt out when the silence stretches too long.

"Why?"

"I was wondering if you've always been this *loud*."

"What's that supposed to mean?"

"You know what I mean." I sigh. "You're always, like, running around with Aaron or the rest of the Pride Club . . ." I try not to sound jealous when I say Aaron's name. There was a time he was one of my best friends—until my mom got involved.

"Why can't I hang out with the Pride Club?"

"You can," I say. "But, like, you're always with them, or, like, even that shirt you had on earlier—"

She glares at me. "What was wrong with my shirt?"

"It said *I CAN'T EVEN THINK STRAIGHT* in giant rainbow sequin letters."

"And?"

"I was just wondering . . . do you always have to advertise it? Because we all get it. You like girls. Have you ever tried being more like—"

"Like what?" she snaps.

"I don't know, like Lydia?"

"You mean in the closet?"

"No, just . . . why does it have to be a thing that you shove in everyone's face? The Miller twins probably wouldn't have even done that shit today if . . . I mean, I don't get why—"

"No, clearly you don't. Stop the car. I'll run from here." She pops her door open before I can even pull over.

"Jesus. Close the door. You're letting in the rain."

"No!"

I pinch the bridge of my nose. "It's not safe to be running in this!"

"Why do you even care?" Morgan shouts.

"Just please. I'll drop you off. You don't have to talk to me the rest of the ride."

"Whatever," she says, pulling her door shut as a low rumble of thunder and a flash of lightning rips through the sky.

"Thank you." We drive in silence for a while, but I can feel her watching me. Trying to figure me out maybe.

Finally, when we get to her apartment, she sighs. "What's your deal? Seriously. It's like you take everything I do personally or something. One second I think we're getting along, and the next you're tearing apart my friends and choice of clothing."

"I wasn't. I . . ." I stare ahead, trying to decide how much I'm willing to admit or if I even want to answer. "Don't you think your life would be easier if you . . . Can't you just be quiet about things sometimes? At least until you get out of here, and you're at your fancy college, where guys like Chad and Clayton can't get to you?"

"There are always going to be more guys like Chad and Clayton." She gets out of my car, pulling her backpack after her. "I'm not spending my life pretending I'm something I'm not, or making myself smaller and quieter, just because someone else thinks I should."

I shut my eyes, swallowing hard, her words spiraling around my head in ways that somehow inspire and confuse the hell out of me all at once. I look at her, words on my tongue that I don't even recognize, right as she shuts the door.

Morgan darts up the steps, flashing me a little wave that I don't return. And it's fine. It's okay. I shove the words down deep, where they can't hurt anybody, least of all me, and lift my chin. It's better this way.

I can't let one girl and her stupid perfect haircut and her

stupid perfect face and her stupid perfect brain derail the one shot I've got at making something of myself. People might be willing to look the other way for an out-of-town track star, but crowning a queer beauty queen will never be in the cards around here.

Not if people know they're doing it, anyway.

16

MORGAN

I couldn't sleep last night.

My mom called after dinner saying there was yet another complication with the "St. Mary's thing," as she's taken to calling it lately, and that my team needed another essay about what happened and the impact it had on my "emotional well-being."

Between that and my earlier conversation with Ruby, I was so riled up that I spent the next two hours writing countless drafts, until it turned from a short, professional statement into a rage-filled ten-page missive about everything effed up at St. Mary's and how the culture of conservatism and homophobia in such an elite academic atmosphere impacted not just me but other kids that I won't name out of fear for their safety. Kids that turned their backs on me so fast when things went down. Kids like Molly Valentine, my first kiss and longest friend, whose parents made her block my number before the ink was even dry on my transfer.

Turns out, spite is a powerful motivator.

But when I finally closed my laptop and regained some semblance of calmness, I *still* couldn't stop running through my conversation with Ruby. I lay in bed, tossing and turning, trying to shove all the puzzle pieces of our interactions together—though at this point I'm not even sure if they're from the same set.

By midnight, I resolved to ask her flat out. But by two a.m., the doubt slipped back. *What if you make a fool of yourself again?* it whispered. *Or worse?*

And yet this morning, I'm still searching the hallways between classes, hoping for a glimpse of her—as if seeing her again will somehow make it all make sense. Or maybe the truth is, I don't care if it all makes sense. I just want to see her. I try to will away the excitement as I walk into Government, our only shared class and the one place she can't avoid me, because I know Dylan is right. I deserve more. But...

Allie sits down beside me, and I'm only half listening as she goes over the logistics of our next meet, which I'm still not allowed to compete in. There has been absolutely no movement with my waiver—it's like St. Mary's hit pause on my entire future—but I really can't think about that right now.

I try to keep up with the conversation, nodding and saying

"uh-huh" at appropriate intervals, while keeping my eyes fixed on Ruby's empty spot, my heart thrumming double speed while I wait for her to appear.

She eventually bustles in with her headphones on, her backpack bumping against my elbow as she pushes past without so much as an apology. I want to know what she's listening to. I want to know what she likes.

My mind wanders, imagining us lying side by side, sharing her knockoff AirPods. Ruby with her hair splayed out beneath her. Me on my side, propped up on my elbow to see her better, waiting for just the right moment in the song to lean forward and—

What? Ruby mouths from across the way, her forehead crinkling. Crap, I've been staring this whole time. I look away, squirming in my seat and turning my attention to Allie.

"So, um, will Coach put Lydia in the sixteen hundred again since I'm out?"

"Hello, Morgan, welcome to the conversation." She raises her eyebrows. "Glad to know I've been talking to myself for the last five minutes."

"Sorry, I was zoning out."

"Yeah, I caught that," she says with a pointed glance in Ruby's direction. My face must look nothing short of terrified, because she quickly adds, "Or whatever," and pulls out her book. Lydia drops into the seat beside us just as the bell rings.

"Okay, class, let's get started," Mrs. Morrison says with a huge smile. "You know what today is, right?"

A couple students, including Ruby, groan in their seats. I lean toward Allie and whisper, "What's today?"

"Group project," Allie whispers back. "She's been teasing it all year. Lucky you, you transferred in just in time."

"Group project for what?" I ask, trying to figure out what we could possibly be doing for an easy class that I was told only required, like, one more essay, max.

"That's right! It's the best time of the year, teamwork time!" Mrs. Morrison continues, passing back some handouts. "For now, I'll let you choose your own groups of two or three, but if you can't figure it out, I'll assign you to one. Now, drumroll, please." She pauses, like we're actually going to do a drumroll, before continuing on.

"Okay, then, since we've been studying the different ways the American government works all semester, I'm going to ask that you choose a major act of legislation that was successfully passed from our history and explore it more deeply. You'll see a list of approved options on the handout, along with important dates. Now, remember, as you do this: I'm not just looking for information on the act itself. I want you to use your critical thinking skills, which means I want to understand context. I want to see the reasons it came to be and society's reactions to it. I want to know everything. We'll be in the research phase for the next two weeks, which will culminate in a written essay by each student—so if you're the group project slacker, I *am* going to find out—and also in a shared presentation to the class."

I glance across the way at Ruby, who is looking very

uncomfortable in her seat, and then at Allie, who's already eagerly circling acts and making notes in the margin. I look down at the page in front of me, seeing everything from the Judiciary Act of 1789 to the legalization of gay marriage.

"The presentation should run about eight to ten minutes in length," Mrs. Morrison says. "Use visual aids like a Power-Point, or write a song, recite poetry, reenact key moments! The sky's the limit!"

I scan the room. Most people are already frantically gesturing to one another to secure their groups for this exercise in ridiculousness. Who would ever voluntarily recite poetry in front of the whole class?

"Okay, I'll give you a moment to split into your groups," Mrs. Morrison says. "I also have some books up here to help you choose, although I trust you all have your phones in your pockets and thus access to Google. You have the rest of the period to settle on partners and topics, and then I want one member from each group to come up to have it recorded. If someone else has already selected your topic, you will be asked to choose another, so decide fast."

Allie grabs my arm, along with Lydia's. "Got my group," she says, and Lydia nods. "So what do we want to do? I'm thinking the National Minimum Drinking Age Act or the Animal Welfare Act, but I'm definitely open to any of the others. Those two just sounded the most fun."

I flick my eyes over to Ruby, still sitting there alone, as Lydia looks over the list. "I like the Endangered Species Act," she says.

"Ooh," Allie says, "that's another good one. What do you think, Morgan?"

"Hmm?" I ask, still watching Ruby. She doesn't get up, though, doesn't even try to join a group, and that's so frustrating. *Just get up, Ruby. Get up. Go after what you want. Is that really so hard?*

"Class, do we have any group of two willing to take on a third or a group of three that will possibly split off?" Mrs. Morrison asks after a minute or two. When no one says anything, she sighs. "Please don't make me assign groups."

Maybe I should take some of my own advice.

I shoot my hand up into the air. "I'll switch, Mrs. Morrison." I grab my stuff with a quick apology to the girls and then move next to Ruby. And yeah, maybe working on a presentation together isn't exactly the same as asking her if she *like* likes me, but it's a start. Or it would be, if Ruby didn't look so pissed right now.

"I don't need a pity partner," she grumbles. "I can do it on my own."

"It's not pity," I say, remembering her words from yesterday. "It's my civic duty."

Her lips curve up for a second, like a smile tried to escape before she thought better of it. "So which one do you want?"

"I was thinking about the Marriage Equality Act."

"Of course you were." She rolls her eyes. "And no."

"Let me guess, you want Don't Ask, Don't Tell?" I mean it as a joke, but her face goes hard.

"What's that supposed to mean?"

"I was . . . You know, what you said yesterday in the car."

She narrows her eyes.

"About me being loud and quiet being easier. It was a joke. Sorry. I just picked a super-gay one, and yesterday you were telling me to shut up about being super gay, and so the joke was—"

"Please stop talking." She sighs. "We'll do the Endangered Species Act." She says it so matter-of-factly that I almost agree right on the spot. "Almost" being the key word.

"I think Allie and Lydia want to do that one. Maybe we could do—"

"Then I better get up there first." Ruby stands up, and I swear to god, she's not full-on stomping to Mrs. Morrison's desk, but it's close.

Mrs. Morrison glances at me and then writes something down with a smile before handing her a packet. Ruby carries it over, looking smug.

"What?"

"We got it," she says. "The Endangered Species Act. All ours." And she's absolutely preening over the idea of getting one over on Allie and Lydia. I should feel guilty about that, probably. Especially when I see them walk up to Mrs. Morrison's desk a few minutes later and she shakes her head no. But I kind of don't. I like seeing Ruby this way.

"So, what's all this?" I ask, gesturing to the mammoth packet of papers in front of us.

"We have to fill all this out for the research portion. There's a bunch of different questions to guide us or whatever."

"Got it." I scan through them quickly. They seem pretty straightforward but also like a lot of work. It clearly says on the top that while class time will be given to complete the assignment, students are expected to meet outside of school or during activity period in order to complete whatever we don't finish in class. "Want to meet me at the library Saturday? There's a meet that day, and I can't go. I could use the distraction."

"I'm . . . busy Saturday."

I wonder if it's another pageant but don't ask. She wasn't exactly receptive when I showed up at one the first time. "I guess then another time?"

"Yeah, maybe."

And, oh. Oh. Nooooow I get why nobody else wanted to partner up with her. Well, it's not my first time doing all the work in a group project, and it probably won't be the last. Mrs. Morrison will have to figure that out on her own during the essay portion, though, because I'm not about to let Ruby sink my grade on the research end.

"You know what? I'll get a jump on things by myself. It's fine," I say. "We can compare thoughts during activity period or something. I need the info for my essay anyway. It doesn't matter."

"Obviously, it matters."

"Look, I know how it works. I don't mind doing all the research stuff, but I'm not writing your essay for you. And you have to pull your weight during the actual presentation, so you don't screw over my grade. Deal?"

"I'm *going* to help with the research. I just . . ." She trails off, shaking her head.

"I said it's fine."

"Will you stop?" She huffs out a breath. "I'll be there, okay? It's just gotta be later, like four. Can you at least wait until four to get a 'jump on things'?"

"Yeah, I can wait until four," I say slowly. Because I thought I at least had *this* part of her figured out. But nope, Ruby Thompson remains an enigma.

"Okay, awesome," she grumbles. It does not actually sound like she thinks it's awesome, though.

"It's a date," I say cheerfully, out of habit and instinct and nothing else, I swear. But she scowls anyway. "I mean not a *date* date, obviously. Just a date, as in a date and time. More of an appointment, really. An appointment to complete an assigned task."

"Stop talking," she says again.

And, right, yes. That's probably a good idea.

17

RUBY

"Oh!" Morgan says when I unceremoniously drop into the seat across from her at the library. "I was starting to think I'd been ditched." She looks at me for half a second, her cheeks flushing when our eyes meet, and then quickly looks away.

I scrunch up my forehead and then remember the makeup. As in, the metric ton of pageant makeup currently covering my face. I'm still picking up extra classes, and today I was stuck working with Charlene's littlest students. I bribed them by offering to let them watch me do a full face at the end of class if they behaved. To them, it's not a burden. To them, it's magic. Unfortunately, it also made me late.

"Yeah, sorry. I know I look like a clown," I say, pulling a pencil out of my backpack and trying to shove down the embarrassment. "I would have been another hour if I actually—"

"I like it," she says, all quiet, and for a second the embarrassment mixes in with something else. "You do a pageant every weekend, then?"

"No." I scribble my name on top of the packet and slide it back over to her. "This was actually for a class I'm teaching. I'm sort of bartering with my pageant coach right now for extra lessons. I help her lead classes and demonstrate makeup techniques, and in exchange she helps me not bomb the interview portions of my competitions."

"Wow, that's dedication."

"Hardly," I mumble.

"What does that mean?"

"Don't worry about it."

She writes her name neatly, right under mine. "If you don't really love it, then why do you do it?"

Her question startles me, both the assumption that I have a real say in the matter and the suggestion that if I did, I wouldn't choose this.

"Who says I don't love it?"

"The expression on your face."

I sigh. "Fine. My mom was a beauty queen before she had me. It means a lot to her that I follow in her footsteps." I tack on that last part, like that covers it. Like we'll just skate over all the other complicated crap that goes along with living with and loving my mom and just leave it at that.

"Do you always do what people want you to do?" Her face is so sincere, so honest. She's not just making boring conversation; she really, truly wants to know.

"Only when it comes to my mother. Life's a lot easier that way." And I'm so grateful that my caked-on makeup covers the shame that comes with admitting something like that. Especially to someone like Morgan. Someone who lives so loud and real, in ways I could never dare.

"I'm sorry," Morgan says, turning back to the book in front of her.

"Don't be; it's fine."

"Okay, then I'm not," she says, and flips one of the pages.

I bet she's giving me a chance to change the subject or challenge her on it or something. And for some reason—I don't know why—I desperately want her to know that I *do* try, but I have to work with what I have, to fight the battles I can actually win.

"I'm entering the county pageant, though," I say, and she looks up. "That one I do want to win. For me."

"Really?" She taps her pen against her lips like she's trying to figure me out. I almost think about letting her.

"Yeah. The top six finishers get a scholarship to the community college. There's an automotive program there, and if I got accepted and could afford to go . . ." I trail off, losing my nerve. I've never said this out loud before, not even to Everly. What is it about Morgan that makes my mouth run off like this? "Forget it, it's stupid."

"It doesn't sound stupid." She leans back in her seat, still studying my face. I can tell when her eyes catch on my lips, overglossed and brightly colored, lingering just a little longer than necessary and sending a jolt of electricity down to my toes. Her expression right now . . . I don't know. It's like she's fascinated. Like she's discovering a new species or something and really, really excited about it. Like I'm some great find or something.

I look away before I do something we'll both regret.

"What's stupid about it?" she presses.

"You're probably going to a really great school, so."

"It sounds like you are too."

I raise my perfectly painted-in eyebrows. "I'm sitting here telling you that I'm trying to scam my way into having a pageant pay for an automotive program at a community college, and you're, like, a D-I athlete or whatever."

"Not yet. And maybe not ever if I don't play nice with my old school."

I flick my eyes to hers, a question on my lips, but she waves me off. Fine. Let her. We should be keeping this conversation to the assignment anyway.

"I think the automotive program sounds awesome," she says suddenly, her face breaking into a smile so warm and genuine it ties my stomach up in knots. "I'm guessing by your car you have the skills to pull it off. I'm, like, completely in awe of you right now."

"Why?"

"Because you're doing something that matters! You fix

things and make them whole again. That's important! It's kind of amazing." She blushes and bites her lip. "All I do is run really fast."

I clear my throat and look away, her attention suddenly feeling too heavy. I don't want it to stop, but I need it to.

"Okay, the Endangered Species Act," Morgan says, turning to the first page of the packet. Like nothing is happening. Like we're just two students working on a project again instead of... whatever that just was.

Or maybe that was nothing.

Maybe heat doesn't pool in her belly when she looks at me, the way mine does when I look at her. Maybe she doesn't think of me at night when it's quiet. Maybe this is all in my head.

That would be for the best, honestly. Because the alternative is that she's just that perfect. That she can read me already, can tell when I get lost in my own head, and knows exactly how to get me out of it. That she knows when to push and when to give me space.

I pull out my phone, not willing to fall any farther down this rabbit hole.

"Here," I say, pulling up some websites I saved last night and rambling off some facts I learned. She smiles again, occasionally looking up as she writes down the answers I already found.

"What?" I finally ask when her smirks and glances become too much to ignore.

She keeps writing, not even missing a beat. "Nothing."

"No, seriously. What?" I ask again, the good feeling bleeding into self-consciousness.

She still doesn't look up. "You're just really full of surprises."

And yeah.

I kind of like the sound of that.

18

MORGAN

"Is working with Ruby the worst or what?" Lydia asks. She's walking me to the Pride Club meeting on her way to sports study hall.

"We actually got a lot done," I say, feeling marginally defensive.

She scoffs. "You mean *you* got a lot done."

"No, she helped a lot."

"Ruby Thompson helped? As in, pulled her weight? As in, actually showed up to the library and didn't just sit there complaining and waiting for you to find the answers?"

"No," I say, pausing by the door. I still wish Lydia would come in, but I'm trying really hard to get over the fact that she won't.

"Really?"

"Really," I say in a slightly exasperated tone. "We got through most of the packet, and she probably did more than I did. It was actually kind of fun. She was super nice the whole time."

And that, that sends Lydia's eyebrows to the sky. "Ruby Thompson is *not* super nice. Wait, did we slip into another timeline? Is this some butterfly effect thing? Are you feeling okay?" She puts her hand to my forehead. "Hmm, no fever."

I push her hand down. "Oh my god. No fever, no slipped timelines, seriously. I think you've got her all wrong. I even offered to do it on my own, and she was pretty firm about helping." I lean against the door frame, shifting out of the way when Anika and Aaron walk in together laughing. "I don't think you know her as well as you think you do."

Lydia snorts. "I've known Ruby since the fourth grade. Maybe she can fake you out for a little while, but—"

"But what?"

"Just be careful, okay? I'd hate for you to get all caught up in her drama."

Ms. Ming walks past me and into the room then, her presence cutting me off before I can respond.

"Are you sure you won't come in?" I ask. Lydia shakes her head. "Even if you don't want to be out, you could still—"

"Don't," Lydia says as she walks away. "Have fun at your club. I'll see you at track."

I don't miss the way she says "*your* club."

"Yeah, see you at track."

. . .

Brennan kicks the meeting off with the usual things—approving minutes from the last meeting and going over old business, by which I mean designing some new bulletin boards and club posters for the school—and then turns the floor over to Ms. Ming to go over new business.

She hops up onto her desk and claps her hands together. "Okay, it's time to get serious about our end-of-the-year service project. Thoughts?"

Everyone goes quiet.

"It doesn't have to be something huge or even fully planned out. Just say whatever you're thinking, and then we can build from there. I think we've had an excellent year overall, but are there any opportunities we missed? Are there any ways we could expand our reach or our focus to help others?"

Aaron clears his throat. "I don't really know how or what yet, but I would love to do something that addresses the issues that trans kids face. My parents have been super cool about it, but that's really not everyone's experience."

Anika sits up straighter. "And the club could definitely be doing more to address the impact race has on things too. Like the whole centering of whiteness in queer spaces and stuff."

Ms. Ming nods. "Those are both excellent notes. How can we turn them into a serviceable project? What can we do on our level to add to the conversation and be part of the solution?"

We search one another's faces like we'll find the answers there, and that sinking feeling comes back, that utterly helpless not-doing-enough feeling I can never seem to outrun.

"No clue," Drew moans, breaking the silence and making a few people laugh.

"Okay," Ms. Ming says, hopping down and writing *What is the issue and how can we help?* on the whiteboard. "Can our school club solve all of the complicated issues surrounding transness or racial inequality in the queer community during one afternoon? Of course not. So let's try to break it down into something more manageable instead. Can anyone think of a specific problem related to these topics? Once we identify that, it should be easier to brainstorm solutions."

Anika taps her fingers on her desk as she considers this. "Homelessness," she says finally. "It really impacts LGBTQ+ youth in general, but I was reading something the other day that said it hits the trans and queer POC communities the hardest."

Ms. Ming writes *homelessness* on the board.

"Yeah, that's true," Aaron says. "We have a lot of people drop in at the center looking for resources for that. Kids get kicked out by their parents or run away because they're scared of their reaction."

I shift in my seat, thinking about all the books that Izzie said were from various donors, and it hits me. "What if we do, like, a clothing and food drive?"

Ms. Ming looks thoughtful. "And how does that answer the problem of queer youth homelessness?"

"We could ask for donations of food, clothing, toothpaste, gift cards, whatever," I say. "And then Aaron and I can take them to the center to hand out to teens who come in needing help."

"That actually sounds really cool," Anika says. "Maybe we could even get people to donate their old backpacks too. We could make, like, bug-out bags for teens."

"I'm sure Izzie would love it, and she doesn't have a program like that going yet," Aaron adds. "She'd probably let us have a display in the main area for people that just want to come in and grab stuff. Like, even if you don't want to formally say you need the help, you can have access."

"Won't that lead to people just stealing the stuff, then?" Brennan asks.

Aaron shrugs. "If somebody seriously wants to steal toothpaste from a queer community center in our crappy town, then let them. They probably need it. And even if they don't, it's a risk I'm willing to take."

"Could we put up donation bins in the cafeteria?" Anika asks.

Ms. Ming nods. "I think the school would be amenable to that. And I can also reach out to Mrs. Hall to get some of her National Honor Society kids to pitch in if we need help sorting stuff. They're always scrambling for extra volunteer hours this time of the year. What do you say? Should we vote on it?"

"Hell yeah," Drew says. And I grin because this finally feels like making a difference.

"All in favor?" Mrs. Ming asks.

Every single kid raises their hand.

19

RUBY

I look down at my phone, frowning at the text from Tyler:
you busy tonight?

I know he's got another big game coming up, which is our usual arrangement, but I heard a rumor that he's been "blowing off steam" with Allie Marcetti ever since I started ditching him. I wish he'd just text her and keep me out of it.

"Something important?" Morgan asks, and I flip my phone over before she sees.

"Nope." I smile.

We're lying on a giant fuzzy rug on her bedroom floor, face-to-face with our books and laptops—well, her laptop; I don't actually have one—spread out between us, along with some papers and the rest of our packet, which is just about finished.

I have another pageant in a little while, one of those crappy mall ones where you just get dressed up and stand in a line. We're supposed to look hot and hope maybe there's a modeling contract in it for some of us—but there never is. Mom says it's good "for experience." If I could roll my eyes any harder, I would.

When Morgan heard I had one today, she offered to come to my house to study instead. She thought it would be easier than me carting all my stuff here, but I said no. She might live in a little apartment, but it's a *nice* little apartment. Quiet and meticulously clean. And my place is rarely the former and never the latter. Especially not with both Chuck and my mom around.

"Okay, so I think we have everything we need to write our essays," Morgan says, filling in the last answer. "Which means we officially need to figure out what we want to do for the presentation."

I sigh. "Not looking forward to that part."

"Seriously?" She bites the eraser on her pencil with an incredulous look.

"Wait, did you think I actually *liked* class presentations?" I crinkle my forehead. "Nobody likes them."

"Well, not normal people, but I thought . . . I mean, you're not . . ."

"I'm not what?" The implication that I'm not normal instantly raises my hackles.

"Not like everybody else," she says.

"How?" I ask, my heart nose-diving into the dirt. Everybody else around here knows I'm trash; I guess it was just a matter of time before Morgan figured it out too.

"Oh, come on." She sits up and kind of waves her hands in front of me like I should know what that means. "You're . . . You do pageants and stuff. I saw you onstage; you're a born entertainer! It was . . . You were amazing."

I look away, blush creeping up my neck, my ears, my cheeks, and down to my toes from the sound of her voice. Because "amazing" is not a word used to describe me, and she keeps throwing it around like it's no big deal.

"Thanks," I mumble, sitting up quick. It suddenly feels a little warm in here, a little too close, with her soft eyes and her smile just a few inches away from mine. I scramble backward until I hit her nightstand, grabbing my notebook after and trying to make it seem deliberate.

She lets out a little laugh as she pulls out a fresh sheet of paper. "So, I think for the presentation—" The alarm on my phone cuts her off.

"Shit."

"What?"

"I have to get ready. Sorry." I can't tell if she's disappointed or relieved when I jump up and grab my bag. I can't tell which one I am either.

"Can I watch you?" Morgan asks, padding after me toward the bathroom, and her question sounds so innocent but feels so heavy.

"Sure," I say, like my heart isn't pounding in my ears at the thought. She perches on the edge of the tub, watching me intently as I pull out my arsenal: my contouring tools, eye shadows, setting sprays, primers, blushes, lipsticks, lip liners, lip glosses, and everything else it takes to transform me from regular Ruby to Pageant Ruby™.

"Wow," Morgan says, reading the back of a bottle of setting spray. "This looks intense."

"Yeah, I guess it takes a lot to make a girl like me look presentable." I mean it as a joke, but it clearly doesn't land.

"No." She frowns and sets the bottle of setting spray down. Her response hangs in the air, and I'm not sure how to respond.

Instead, I set to work laying the foundation and contouring myself until my cheekbones look sharp and my nose looks perfect, and then I fill in my eyebrows, change the color of my eyelids, and glue on fake eyelashes to boot.

Morgan's quiet at first—watching me like a hawk—but soon starts chattering away, telling me how stir-crazy she's going having to sit out meets, and finally filling me in on the whole waiver thing.

I hate her old school.

Halfway through, I work up the nerve to ask Morgan why she likes to run so much. My question is met with a long silence.

"I sort of fell into it after my grandma died when I was eleven," she says finally.

My brush stills. "That seems like a weird way to get into running."

"We were very close." Morgan shrugs. "She lived on the edge of this amazing preserve. She used to swear there were wolves, but I never saw one. We used to make little fairy houses together and then wander through the deer trails, hiding them. I was convinced the preserve was magical."

"Cute," I say, tilting my head back and forth in the mirror to make sure I'm blended well from every angle.

"It was, until my grandma died."

"Right." I forgot where we were going with this.

"After the funeral, I ran back to the preserve. Dylan chased me as far as he could until the woods 'swallowed me up.' His words, but that's what it felt like. He never came with Gram and me on our walks, so he didn't know the trails like I did. I was happy to get lost in there. I could pretend Gram was just around the corner or beyond the next fork. But of course, she wasn't. I ran until I couldn't anymore. And then I walked out exhausted, with my funeral clothes all muddy and sweaty. Dyl was lying in the grass waiting. He wasn't mad or anything. He just said, 'Come on, Usain, let's get home.' And that's when I realized I was *fast*."

"You definitely are that," I say. Our eyes meet in the mirror, and she smiles like it's the most natural thing in the world, and I smile back. Like it's fine. Like I'm allowed too. I look away, messing with all my bottles and containers. "Do you still run in the woods?"

"For cross-country, yeah. Otherwise I stick to roads, unless I'm upset. Getting lost in the trees still calms me down, I guess."

My eyes linger on hers for a second too long. On some level, I know I'm only here to do schoolwork, and that I'm doing my makeup the same way I've done it ten thousand times around ten thousand other girls—but I can't shake the feeling that this is different somehow.

I lean closer to the mirror and put the tiniest dab of highlighter over the lipstick on my bottom lip, making it look extra plump and kissable. I'm playing it up; I am, but I haven't been able to stop thinking about how she looked at the library, no matter how hard I try. I flick my eyes to hers, and her mouth pops open with a little huff, telegraphing her feelings loud and clear. She's always, always so loud, even when she doesn't mean to be. *Especially* when she doesn't mean to be.

I revel in her expression, just a little bit, before shoving my highlighter back into my kit.

What am I doing?

This is just a group project, I remind myself. For school. That's all it can be. She can pretend it doesn't matter that she's a girl who likes girls. She can act like it's fine and normal. But that's not how everyone sees it. Not how my *mom* sees it. Not how the judges see it. And yet looking at Morgan Matthews right now, and the way she just licked her lips, I almost want to—

"What are you thinking about?" she asks, and I desperately try to shove every thought of kissing her out of my head.

"Just . . ." I try to shake off the confusion that's spinning spiderwebs in my head. What if I've been the fly and not the spider all along?

"Just . . . ?"

I look down, pretending to take an inventory of the mess I've made of her bathroom. And I haven't even done my hair yet. "Just that I forgot the clips I use while curling my hair. You don't happen to have any, do you?"

"I have, like, bobby pins, if that helps. But I don't really have hair anymore, you know?" She angles her head and points to her pink pixie cut, which only serves to make her neck look extra delicate and touchable.

I'm so screwed.

I scrunch up my eyes and exhale, cutting off that line of thought. "No, like the big clips," I say when I'm finally back in the driver's seat of my brain. "The ones they use at hair salons and stuff to section off your hair."

"People actually own those?" Morgan asks, looking a little bit scandalized. "I thought that was strictly a salon thing. I don't even know if Dyl has them at his *shop*. You're saying this is, like, a common household good?"

"Maybe not *common* common, but yeah, people own them. A lot of people." I laugh. "It makes it a hundred times easier to curl your hair when some of it's out of the way."

"If you just need it out of the way, then I could hold it, right? I'm happy to be your living, breathing hair clip."

"Sure," I say, even though everything inside me is screaming that this is a bad idea. I plug in my curler, waiting for it to heat up, and cordon off part of my hair. She steps up close, so close I can smell the spring-fresh dryer sheets on her clothes.

"Let me." She sweeps the hair up from my neck, and I shiver from her touch—I can't help it. In the mirror, I watch her fingers card through my hair, her eyes fixed on the little scar on my shoulder that I got from tripping at a pageant when I was six and hadn't fully realized how slippery new tap shoes were yet.

Morgan looks up, and I look away, picking up my curling iron. It takes us a minute to get the rhythm right, but by the end, she's anticipating my next curl before I am.

"Wow," she breathes when I'm finally done. And I think I want to live here, in the space of that "wow," in that one little syllable she's managed to stuff so full of adoration and joy.

But my phone's *seriously now, you have to go* alarm screeches, bursting the little bubble we've made. I excuse myself and grab my dress off the hanger in her room. She follows me out, sitting on her bed while I disappear behind closed doors. I shimmy into my body shaper before taping and twisting myself into as much of an approximation of this industry's "ideal female form" as possible.

"Morgan," I call, pulling the bathroom door open. "Can you?" I gesture to my back, where the zipper is still undone, as if closing my dress isn't something I've been able to do blindfolded and upside down since I was five.

I'm playing with fire here, and her hands are like gasoline.

I turn around when she comes closer, holding my breath as she slowly pulls the zipper up, one agonizing second at a time. A zing ripples down my spine, setting the baby hairs on my neck on edge as I imagine what would happen if I asked her to pull it the other way instead.

A heavy breath brushes against my neck as she finishes, and I lean back, just a little, into her touch.

"People keep telling me to stay away from you," she says softly, and some of the warm, fuzzy feeling in my head clears.

"Right," I say, putting space between us.

She tugs my hand gently, turning me until we're face-to-face. "Do you think I should? Because I really don't want to."

I don't want her to either, but what right do I have to say that?

I pull my hand back slowly, not sure how to answer. "I'm going to be late."

20

MORGAN

My parents surprise us and come up for brunch today instead of dinner, which I'm actually happy about. With my volunteer hours at the center later, I would have missed them otherwise, and I really need a hug from my mom after my confusing study date with Ruby. There's nothing new to report with our case, so for once we get to just relax and laugh in between bites of my mom's French toast casserole and my dad's scrambled eggs. It's kind of perfect.

When they head out for their long drive home, I flop onto my bed and go back to obsessing over my latest interaction with Ruby. It's becoming an unwelcome habit, which is why I decide to ditch my bike in favor of a nice long jog to the center. Nothing clears my head better than running.

I turn the volume up higher on my headphones and push my pace, doing my best to forget about Ruby with every slap of my sneakers on asphalt. But then again, watching her essentially put different dots of paint on her face to turn it into, well, a whole other face, was pretty damn impressive. And the way her breath caught as I pulled up that zipper . . .

I shake my head and keep running because everything after—the way she pulled back, the way she didn't answer when I asked if I should stay away—sucked. And god, I need to stop. I need to focus. There can be absolutely no more *star-crossed lovers staring in a bathroom mirror* crap, no more searching for her in the hall. She's being downgraded from girlfriend material to random student that's nice to look at. Because there's no denying she is *really* nice to look at. And to talk to. And . . .

I run even faster—all out sprinting now—trying to outrun any thoughts of Ruby's completely dreamy lower lip. I need to get a grip. This is just a ridiculous chemical reaction in my brain. That's all it is. That's all I'm letting it be.

Except I'm so utterly lost in my thoughts, trying to convince myself that's true, that I nearly run right past the center. I bank left and cut into the parking lot at the last second.

"Hey," Aaron says when I walk in all sweaty and out of breath. Running here, though effective, was possibly not my best idea.

"Hi." I bend over with my hands on my thighs. Definitely should have skipped that whole sprinting-at-the-end part.

"You ready, or do you need a minute?" he asks. "Your appointment is already here."

I stand up, bolstered by the news. Today, I'm meeting "Danny," the student athlete they told me about before. While Aaron is going to pop in and out a few times, I'm going to be running the show mostly on my own for the very first time.

"I am definitely ready." I grin.

Aaron leads me into the counseling room, where a boy about my age is seated. He nods beneath a thick mop of brown hair when I walk in and then fixes his eyes directly on mine. His body is tense, his knee bouncing a mile a minute, like his entire psyche is deciding between fight or flight.

"Danny, this is Morgan. Morgan, Danny. I'll let you two get to it, but I'll be just outside if either of you need anything." Aaron leaves with a little wave, and I drop into the comfy chair across from Danny.

The room is small, but not too small, the overhead fluorescent lights flicked off in favor of warm floor lamps. It has a desk and chair in the center of it, but I've been sitting in these overstuffed recliners when I observe Aaron and Izzie's meetings, and I like them better. Being next to the person I'm talking to feels a lot more natural than sitting on opposite sides of a desk.

Danny shifts in his seat, and I smile. "So, what do you play?"

He looks at me suspiciously. "Does it matter?"

"I guess not." I don't bother telling him that I already know it's football and that his name—even though I'm not sure what it is—definitely isn't Danny. I also definitely don't tell him that I've seen him play against my old school, more than once. "What would you like to talk about, then?"

"Why's your hair pink?" he asks.

"You want to talk about my hair?" Somehow this is not how I envisioned this going.

He smirks. "People don't dye their hair weird colors if they don't want anyone to notice."

"Fair enough." I cross my arms. He has a point. "I transferred from a superstrict private school that didn't allow 'unnatural hair colors.' Unfortunately, it also didn't allow girls kissing other girls—something, you know, I really like doing. So now I'm here, living with my brother, who happens to own a barbershop full of hair dye, trying to grab on to my fresh start however I can."

Danny raises an eyebrow. "And pink hair does that?"

"Kinda. It's something completely new to me. Besides . . ." I twist my face up in mock confusion. "Do you see how cute this looks? Everyone should go pink. In fact, I can text my brother and see if he has an opening if you—"

Danny laughs and shakes his head. "No, I'm good."

"Okay," I say. "Well, if you're not here for a makeover, maybe we should talk about what you are here for."

He sucks down a deep breath and braces himself as he nods. And then the words pour out of him. He's gay, he says. And he's freaked that if he comes out, his teammates will be all weird about it. I resist the urge to reassure him with platitudes like *They won't*, or *It will all be okay*. I know that may not be true. People might be weird. They will probably be weird. They were weird to me.

So instead I tell him what my mom always tells me: "If somebody doesn't think we deserve to love and be loved the way we want, with whatever person we want, then they don't deserve our time or attention anyway."

He doesn't look convinced.

I don't sugarcoat it. I tell him it probably will be hard and uncomfortable at first, but that everyone should live their truth. And that if he feels ready to come out, he should. Aaron smiles from the doorway—one of his quick pop-ins—and gives me a little thumbs-up before disappearing again.

"What if I come out and they kick me off the team?"

"They could try," I say, "but hopefully they wouldn't get very far." He looks at me in confusion, and then I tell him my story. He says he's heard of me and seen my family on the news. I pretend to be surprised when he tells me he goes to a private school not too far from where I used to live.

And then I tell him that hopefully one day, once this lawsuit is settled, schools won't dare pull this crap—not even overpriced, overblown private schools like ours. He says he wishes that day were today.

And, yeah, me too.

Dylan comes home late with a pizza. He excitedly tells me that he finally asked out that woman he's been crushing on, and she said yes. I try not to think too hard about how much

I wish that were me and Ruby. He heads off to bed early, but I stay up watching Netflix all night and obsessing.

And then, sometime around midnight, throwing caution to the wind, I grab my phone and send her a text: **Hope the pageant went well!** ☺

21

RUBY

I read her text about ten thousand times, think of about a hundred different ways to answer, but in the end, I do nothing. Not even a quick low-key "thanks." I just leave her hanging. Like an asshole.

On Monday, we have the entire class time to work on our presentation. My stomach is in knots waiting to see what she says. But she says nothing. Morgan acts like there isn't anything between us. Like I'm just another classmate or coworker or something. She doesn't get mad. Or crack a joke about it. Or acknowledge it at all. She's just . . . completely fine, and I hate it.

I know that I don't have the right to hate it, that I deserve worse than this for both rushing off and not returning her text, but I'd take annoyance or anger to this indifference any day.

On Tuesday, she flat-out ignores me, looking right through me in the halls, and I can't take it. I get lost on my way to my car after school and accidentally end up at the track watching her practice. Everly is there snapping pics of the guys and grabs another candid shot of what she calls my "moony-for-Tyler face."

Good. Let her think that.

Unfortunately, this confuses the hell out of Tyler, who seems to think I really *was* there to watch him practice. That night, I reply to his booty-call text with a picture of lotion and some tissues.

Oh, and Morgan? She didn't look at the stands once the entire time.

By Wednesday night, after another long day of being ignored, I lose it a little. I text her an article I dug up about some runner who did an ultramarathon. I don't even know what an ultramarathon is, but I figure she'll like it.

She doesn't respond, because karma.

Meanwhile, Everly is up my butt asking me why I'm such a sad sack, and even Billy called me to check in since I hadn't been around the shop all week. I admit to neither of them that besides homework, working for Charlene, and pageant prep, I've just been home licking my wounds.

In class on Thursday, I ask Morgan if she got my text. She says yes and that it was interesting, but she sounds weird when she says it. Like, not unfriendly, but politely unfeeling. Like I'd said, *Nice day out, eh?* instead of googling fifty different running articles to try to impress her. She's not even asking *how* or *why* I found it.

It's difficult to focus on a speech about the Endangered Species Act when I feel like a time bomb about to explode.

That night, I try the text angle again: **Ready for our presentation tomorrow?**

This time she writes back, just a simple one-word answer, but I'll take it: **Yes.**

The next morning, I'm through-the-roof antsy. Like I just drank a dozen black coffees and topped them off with a Monster. I don't know why. Scratch that, I know exactly why. Because Morgan responded.

But it was only one word, and I can't work out the tone. A reassuring yes? Or an annoyed yes? The period at the end doesn't instill confidence.

I may not know what she's thinking, but I know what I want her to be thinking, which is that she definitely should *not* stay away from me, even if it's for the best. I flip between wishing I had told her that to her face . . . and wishing I had let her run home in the rain that day.

But her hands, Jesus, her hands on my back. And the way her breath hit my ear featherlight. And now we have to talk about protecting endangered species while I'm frustrated and confused and tied up in knots.

"Are you okay?" she whispers to me as Lydia and Allie walk up to present the Animal Welfare Act.

I shrug like it's no big deal, even though it is. Because I realized last night that she might never speak to me again after this group project ends. Who goes to a pageant by choice *and also* doesn't want a dumb group project to end? The new me. Apparently. But only for nefarious reasons, so it still tracks.

I'm so lost in my head that I don't register it at first, Morgan's hand drifting lightly over mine and squeezing, like she did when I was scared of the cop. My eyes snap to hers, searching. Because indifferent classmates don't hold hands. Not even under the table. A small smile crosses her lips, and she whispers, "Relax, we've got this."

I squeeze back, nodding even though I know she's talking about the presentation and not . . . *us.* The warmth from her hand spreads up my wrist, swirling through my veins until it pools deep inside me, in the place where all my "girl crushes" stick the landing, that little corner of me that gets a little swoony and maybe a little something else too.

I sit very still. I can't decide if our hands should move or stay, but I don't want to be the one to make that decision.

Morgan squeezes once more and then pulls away, organizing the note cards into two separate piles in front of her. One for me to read and one for her. Like two girls can just hold hands and then go on with their lives or something.

And that's when the shame creeps in. That awful *I should not want this, my mom is going to kill me, what the hell am I doing, people will get ideas* shame for how much I like—

"Ruby? Morgan? You're up," Mrs. Morrison says, and holy shit, I just obsessed through Lydia and Allie's entire presentation.

Morgan looks at me sort of expectantly, so I scoop up the note cards and march up to the front. Mrs. Morrison has already loaded our presentation onto the screen and holds out the little clicker thing to change the slides. I take it with slightly shaking hands as Morgan comes to stand beside me.

But she stands a little too close, like *I can smell her shampoo* too close, and all rational thought leaves my head when I inhale a little more deeply. I step to the side just a little bit. Just enough to remember we're supposed to be talking about endangered animals and not writing love songs to fruity shampoo and lavender body wash. But then she follows me, smiling like I was making room and not trying to escape the scent of . . . What is that, even? Peaches? Can people's hair really smell like peaches?

"Ruby?" she whispers out the side of her mouth, smiling at the class. Right. I have the first card.

I try to flip the title card and read the next one, but I drop them all instead. They spill out in front of me, and I kick some in my rush to scoop them up. A few people in class snicker. My cheeks flame.

This is why I don't do presentations.

This is why I don't do group projects.

This is why I have a barely passing average.

I'm a joke here. A mildly amusing piece of trash that makes everybody else feel better about their lives.

It's different on the pageant stage. I'm good at that. A switch flips, and I become someone else. Confident. Smart.

Witty, even. But this is insecurity and indignity and every-thing I suck at, all at once.

Mrs. Morrison shushes the class as Morgan drops beside me and helps me organize the cards. She hooks her pinkie around mine just for a second, so quick I almost think I've imagined it, and whispers, "You can do this, Ruby."

And I don't think I can, but I also don't want to disap-point her.

I take a deep breath and stand up a little taller, a little straighter, pretending I'm on a stage. I smile and focus on a spot on the back wall after glancing at my note cards. And I perform.

I don't see her again until after the final bell, when I'm rushing to my car to get to a class I'm covering for Charlene and she's walking to track, her spikes dangling loosely over her shoul-der. Lydia and Allie are walking ahead, but Morgan slows her pace, dropping back to match mine as soon as she sees me.

"You were amazing today," she says, tilting her head toward me as we walk.

And there's that word again. *Amazing.* "You did the hard parts," I say, because it's true. She assembled the PowerPoint *and* kept me from losing my shit.

"Nuh-uh, you don't get to do that."

"Do what?"

"Downplay how hard you worked on this and how much you killed it up there. I was a wreck, and you nailed it."

"You were nervous?" I ask, arching my eyebrows. "I couldn't tell at all."

"Well, good, then maybe we'll actually pull off a decent grade. You turned in your essay, right?"

"Yeah." I leave out the fact that I had to stay after class twice this week to get help from Mrs. Morrison on it.

She stops walking and gestures over her shoulder toward the track. "Well, I have to . . ."

"Yeah, I have to too. I have to cover a class for my pageant coach, and then after, I have another session of my own."

"Sounds intense."

I flip my hair back with an exaggerated sigh. "It takes a lot of work to be this amazing, you know."

"Nope," she says, and when I look at her, her eyes look so serious. "I doubt that very much."

"Matthews!" the coach calls, blowing her whistle. "Get your ass over here."

Whatever spell we were under is broken. Again. Every time.

"I better . . ." she says.

"Right."

"Hey, are you going to be around this weekend?" Her question catches me off guard.

"W-Why . . . ? The project's over," I stutter out, and her face falls. I didn't mean it like that. I didn't. I was just surprised that *she* still—

"Yeah, true," Morgan says, walking backward toward the track. "I was just thinking of studying or something." She's acting all nonchalant, but I can tell she's embarrassed.

"There's a lacrosse party tonight," I blurt out.

"Oh yeah?"

"You should come," I say, which earns me a head tilt. "I mean, it's open to the general public, so you don't actually need my invitation. But it beats studying. I mean, if you get bored."

"Yeah, if I get bored," Morgan says, and bites her lip, which just—

"Matthews!" Coach shouts again.

"You better go."

She smiles so big her eyes crinkle. "Yeah, I better."

22

MORGAN

"Why are we going to the lacrosse party again?" Lydia whines, swiping another coat of mascara on her eyelashes.

"Come on, it's a rite of passage, and Morgan's never been," Allie says. "Everybody should experience the splendor of hanging out with a bunch of drunk lacrosse bros at least once in their high school years, right?"

"But why do I have to suffer along with you?"

"Wow, you guys are not exactly selling it here," I say, trying to sound cool about it even though I really, really want to go. Just the idea of seeing Ruby again, especially Natural Habitat Ruby and not Freaking Out Over a Group Project Ruby or Beauty Queen Ruby, has me ridiculously intrigued. So ridiculously intrigued, in fact, that I'm willing to risk running into the Miller twins again to do it.

"Lydia's just being dramatic," Allie says, shimmying into a tight gold tank top. "They're always fun, plus free booze for the girls. Only the guys get charged."

"That part is nice," Lydia admits. "Though self-serving and mildly to moderately dangerous at the same time."

"So . . . what are you wearing tonight?" Allie asks me, pointedly changing the subject.

"Uh, this?" I gesture to the clothes I have on.

"Uh, no," she says, teasing me. "You cannot go to a party in track shorts and a band T-shirt. Sorry."

"I like track shorts and band T-shirts," I say. Except then I think about Ruby and how she might want to see me out of my uniform just as bad I want to see her out of hers. Wait, that came out wrong . . . Or maybe it didn't. I don't even know anymore.

"I've got something better," Lydia says, disappearing into her closet and coming out with skintight black jeans and a tank top that's barely there.

"I think this is too small," I say, and then realize it laces up the whole entire back. "It's not even a shirt. It's like half a shirt. That's—"

"Entirely the point," Lydia says, shoving me into her bathroom to get changed.

Twenty minutes later, we're all piled into Allie's car.

"Where is this party, anyway?" I ask.

"Oh, not far," she says. "We could walk there if I weren't in these shoes."

"Yeah, it's at Tyler Portman's house," Lydia says. "His dad travels a ton for work, and his mom usually goes with him, so it's just him. He's been hosting killer parties since we were fourteen."

"Tyler Portman?" I ask, my stomach twisting. As in the Tyler Portman that Ruby was, and possibly still is, hooking up with?

I tug at my clothes, suddenly feeling even more exposed and off my game. At least if I were still wearing my old stuff I could hop out and run away. In this, I'm effectively trapped. But seriously, what is Ruby trying to pull?

"He's an epic dude-bro, but what can you do?" Allie says. "He has the best parties, and he's actually pretty sweet once you talk to him."

"Since when do you actually talk to him?" Lydia scoffs.

"Since sometimes," she says with a smirk.

"Oh my god, are you hooking up with Tyler now?" Lydia groans and shakes her head, but Allie just laughs.

"I can neither confirm nor deny. But *if* I were, it would just be a super-casual, no-strings-attached thing. Like, we're not exclusive or anything. Not yet, anyway."

"You little shit," Lydia says, punching her arm. "I can't believe you didn't tell me!"

"It's new. Very new."

And I flop against my seat with a smile. Maybe it's a coincidence that Ruby's first real invite to me was to *his* house. Maybe she's done with Tyler, and this is her way of telling him that. Maybe, maybe, maybe.

Granted, I've never been to a house party before, but I thought I had a pretty low bar for being impressed. Now that I'm here,

I realize it should have been even lower, like to the basement floor. It's super crowded as we push through the house to the kitchen, Allie leading the way, laughing and shouting, "It's beer time, bitches!"

The music thumps hard enough to make the walls rattle, and everything's sticky and smells like sweat and stale beer. I have never wanted to be someplace less—and that's before I notice Ruby grinding against a bunch of the lacrosse guys.

Okay, scratch everything I thought in the car. I'm out.

I turn to leave, but Allie stops me, two beers in her hands. She gives me one and raises the other one in the air, dancing into the middle of the living room to a chorus of catcalls. Charming place, really, this house full of dumb boys.

Lydia comes up beside me then with her own cup, raising an eyebrow at our dancing friend. "Allie eats this shit up," she says, taking a hefty swig of beer. I follow suit, trying not to cough when the warm, foamy liquid hits the back of my throat.

"Is it always this gross?" I shift my weight to unstick my feet from the floor, not entirely sure if I'm talking about the beer or literally everything else.

Lydia nods, downing the rest of her beer in a gulp while watching Allie in the crowd, her jaw slightly tense, head tilted . . . and a longing in her eyes that nearly matches mine.

"Holy shit, Lydia, do you like—"

"I'm going to get more beer." She cuts me off with a look that says *Drop it* before disappearing into the crowd.

Interesting. Maybe I'm not the only queer girl with a hopeless crush tonight.

Anika and Drew are off in the corner, and as soon we notice one another, they start beckoning me over. I'm moving through the crowd, getting jostled here and there. When I'm almost to them, I do a little half wave thing in greeting at the exact moment some kid steps back, sending what's left of my beer sloshing all over us both.

"What the hell!" he shouts, turning around like he intends to maul me . . . which is the exact second a hand wraps around my waist and pulls me backward.

"Sorry, Travis," Ruby calls over her shoulder, leading us away. "She didn't mean it."

The kid, Travis, apparently, shakes his head, picking at his beer-soaked shirt and wringing it out.

"You came!" Ruby shouts over the din of the music, pulling me to the opposite corner of the dance floor. I can tell right away she's drunk, but I try to ignore it because she looks so legitimately happy to see me. I glance over at Anika and Drew, who give me twin puzzled expressions, and mouth a quick apology.

"I guess I was bored," I shout back, and the song switches, the beat throbbing against the dance floor. Ruby smiles so big and wide I almost drown in it. I am so screwed, so absolutely lost in this girl in front of me, this girl who's grinning like seeing me is the best thing that happened to her all day.

Ruby catches her long hair in her hands, pulling it up to the top of her head and letting it cascade down over her shoulders as she starts to dance. *Thanks for that, universe.* I'm definitely never forgetting this moment for as long as I live.

"I love this song!" she shouts, moving even closer until she's brushing up against me with every move. I stand still and awkward, not sure what the rules are in this situation, if this performance is for me . . . or for everyone else.

"Dance with me," she whispers in my ear, spinning me around so she's behind me, and a full-body blush shoots fire down my skin.

She puts her hands on my hips, pushing and pulling me until I find the rhythm, her body pressed against my back, her breath on my shoulder as she sings along. She slides her fingers from my hip to my hand without warning, interlacing our fingers and then running them across my stomach. My breath catches as she dips them a little lower, just beneath the waistband of Lydia's too-tight pants, before twirling me around to face her. I lose the beat then, laughing as she bites her lip. She releases my hand, grazing her fingers up my sides and then down my neck, her hands everywhere and nowhere until it's just us on the dance floor, her leg slotted between mine as the whole world falls away.

"I know you like me," she whispers into my ear. And I . . . I don't know what to do. She pulls my hands around her neck and dips her head onto my shoulder, a flick of her tongue against my skin before she pulls back, wiping her lip like it was just a stray drop of beer. I am lost, utterly, in the feel of her body under my fingertips . . .

And then people start whooping and catcalling, and I realize just how many of the lacrosse boys are watching, cheering and clapping at the spectacle of us. I hate it.

Ruby is still dancing, reveling in the attention and not noticing I've lost the beat. And then Tyler comes up behind her, turning our twosome into a threesome, and I stop dancing altogether. The beer churns in my stomach, drowning all the butterflies as his hands touch her skin.

Tyler grabs Ruby's hips and pulls her toward him. She laughs, never missing a beat, and I dart off the dance floor and up the stairs, like some girl in a horror movie, not knowing where I'm going but just needing to get away. Fitting for this nightmare scenario. I find an empty room and run to the window, flinging it open and gulping down the cool night air.

A hand comes up and rubs my back, and I jump, my stupid hopeless brain praying it's Ruby. But it's not. It's Anika standing there, with Drew behind her shooting me a knowing glance.

"It's okay, it's okay," Anika says, and I don't even realize I'm crying until she pulls me into a hug.

"I just, I don't know." I sniffle into her shoulder. "I don't get it. I thought she liked me."

"She's a mess, Morgan," Drew says, squeezing my shoulder with a sympathetic look.

"But what does she want?" I whine, like they're going to know. I don't even think she knows. "I said I would never do this again—fall for the girl who'll most screw with my head. And I did—like, textbook. What is wrong with me?"

"Hey, hey, stop," Anika says. "There's nothing wrong with you. Why don't we get out of here? We're meeting the rest of the gang at the diner. Come with us."

"I dragged Allie and Lydia here just so I could see Ruby." I laugh, short and bitter. "I can't ditch them."

"Really?" Drew asks, looking hesitant to leave me. "I'm sure they'll understand."

"I can't." I don't want to admit that a tiny part of me is still hoping Ruby will magically appear and apologize.

Anika and Drew exchange a look. "I know we aren't best friends or anything," she says. "But even I can tell how much this is upsetting you. Just come with us, please? We'll talk it out over bad food and worse lighting. Aaron's coming too. He can go full peer counselor on you."

I shake my head. "I just need a minute to pull myself together. But go, have fun. I'm good, I swear."

Anika pulls me into an awkward hug. "Okay, well, text us if you need us."

"Will do," I say, and I force out a smile.

It turns out "a minute" was a poor estimation. I take more like fifteen, actually, sitting on the floor, calming down my stomach, nursing my whiplashed libido, and trying really hard not to cry over the fact that the most intense romantic experience of my life may have just been a show Ruby was putting on for her bang buddy, Tyler, and his friends.

The hopelessly naive part of me still hopes that I'm wrong and that Ruby never came up because she's still downstairs looking for me. Maybe she already told Tyler off, but I have no idea because she can't find me while I'm up here pouting instead of fighting for the girl I want.

I scrape my ego off the floor and head down, taking a deep

breath as I turn the corner, only to immediately bump into Lydia.

"There you are!" She looks pissed. "I've been looking everywhere for you!"

"What's going on?"

She links her arm around mine and pulls. "We're leaving. Now. Allie's in the car sobbing her brains out."

"Why? What happened?" I swear to god, if any of these boys touched her or hurt her in any way, I'll—

"That happened," she says, pointing behind us.

I turn my head just in time to see Tyler dip Ruby on the dance floor, nuzzling her neck and kissing her behind her ear. Her head turns as he pulls her up, her sleepy eyes meeting mine, widening just a bit before squeezing shut when he kisses the corner of her mouth.

"That fucking asshole," Lydia says, glaring at Tyler as she pulls me out the door. "Leading Allie on like that, making her think it was more than it was."

"Yeah," I whisper. "That asshole."

23

RUBY

I wake up the next day in Tyler's bed, my head pounding, my clothes from last night sticking to me in uncomfortable ways. Shit. I scan the room with sluggish eyes and run the math on whether I can escape out the window without him noticing, which is when I realize he's not even here.

And then it all comes rushing back, the dancing, Morgan, the look on her face when she saw Tyler and me. Shit, shit, double shit.

Footsteps at the door have me scrunching my eyes shut and feigning sleep, but I open one at the sound of a cup being set down on the nightstand and the scent of coffee wafting into my nose.

"I know you're awake," Tyler says, crouching down near

the bed and pushing my hair out of my face with a level of affection we don't typically share.

"Morning," I say with a little wince.

"You stayed the night." He hands me the mug. "This must be some kind of a record. Should we alert the media?"

I sip my coffee, eyeing him. "Yeah, sorry about that. Didn't mean to break protocol."

"No, it was nice for once," he says, standing up to grab a bottle of Advil off his desk and toss it onto the bed beside me. "Or it would have been nice if you weren't crying half the night."

"Um," I say, my stomach sinking, because I don't remember that part. "I had way too much to drink last night."

"I noticed."

I shift uncomfortably, wrapping the blanket a little tighter around myself. "Did we, you know?"

He looks absolutely horrified. "Jesus, Ruby. Do you really think I'd try to hook up with you when you were that drunk?"

I look away, because the truth is, I don't really know him all that well. We don't talk much outside of the whole quick-release thing we've had going for the last year or the occasional text or high five in homeroom.

"Wow." Tyler pulls some shorts on over his boxer briefs. "On that note, I'm going to the gym. Why don't you slink out like normal before I get back? We'll pretend last night never happened." He looks actually wounded right now, and I hate this. I hate that I'm hurting everyone who seems to have even a modicum of concern for me.

I'm the fucking worst.

"I'm sorry," I say, "but I had to ask. Not everyone is—"

"I would never do anything without your consent." He looks serious. "And last night, you were in no shape to give it."

I look down again.

"You don't remember anything, do you?" he asks. "Christ, how much did you drink?"

"A lot," I say. Enough to drown every conflicting thought I had in my head, or at least try to. "Fill me in? Please?"

He sighs, staring at me for a second before sitting on the bed. "Well, you basically dry-humped that girl Morgan in the middle of my living room."

"I remember that part," I say, because that's not something I will ever, ever forget.

"And then we started dancing, which pissed off Allie and confused the shit out of me."

"Allie Marcetti? She was here?"

"Yeah, I didn't even know. We've been kind of hooking up since you dropped me. I like her and all, but she's not you. When you danced with me last night, I thought we were back in the game or whatever. Until I realized how drunk you were when you started bawling on the dance floor after I kissed you."

I wince. "Sorry about that."

"Yeah, that was not great for my ego or my reputation," he says, but with enough teasing in his voice that I know he's not mad. At least not about that part.

"I brought you up here and tried to put you to bed, but you were really upset. I ended up staying with you until you finally fell asleep, but by then everyone else was really drunk, and I got worried someone might come in here while you were passed out, so . . ." He gestures to a sleeping bag and pillow on the floor. "I decided to hang close."

I look away. Showing weakness to Tyler and him actually being cool about it somehow makes me feel even more vulnerable, like maybe I lost a little skin when he was peeling back the layers.

"Listen, Ruby, we definitely don't have to be fuck buddies or whatever you want to call it anymore, but you don't have to shut me out either. I don't mind being your friend. I'd actually like that."

My startled eyes meet his, sure this is just a plot to keep me close, but I find only sincerity in them. "Really?"

"Really. It sucks a little, because you're really hot and we've had a lot of fun together, but last night . . . Look, I don't think I'm the one you want, and being friends wouldn't be the worst. That's all I'm saying. If you ever want to talk about what had you crying your brains out last night, I'm here."

I scratch the back of my neck. "Thanks, I'll think about it," I say, because I have a really good idea what I was crying about last night, but I'm not ready to share that with anyone yet.

Except maybe her.

My hair is still wet when I get to her apartment and ring the buzzer. I tried pulling it into a messy bun, but that just left the back of my T-shirt—a borrowed one of Tyler's that I've knotted up above my hip after my shower—soaked for no reason.

Everly has texted me about a dozen times this morning, and I'm supposed to meet up with her in an hour and a half to help her pick through some photos for her senior project. But I can't shake this sense of doom in my chest every time I think of Morgan, like I ruined it all before I figured out what it even was. And it's that feeling that has me standing on her porch right now.

I hit her buzzer a second time, and finally there are footsteps on the other side of the door. I wave at the peephole, figuring someone's staring at me. I don't know if it's her or Dylan, but judging by the amount of time that passes with the door not opening, I'm guessing it's her.

"Hey," I say to the still-shut door. "Can we talk?"

A lock clicks, and the door cracks open. She doesn't undo the chain.

"Hey, Ruby," she says slowly, eyeing me warily. "What are you doing here?"

"Can I come in?"

"Why? The group project's over," she says, repeating my words from yesterday.

"I thought maybe we could study," I say, echoing hers right back with a hopeful smile. She just stares. "Or not?"

"What do you want, Ruby?" Her voice is hard.

I bite my lip. "I just want to talk."

She closes the door just enough to slide the chain off, and shame creeps up my spine—not for liking her, this time, but for letting her down. Again. "What's there to say?"

"Nothing happened between me and Tyler last night, I promise."

She swings the door open wider but still doesn't let me in. "Why would I care what happens between you and Tyler?"

"You know why."

She narrows her eyes. "Do I?"

"I can go, if you want," I say, turning to leave, caught between the sudden panic that I read everything wrong and the sudden panic that I didn't.

Either way, this isn't working.

"I guess you can come in, since you drove all this way," she says, like her apartment isn't smack in the middle of town.

I'm four steps from the safety of my car, four steps from maintaining the status quo, four steps from lying low and getting through . . . but I've never spun around so fast in my life.

Morgan holds the door open for half a second, giving it a good shove so I have time to catch it after she disappears inside. I find her sitting in the living room, the TV on mute. She's got a perfect view of the parking lot through her curtains, which means she definitely saw me pull in. Is that better or worse? Like, she hesitated, but also, she ultimately unlocked the door.

Morgan stares at me expectantly, and I don't know what to say. I don't know why I'm here, beyond the fact that I feel totally guilty about last night, even though I technically have no reason to. But also, I have *a lot* of reasons to. My heart jumps into my throat.

"I take it no pageant today?" she asks, flicking through channels on the still-muted TV.

"No, not today." I can hardly believe she's even talking to me. "I have to meet Everly in a little while, though."

"Oh," she says noncommittally, not taking her eyes off the

TV. "I guess that doesn't leave much time for studying, then. We should get started."

"I didn't really come here to study." I move to the coffee table, blocking her view of the TV. "But you know that." I need her to look at me, I need her to see how sorry I am for last night. I need her to feel what I can't say.

Morgan just sighs and looks away. "What do you *want*, Ruby?"

"I don't know," I say, answering honestly. What do other people say in moments like this? I don't get crushes. I don't do relationships. Especially not with girls. This is uncharted territory for more reasons than one.

Morgan stands up. "Cool, well, thanks for stopping by, then."

I scoot forward on the table, reaching for her hand and trapping her legs between mine. Morgan hesitates, searching my eyes, and then sighs. "I can't play these games with you anymore. Not after last night."

"I'm sorry," I say. "I'm so sorry. I should never have—"

"I felt gross."

"Oh," I say. I drop her hand and slide back . . . because "gross" was the opposite of how I felt. I *liked* dancing with her. More than liked it, even.

"How could you do that to me? You obviously know how I feel about you. You even said it!" She shakes her head and drops back onto the couch with crossed arms. "And then you *still* used me to get Tyler's attention? That's screwed up, Ruby!"

"Wait, what?" Because I didn't. *I didn't.* I may not have known what I was doing, but it definitely wasn't that.

"This whole time, were you just like, *Oh, look at this pathetic girl who has a crush on me. I bet I can use that to my advant—*"

I cut her words off with a kiss, trying to show her what I feel, trying to pour everything I can't say into her lips on mine, so she can finally understand. But I've barely started when her hands are on my shoulders, shoving me away.

"What are you doing?" she shouts.

"I thought . . ." I trail off. I don't know what I thought. I didn't think, actually. And, oh no, oh no. Her eyes well with tears before she runs down the hall and slams the door.

I sit there for a second, trying to figure out what to do and how I read all of this so wrong, and then I follow her, knocking softly on her door.

"Go away, Ruby," she says, and I can tell she's still crying.

Shit.

I reach for the handle but stop myself, remembering my conversation with Tyler earlier about consent. I turn around instead, sliding down the door with my back against it. I stretch my legs out, and I pick at my nail polish. I suck at feelings. I suck even more at talking about them. Why won't she let me just show her? "Morgan—"

"Why are you still here? Go!"

I tip my head back against the wood. "I will if you want me to. But I really don't want to."

"What *do* you want?" she asks, her voice more frustrated than I've ever heard.

176

I take a deep breath and cut open that little box of feelings inside me. If she needs me to bleed for her, I'll bleed. "I've never . . . Tyler and I used to hook up or whatever, but I don't . . ." I sigh, already frustrated with myself. "I mean, I don't worry about him when he's not around or anything. But you? All the time I want to know what you're thinking. All the time I want to be around you. Every other thought in my head is about you now! And sometimes I hate it. And other times I like it. Too much. And I don't know what I want, I don't, but I do know that I don't want to be the one to hurt you. I didn't do what you think I did last night. I wouldn't. I—"

The door clicks open, and I sprawl backward onto her bedroom floor.

She lets out a huff that could maybe turn into a laugh if I play my cards right. But it's gone before I'm even up off the floor.

"Explain that last part," she says, crawling onto her bed and wiping at her eyes.

"I swear I didn't use you. And I'm sorry for making you feel like that. It wasn't my intention, I promise. I had way too much to drink, and you were there looking so . . ." I shake my head.

Morgan scrunches her forehead, waiting.

"So *good*." I look away, my neck and ears going crimson.

"Then why did you dance with Tyler?"

"I don't know! Everything got so jumbled up!"

"Why did you kiss me just now?"

"I wanted to show you!" I say. "I can barely even talk right around you. You mess with my head so much."

"*I* mess with *your* head?"

"Not like . . . That came out wrong. Let me show you," I plead, taking a step closer. Maybe another kiss, a better kiss, will fix this. I take another step, and another, until I'm right in front of her. "Can I kiss you again?" I lean down so our faces are only inches apart.

"Why?" she asks, and I feel the word on my eyelashes as my heart taps *I don't know, but I want to* against my ribs.

I tip her face up until our noses touch, smiling at her shaky exhale, and say, "I just want to try something."

Morgan jerks her head back at my words, her entire body following suit as she scrambles away and climbs off the bed. "You need to go. Now," she says, her voice cold.

My hazy smile is replaced by a look of confusion. "What? Why? Morgan—"

But she's already marching out of her room and to the front door, holding it wide open by the time I get there. And this time, this time I can tell she means it.

"Morgan—"

"I'm not something to try. I'm not your little experiment. Stay away from me, Ruby. Okay? This is a mistake."

I don't even have a chance to respond before she slams the door in my face.

24

MORGAN

"She called you an experiment?" Anika all but shrieks midbite into her chicken tender.

We're all at the diner—might as well call it an unofficial Pride Club meeting at this point—and Drew and Anika have been nice enough not to pry about why I showed up sniffling and tearstained, even though I'm sure they can guess after last night.

It's taken me an hour to work up the courage to fill everyone else in.

"Seriously?" Drew asks. "That seems ridiculous even for her."

"She didn't use the word, but that was the gist. She said she wanted to 'try something' and then went to kiss me." I grab a soggy french fry. "After seeing her and Tyler last night, even if she says nothing happened..."

"Yeah, she can go 'try something' with someone else," Anika says.

"Dude, what if it just came out wrong?" Aaron asks, and I snap my head toward him.

"You're standing up for her?"

"What, because she's your neighbor, you're going to take her side now?" Drew snorts.

"You're her *neighbor*?" I practically shriek. Sure, I've never been to Aaron's house, but still, this feels like crucial information.

"Yep," he says, popping the *p* like it's no big deal. "And look, if I'm sticking up for her, it's only a little. I'm just saying, I did a lot of messed-up things when I was working through my identity stuff too. I was clumsy as hell about it. I'm not saying she's not a megabitch or that you have to be the one to put up with it, but it sounds like she's legitimately floundering. And her mom is just..."

"What?" I ask. Ruby's mother has always been a bit of a question mark to me.

Aaron looks uncomfortable. "I don't want to seem like I'm talking shit, but you hear a lot when you're living as close together as we are. Let's just say our upbringings couldn't be more different. We were actually really close once, but when I came out as trans, her mom stopped letting me over. She didn't want 'that stuff' around her kid."

"Wow," Brennan says.

"They have a weird relationship. Her mom's super controlling and closed-minded. I don't know what Ruby's doing, but if she *is* part of our team, it can't be easy in that house. I'm sure that's constantly in her head."

"Wow," Drew says.

Aaron slides the chicken tenders closer to me. "Not everybody's journey from A to B can be as clear-cut as yours was, Morgan."

"Clear-cut?" I snap. "I had to switch schools in the middle of my senior year! None of my old friends will talk to me! I can't even run track right now! I took a chance on owning who I am, and I could lose *everything* for it. How can you possibly say it was easy!"

"I didn't say it was easy," Aaron says. "I said it was clear-cut. And it was, because you know who you are and what you want. You have parents who are behind you, a brother who lets you stay with him, and"—he gestures around the table—"new friends who will always have your back. I got really lucky too; my parents are the most supportive and open-minded people in the universe! When I told them I was changing my name to Aaron with an *A*, my mom literally ordered a bunch of blankets and ornaments and everything she could find with the new spelling. She even wanted to have one of those stupid gender reveal parties to announce it to the extended family—you know, the ones where all the blue balloons shoot out? Luckily, I squashed it."

"God, I love your mom," Brennan says.

"Me too," he says. "But we need to remember that not

everybody has that, especially not from the jump. I mean, our end-of-the-year Pride Club project is literally a food and clothing drive because so many kids get kicked out of their houses for this shit."

I cross my arms. "Why do I suddenly feel like I'm the one being judged here?"

"You're not," Aaron says. "All I'm saying is, if you care about her, and she's worth it to you, cut her some slack. This is the first I've ever heard of her having an interest in anybody but guys, and I'm pretty plugged into the rumor mill at the park."

"Yeah, and she's certainly had *plenty* of interest in guys," Anika snarks. "No rumors needed on that front."

Aaron raises an eyebrow. "What we're not going to do is slut-shame her."

"What are you, like, her protector now?" Anika snorts. "She's messing with Morgan's head!"

I frown, my heart sinking just a little bit more. Because even though I'm really pissed at Ruby, hearing Anika talk crap about her isn't helping.

"How long have you all known her?" I ask, trying to change the subject.

"Since kindergarten," Brennan says.

Drew tilts his head. "Same, I think."

"Uh, basically since birth," Aaron says. "Our parents moved into the park at the same time."

"Since third grade," Anika says.

"And she's really never shown any interest in a girl before?"

Aaron shrugs. "Not that I know of. But then again, she doesn't really date guys either."

"Yeah, she just hooks up with them." Anika grimaces. "A lot."

"Will you cut it out?" Aaron asks. "Please?"

"Sorry," she says, looking properly admonished. "You're right. I'm being an ass. I'm just pissed for Morgan."

"This was supposed to be my fresh start." I sigh, dropping my head into my hands. "And instead it's just the exact same thing all over again. Falling for yet another girl who doesn't know what she wants. Good job, Morgan."

"Wait, falling for her? Like *falling for her* falling for her?" Brennan asks, his eyebrows scrunching together.

I peek up over my hands. "Why is this my life?"

"Because you're super cute," Drew says with a little smirk when I look up at him. "Oh, woe is Morgan. All the girls want to kiss you, even the ones we *thought* were straight. You'll probably find Anika on your porch next, banging on your door."

Anika punches him on the arm, and then everybody starts laughing. Even I do, for a sec, before the dread of *What's it going to be like seeing her at school Monday?* comes back. At least the project is over, so I can move my seat back next to Allie and Lydia. But now that her lips have been on my lips . . .

"Earth to Morgan," Anika says, flinging a fry at me.

"Sorry." I fake a smile. "I think I'm going to go for a run, actually." I toss some money on the table and slide out of the booth, grateful that my daily attire consists of running gear and little else.

"But there's still food!" Drew says.

"I need to work this out of my system, you know? I'll feel better after."

"Are you sure?" Aaron asks. "I didn't piss you off with my truth bombs, did I? I know sometimes they don't land."

"No, we're good. You made a solid point. I just don't know how to deal with it yet."

He nudges me with his elbow and gives me a reassuring smile. "Hopefully, you'll figure that out on your run."

"Yeah." I hope so too.

My feet hit the pavement, their steady rhythm against the asphalt as familiar as my own heartbeat. I start off slow, warming up my hip until the endorphins squeeze out the ache, and then I push myself harder and faster through the town, trying to forget the tingle of her lips on mine, and how I let myself feel them, just for a second, before I pushed her away.

I run until the businesses give way to houses, which give way to trees, and then I dart into the woods, cutting through what looks to be a path. I can't tell if it was made by a deer or a runner or maybe, hopefully, both.

I perform best on the track—a lot of us do—but there's just something about racing through the trees, branches flying past, squirrels jumping, and snakes slithering out of my way. Nothing else matters except my feet and my body and the dirt that holds me up, as I strike and push off, my pace quickening until finally the world fades away, a blur of nothing but adrenaline, endorphins, and peace. I linger there, all thoughts chased out, just a body in motion staying in motion, swimming in the chemicals in my brain.

But then my left foot snags a root, which sends me sprawling onto the ground. My headphones fly off as I shift my fall to save my ankle, smashing my cheek onto a rock as I come to a halt in a big pile of leaves.

"Ouch." I grunt, slowly sitting up to assess the damage. My head already hurts, and I'm pretty sure my cheek is bleeding, but I'm more worried about my ankle. I slide my foot up and touch it gingerly. It's going to bruise, definitely, but nothing seems broken. A mild sprain at worst. I flop to the ground, smiling. I've run with much worse. This is why the universe invented KT Tape and ice and ibuprofen. Finally, something I actually know how to handle.

It's nearly dark by the time I limp all the way home, my ankle screaming as the blood dries on my cheek. I find a note from Dylan saying that he went to a concert at a bar called the Screeching Weasel in the next town over, and that he left me money for pizza in the usual spot.

The usual spot is under the bread on top of the stove, because "bread hides dough," apparently. But why he thinks he needs to leave cryptic notes and hide cash is beyond me. If a burglar broke in, they'd probably be a lot more likely to steal his giant TV and gaming systems than to try to puzzle out the clues and hunt for twenty bucks.

I reach into the freezer and stop, my hands pausing at the bag of frozen peas.

Nope. Not going there.

I shove them out of the way and grab my favorite ice pack instead, before heading to the bathroom. I need a quick shower, some antiseptic for my cheek, and sleep.

Tomorrow will be better. It has to be.

25

RUBY

I'm drunk again. I didn't mean to be drunk. Especially not two nights in a row. But I am. So drunk. Drunker than drunk. All of the drunk. Very wickedly drunk.

"You know you're saying that out loud," Everly says, poking me with her foot. We spent the last few hours picking out photos for her senior portfolio project, which she's calling Heart Eyes. She's been snapping pictures of people when they're not paying attention, specifically when they're looking at someone she thinks they care about. Apparently, it's not an invasion of privacy as long as she does it in public. Great. She's mostly got a good mix of parents looking at their children, people looking at the people they're dating or married to . . . and then there's me. Fucking heart eyes for days over Morgan Matthews. Not that Everly knows that.

She's curled up behind her now-official boyfriend, Marcus, her chin resting on his shoulder as he plays Xbox with his headset on and occasionally takes a swig of whiskey. Living the hetero dream, I guess, while I sit here, lonely and drunk. Drunk. Dunk. Dink. Dank.

I roll over on my back and stare at the sky. The ceiling. Whatever you call it. I don't even know. I just look up and try to think about anything else. Because somehow, around hour two, Everly convinced me to let her put my picture in her showcase. She still thinks I was looking at Tyler. I'd be laughing if I didn't feel so much like crying.

So here I am. On her floor. Trying to forget Morgan's soft lips and angry face. And the fact that photographic evidence exists of how she makes me feel.

"Wait, whose lips?" Everly asks.

Shit, am I *still* talking out loud? I reach out my hand, taking the bottle from where it rests on Marcus's hip, and gulp down some more, wishing the alcohol could burn every last thought out of my skull.

"Morgan who? Morgan Matthews?" Everly asks, sitting up a little straighter, which jostles Marcus.

"Damn, baby," he says. "You made me miss my shot." But he smiles when she kisses his temple before crawling over to sit beside me.

I turn my head away from her, but she turns it back.

"Morgan Matthews? Really? That's who has you showing up on my porch with two bottles of whiskey? I thought this was about Tyler! Ruby, Morgan is a girl."

I take another swig. "Don't I friggin' know it," I say,

curling away from her again, because I will not get emotional over this. I can't.

"Oh my god," she says softly. "That picture . . ." Everly tries to pull me toward her again, but I refuse, jerking my shoulder away and staggering to my feet. "Were you looking at *her*?"

"No, it's . . . Forget about it," I mumble.

"Ruby, it's cool. I was just surprised. Don't—"

"I gotta get out of here," I say, picking up the still-unopened second bottle of booze and my keys from the coffee table.

"Uh, no," she says, snatching the keys out of my hand. "You're definitely not driving anywhere."

"I'm fine." I reach for them again, but she shoves them in her pocket.

"Stop. You're not thinking straight right now."

I laugh, and when she looks confused, I add, "Pun intended?"

"Oh my god," she huffs, but I don't hear the rest. I stomp up the stairs and out the front door of her split-level ranch. Unfortunately, she's right behind me.

"Ruby, stop." She darts forward and cuts in front of me, mirroring me when I try to sidestep her. Damn her sober reflexes. Everly doesn't drink. It used to annoy the shit out of me until she told me it was because both her parents are in recovery. She's scared if she starts, she'll never stop. *How responsible,* I think, untwisting the cap on the bottle.

"What do you want from me, Ev?"

"I've been your best friend for seven years. Don't you think it's finally time to let me in?"

"You are in," I shout, raising my hands and then slapping them down to my sides. "You know everything there is to know about my shitty life. What else do you want?"

"Oh, I don't know. Hypothetically, let's just say you had a crush on the new girl. It would be nice if we could talk about that. You know, like best friends? Instead of you coming over and getting all angsty and shit-faced in my basement. If you're afraid I'm weirded out or something, I'm not."

"I don't have a crush on her," I say, which is technically not a lie. She's more than a crush, she's a goddamn . . . I don't even know. A chair-stealing, car-hitting, loudmouthed life ruiner. I take another swig.

"Fine." Everly sighs. "But if you did *or* ever do in the future, I'm here for you."

"It's fine. *I'm* fine. I don't need you to be 'here' for me or whatever. You and Tyler and everyone else can just take all of this pity and concern and throw it right in the trash, because I don't need it!" I punctuate my words with a tilt of the bottle. "Do you hear me? I don't need anything!"

Everly steps forward, wrapping her arms around me so tight that I almost lose my balance. I will not cry. I. Will. Not. Cry.

"Shh, it's okay," she says.

I bury my head in her shoulder as Marcus opens the front door. The light from inside the house spills out onto the driveway, swallowing us whole. "You good?" he calls out.

I step back into the shadows and wipe at my eyes. "I'm going," I say quietly. "But thanks."

"Come inside," Everly says.

I shake my head but hold the whiskey bottle out to her. "Take this away, and please let me go. I'm gonna walk it off."

"Let me drive you home at least. It's like two miles."

"We'll talk tomorrow or something, okay? I just want to walk."

She looks unsure but doesn't move to stop me. And I wonder, is this what coming out feels like? Is it always this bad and drunk and confusing? Does it still count if you try to take it back?

I'm barely to the end of Everly's street when I start to get mad. Mad that Morgan makes me feel these things. Mad that she makes me question things that I thought I knew right down to my bones. Things like *I'll only crush on famous girls I'll never meet* and *I'll never want to be anyone's girlfriend. Ever.* Screw her for stirring this up and then shutting the door in my face. She. Shut. The. Door.

I don't need her. I don't need her shit. Her goddamn . . .

There are other hot people in the world, is all. And if I'm going to end up on the floor, drunk, confessing that I like girls, then it's gonna be over someone who warrants it. And Morgan Matthews doesn't. I deserve, like, Kristen Stewart or Tessa Thompson or, like, every girl in the cast of *Riverdale*. Go big or go home, right? That's big, not Morgan. Morgan is tiny. A blip. A minuscule thorn in my side that just keeps digging and digging and . . . I should tell her that. Right now. Just march up like, *Oh, you don't want to kiss me? Well, guess what? I don't want to kiss you anymore either.*

There's a teeny-tiny part of my brain screaming at me that this is bad idea, but I hang a right anyway and find my way to

Morgan's front porch. Because there is a much bigger part of my brain that wants her to know that I'm done. That I tried. That *she's* the mess that *I* can't be a part of, and not the other way around.

I knock. And when she doesn't come to the door, I knock again, harder. And then I push the buzzer until the door is wrenched open by a very sleepy-looking Morgan saying, "Jesus, Dylan, did you forget your keys or . . ." Her words drop off when she sees me.

I stand up a little straighter. "Hi."

"What are you doing here?"

I scratch my neck, conceding to the little voice in my head that, yeah, maybe showing up drunk on Morgan's doorstep in the middle of the night was, in fact, a terrible plan. But oh well.

"Ruby?" Morgan crosses her arms. She's in a T-shirt advertising some track invitational and the tiniest pair of sleep shorts that I have ever seen. I can tell she's not wearing a bra, and I know I absolutely should not be noticing that, so I look away hard and fast before I stare too long.

I try to tell her that I don't want to kiss her. That she's no KStew. But everything gets jumbled, and what comes out is "I want to kiss KStew."

She scrunches up her forehead. "Okayyyyy? Cool?"

I take a deep breath and hang my head. "No. Well, yeah, but no. I was trying to say that it's fine that you slammed the door. Because there are ten thousand other hot people in the world, and you're just a blip or . . . or . . . a speed bump, you know, because of the whole . . ."

She raises an eyebrow. "*Hitting me with your car* thing?"

"Exactly. You remembered!" A goofy smile spreads across my face. "Anyway, I'm officially raising the bar. So, yeah. You"—I poke her chest—"are out."

"Okay, thanks for letting me know, then." She starts to shut the door.

"You're welcome, little blip," I answer, tilting my chin up as I turn to walk down the steps. But I misjudge the distance and end up skidding down all three of them on my butt.

I try to push myself up, scraping my arm in the process, which is when Morgan appears beside me, barefoot in sharp gravel, and no, no, no, she shouldn't be out here because of me. She should be inside in her little sleep shorts, sleeping.

"Quiet. You're very drunk," she says. It's not a question but a statement. She wraps her arm around me and hauls me up.

"So what?" I mumble, and try to shrug her off.

Morgan tightens her grip, steering me inside her apartment. There's a little scrape on her cheek that wasn't there earlier, and I reach out my hand, grazing it gently, until she unceremoniously drops me onto the couch and leaves.

I'm not sure what I'm supposed to be doing, so I sit still, right where she left me, hoping we'll both hate me less in the morning if I behave. I regret leaving my bottle. Not that I'm anywhere near sober, but I would like to be drunker. A lot drunker. Like, *won't remember any of this tomorrow* drunker.

She returns a second, a minute, an hour later—what is time when you're wasted on stolen whiskey on your crush's couch?—with a washcloth and a little first aid kit. She dabs at the scrape on my arm and shoves a Band-Aid in my hand with a clipped "Here."

"Thanks," I say, choking on a smile. Because I should definitely not find Morgan playing nurse this hot.

"Anything else, or are we done?" she asks, putting distance between us.

I duck my head. "I guess not."

She sighs and heads down the hall, disappearing into one of the rooms. I'm not sure if I should stay or go. Probably go, right?

I'm almost to her front door when she comes back.

"What are you doing?"

"Leaving," I say, turning to see her holding a pillow and a blanket.

"Not like this, you aren't." She drops the stuff on the couch. "Please tell me you didn't drive here."

"Everly took my keys."

"Everly should have taken all of you and put you to bed." She spreads out the blanket and fluffs the pillow.

"She tried, but I'm stubborn."

"I've noticed."

"You don't have to do this."

Morgan puts a hand on her hip. "I'm not letting you walk home alone, and my brother is at a concert with the car. It's this or I get dressed and bike you home, and I really, really don't feel like doing that, okay? Will you please just lie down and sleep this off so I can go back to bed? I'm begging."

"Okay," I half whisper as I move over to the couch. "I'm sorry I woke you up." I search her eyes as I say it, hoping she sees how serious I am. She must see something, because her face softens, just a little.

I think I hear her whisper good night as her bedroom door clicks shut.

26

MORGAN

At first, I think I'm in my old room, at my actual house, with my giant yellow lab, Dusty, sprawled across me. He always used to sneak in whenever my mom forgot to shut my door after she peeked in before work every morning.

But then I hear Dylan shout, "I'm out," the way he always does before leaving, and it all comes rushing back: where I am, what happened last night. The weight shifts against me with a little hum, an arm snaking its way over my side. Definitely not Dusty, then.

I crack open my eyes and find Ruby tangled up around me. I'm trapped under the blankets with her on top of them. I take in her still-sleeping form, torn between being furious she's in my bed and marveling at how peaceful she looks right now with her face relaxed and her hair spilling out around her.

But I can't let this happen.

I take a deep breath and lean into her with a sort of half-stretch, half-shove gesture that knocks her just enough to wake her. I can tell when she really registers what's going on, her sleepy confusion giving way to big, wide eyes. Her entire body goes tense as she scrambles backward to the end of my bed.

I push up to my elbows. "Yep," I say, looking down at her.

"I'm sorry."

"For coming here last night to tell me that you didn't need me, or for ending up in my bed after I put you on the couch?"

"Both?" She runs her hand over her face. "I panicked when I heard your brother drive up last night. I was planning to sleep on your floor, I swear. I don't know what happened."

"Why'd you panic?"

"I didn't want you to get in trouble because I was here," she says, wrapping one arm around her shoulder.

I tilt my head. "I texted him to let him know. It was totally fine."

"Oh," she says, and then we both just sit in super-uncomfortable silence.

"I'm going to hop in the shower," I say when it's clear she doesn't have anything else to add. "Will you still be here when I get out?"

"Probably not."

I nod. It's not like I wasn't expecting that answer.

I take my time in the shower, trying really hard not to think about the fact that in the last thirty-six hours or so, the girl I like kissed someone else, kissed me, showed up drunk on my doorstep to tell me there are other hot girls—which is the part I'm really trying not to cling to, because for her to say "other" implies that she might actually be including me in the "hot girls" category—and *then* slept in my bed all night, which I am too much of a heavy sleeper to even have been able to appreciate.

Cold water forces me out of the shower before I'm ready to face the truth: Ruby will be gone when I get back to my room, and last night will just be another memory to toss on top of the *mixed messages from girls I like* pile.

I wrap myself in a towel and pad to my room, hesitating before I walk in. It's fine that she's gone, I remind myself . . . except Ruby didn't actually leave after all.

"You're still here," I say, clutching my towel a little tighter as water from my hair drips down the side of my face.

She swallows hard, her eyes widening before she looks away. "I'll give you a chance to get dressed," she mumbles. "Can I borrow your bathroom?"

"Sure?" I say, still sort of shocked.

I dress faster than I ever have in my life and then fly around trying to straighten up before she gets back. Not that I didn't just leave her alone in my mess of a room for fifteen minutes. I'm sitting on my bed, trying to look nonchalant, when she opens the door, her hair in a messy bun on top of her head.

"I, uh, borrowed some toothpaste too," she says sheepishly.

"You can keep it," I say, like an absolute grade-A dork.

A small smile spreads across her face. She starts to come closer but then seems to think better of it, folding her arms behind her and leaning against the wall near my door.

"Morning," she says.

"You didn't go."

"Do you wish I did?"

"I don't know. I mean, I'm sure you and KStew will be very happy together, so."

Ruby hangs her head, chewing her lip for a second. "Sorry about all that." When I don't say anything else, she looks at me, her eyes wild. "You constantly make me feel . . ." She shakes her head. "Morgan, sometimes you are the most frustrating person I've ever met."

"Wow, thanks." I frown.

"I'm just being honest." She shrugs. "What happened to your cheek?"

"I fell."

"When? Where?"

"Yesterday, in the woods."

"I thought you only went trail running when you were really upset?" She huffs out a little startled sound. "Wait, did you run in the woods because of me?"

I cross my arms and look away.

"Morgan . . ."

"What do you want me to say? That I like you? You already know that. That it hurt when you made me feel like I was some kind of an experiment? Fine, you win. It hurt. Anything else?"

"No, that's not—"

"None of it matters, though. It doesn't change anything between us."

"It matters to me," Ruby says, pushing off the wall.

"Why?"

"Because this doesn't happen to me!"

"What? Kissing girls?"

"No, relationships!" Ruby practically shouts. "I don't do relationships. Period. With anyone. But you've got me so messed up over here. I don't . . . What do I even do with this?"

"Nothing," I snap, standing up to, I don't know, kick her out again or something. "My days of being someone's experiment are way, way over."

"I'm not experimenting. I really fucking like you, okay?!" Ruby shouts, taking another step toward me. "Why don't you get that?"

I roll my eyes. "Maybe because you showed up drunk at my house last night, crying and telling me how much you don't."

"I wasn't crying."

"Well, you had been," I say, just to get in a jab.

She shakes her head. "Whatever. I told you I was sorry."

"'Sorry' doesn't explain it happening in the first place!"

Ruby laces her fingers over her forehead, never breaking eye contact. "I tried to kiss you, and you slammed the door on me."

"Because I'm not playing your games!" I shout. "You can't just like me when you're drunk."

"I wasn't drunk yesterday afternoon!"

And that I don't have an answer for. But I know this: We aren't working. We aren't in sync at all. "I can't do this with you, Ruby."

Her face falls, all the anger draining away. "Why not?"

And the sincerity behind her question knocks the air out of me. Everything I know and feel about this absolute tornado of a person standing in my room right now starts spinning around my head along with everything Aaron said yesterday, punctuated by her big puppy-dog eyes and the sad slump of her shoulders. So what if she's a mess? Maybe we all are. But what if she's meant to be *my* mess, and I'm meant to be *hers*?

"Do you really like me?" I ask, my voice so small and unsure it barely sounds like me at all.

"I'm not allowed to like you," she says, biting her lip. "But I don't really care about that right now."

"What does that mean?"

She takes another step toward me, so close we're nearly face-to-face. "It means I don't care about anything except how much I want to kiss you and have everything be okay between us."

"Just right now?" I ask as she comes even closer, her nose skimming against my cheek.

"We gotta start somewhere, don't we?"

She pauses right before our lips touch, letting me be the one to close the distance this time, to be the one making the choice. And I do.

It's our first kiss, the first one that really, truly counts, and my toes curl.

She nudges my lips open, her hand tangling in my hair, as we dissolve into a mess of smiles and teeth and tongues. And it feels like nothing exists beyond where our bodies meet. Because Ruby Thompson is the very best kisser, and this kiss is one for the ages, and I want it to last forever.

Ruby walks me backward toward the bed, giggles escaping us both as we fall onto the mattress. Her hands and hair, her lips and nails, are everywhere at once. She kisses like she's dying, like it's our last moment on earth. She pushes up my shirt and brushes her lips against my sides and my stomach so desperately, and then she's back in front of me, so close I can count her freckles before she disappears against my neck, my entire body trembling as her hand snakes down, past the band of my shorts, and then—

"Wait," I say, my hand on her wrist before she can go any farther. She stills, looking at me with a mixture of concern and lust that quickly turns to fear and rejection as she jerks away.

"Sorry, sorry," she says, trying to get out of the bed, but I pull her close until she buries her head in my neck and finally breathes. "I shouldn't have."

"It's okay," I say, running my hand up and down her back.

Ruby pushes herself up to her elbows. "Was it not good?"

I frown at the fear in her face and touch her cheek. "No, it was amazing. You're amazing. I'm just not ready for that yet. Are you?"

"Yes," she insists, looking like she has something to prove as she leans in for another kiss.

"Ruby," I say, tucking some of her hair behind her ear with a soft smile. "I know what you're doing."

"I'm making out with the person I like," she says, and sticks out her tongue.

"I don't want it like this," I say, and she looks confused. "I don't want you to hide your feelings behind sex."

"I'm not," she says, distracting me with another kiss behind my ear.

"Then what?" I ask, when I regain my senses.

She looks down to where her fingers are tracing lazy infinity symbols on my arm and takes a deep breath. "I want to show you how much I like you." She looks up at me then, her eyes a little glassy, her lips a little wobbly. I open my mouth to say something, but she just shakes her head, letting out a self-deprecating laugh as she pushes herself off the bed.

"Ruby, we don't have to have sex for me to know . . ."

She turns around, shrugging as she raises her hands and drops them. "What do you expect? Because this is who I am. I do pageants, I fix cars, and I . . . If you're looking for another, deeper Ruby or something, she doesn't exist. So I don't know, Morgan. Is this just pointless?"

"Ruby," I say, more sternly.

She turns to me, looking utterly lost. "Yeah?"

"I am interested in that."

"What?"

"The cars, the pageants, the . . . rest," I say. "I'm very interested."

"But . . ."

"But I want to know more than the fact you like cars and were a runner-up Miss Tulip or whatever before we go farther than, like, kissing. I want to know what those things *mean* to you. It's not that I'm not interested; it's that I'm not ready. I want to take it slow, and I really, *really* hope you can understand."

She hesitates before answering, like she's really thinking it over, and then nods. "All right, Matthews. We can try. But I'm gonna need more hints about what you're looking for, okay?"

I smile. "I don't have anywhere to be right now, do you?"

She shakes her head.

"Take me somewhere, then."

"Where?"

"Somewhere that matters to you," I say, and her face, it just lights up.

"I can definitely do that," she says, leaning closer. "But can I have another kiss first?"

"One," I say, holding up my finger with a laugh as she tackles me on the bed. "One kiss."

"One kiss." She grins. "For now."

27

RUBY

I forgot that I left my car at Everly's until I stepped outside Morgan's apartment. And with Morgan's sore ankle—
it doesn't matter that she's trying to hide it; I noticed right
away when she got out of the shower—no way am I letting
her walk all the way to Everly's with me. Instead, I convince
her to let me borrow her bike and set her up on the couch
with frozen peas—despite her protestations—and pedal my
heart out.

Everly isn't home when I get there, but a quick text
tells me that she left my keys under the front seat of my
car. I text her back a quick **thank you**, along with a kissy
face, before shoving my phone into my pocket and going for
the keys.

There's something else under there too, and when I slide it out, I see it's the picture Everly took of me, lust-struck on the bleachers. She must have printed it out after I left. There's a hot pink sticky note on it that says, *We need to talk. Love you.* And I know. I know. I run my hand over my face and head behind the car, safely depositing the picture in the trunk. I don't want Morgan to know it exists, to know how far gone I was on her from the start. *It's safer this way,* I think as I shut the trunk.

I recline the passenger seat and hit the quick release on the front tire of Morgan's bike before sliding it inside. I have to take a couple really deep breaths when a little mud gets on my nice leather seats, but Morgan is worth it.

When I get to her apartment, though, I ask her if she's cool with hanging for a little bit so I can get it cleaned up, using a little of the car interior cleaner I keep stashed under the passenger seat—okay, a lot of the car interior cleaner. She laughs and says yes before disappearing back inside.

When everything is said and done and I finally go in, marginally sweaty but feeling a thousand times better, Morgan is carrying plates to the table, pizza and salad already sitting on it.

"You didn't have to do all this," I say, torn between marveling and panicking at the utter domesticity of it all.

"No trouble." She grabs some napkins off the counter and slides into one of the seats at the table. "I just reheated some old pizza and opened a bag of lettuce."

"I know, but—"

"Eat," Morgan says. "This is more of a precaution than a good deed."

I raise my eyebrows.

"I get very, very, very hangry when I don't eat. And I skipped breakfast."

I laugh. "I'm sure I can handle you a little hangry."

"Oh, it's not a little. It's like DEFCON one—run for cover, scorched earth, the whole nine. You *will* cower in the face of a hungry Morgan."

"Good to know," I say, passing her the salad. "Eat up, then. I didn't leave any time in the schedule for cowering."

"So where exactly are we going?" Morgan asks within minutes of us being on the road.

"You'll see," I say, desperately trying to ignore the constant thrum of *What if this is a terrible idea?* spiraling through my head.

"I can't wait." She sets her hand over mine as I shift gears, giving it a little squeeze, and for a second my fear flies out the window, disappearing into the warm spring air.

I'm alone in this car with the person I like. And she likes me back. And right now, that's enough. I flex my hand, catching her fingers between mine, and her lips curve up in a smile.

Roughly ten minutes later, we're pulling up in front of Billy's garage, the comforting scent of grease and gasoline wafting in through my open windows. I glance at Morgan, who stares inquisitively at the building.

"Come on," I say. "I want you to meet someone."

Billy is hunched over his desk, wrestling with a jammed-up stapler and letting out an impressive string of swears, when we step inside his office.

"Here, let me," I say, taking it from him and using one of my long nails to pry out the pile of staples from when he obviously just kept squeezing it and hoping for a different result.

"What are you doing here, kid?" he asks. He wipes his hands on a rag and then leans back in his seat. "I didn't think I'd see you until . . ." He stops midsentence, finally noticing Morgan hovering in the doorway. She gives him a little wave as I set the now-fixed stapler down in front of him. "And who's this?" he asks, looking thoroughly amused.

"This is my . . ." I hesitate. My what, exactly? "Friend" doesn't seem to cut it, but I definitely can't say "girlfriend" either.

Billy eyes me, curiosity dancing across his face. Morgan steps forward with her hand out. "I'm Morgan," she says. "Nice place."

"Your friend's a liar, Ruby," he says. "A polite liar, but a liar nonetheless."

"Hey, in her defense, she doesn't even have a car. She probably genuinely thinks your shithole is what garages are supposed to look like." I smirk.

"You need to teach her better, then," Billy says, narrowing one eye. "Can't send her out into the world thinking that way."

"I will." I laugh. And this would be the perfect moment to

grab her hand, to show Billy exactly who she is to me, but I'm not ready. Morgan tucks hers in her pockets, almost like she knows it too.

"What can I do for you girls today?" Billy asks.

"Morgan wanted to see where I hang out. I thought she could meet you and I'd show her around a little."

"Well, I'm pleased to meet you, Morgan. And, Ruby, you know you don't need my permission to go poking around in here," he says. "I've got about fifty invoices to staple now, though, so I trust you can handle the grand tour on your own?"

"Yeah," I say, relief washing over me.

I don't know if he gets it, if he realizes that this is as close as I've ever gotten to bringing somebody home to meet my family, but if he does, he seems on board—and even figured out a way to give us privacy to boot. Billy hasn't had fifty invoices this month, let alone this week.

I step into the main bay, pulling his office door shut for good measure. The garage is eerily silent—not even Billy's favorite *Best of Johnny Cash* CD is playing, a rarity for this place. I take Morgan to the far corner of the garage, away from the lifts, where I have a little workspace.

"This is my area," I say. She stops at the bulletin board I've filled up with pictures of models posing with cars. All of them are women.

She looks at me, a smirk on her face. "Nice pics."

"I just really like the cars?" I say with a fake wince.

"Mm-hmm, yeah, all of these women have really, really nice . . . cars," she says, then bursts out laughing so hard she snorts, and, oh my god, I love her. I mean, not really, but still.

I slide open one of the drawers once we've reined it in. "These are my tools here, and these are some parts I'm working on. Billy lets me work off stuff for my car. He's a flipper on top of his regular work. He'll bring in these really garbage cars, and then I work on them with him until they can pass inspection and be sold. That's how I fixed up my car, actually."

"There is no way that was ever a garbage car," she says, gesturing toward the parking lot, where my baby sits, its fresh paint job glinting in the sunlight.

"Yeah, she was." I reach into another drawer and pull out what Billy calls my "befores and afters"—pics we take when we first bring a car in and then on the day it's sold. I flip through the pile until I find the "before" picture of my car, all rusted-out and ruined, and drop it on the table in front of her. She picks it up and holds it in view of my baby, squinting as she looks back and forth.

"There is no way that is the same car."

"It's amazing what you can do with an angle grinder and too much free time," I say as we walk to get a closer look.

"I don't believe you."

"Look," I say, pointing to a tiny little dent on the side fender in the picture and then pointing to it on my car. "Same dent."

She scrunches up her eyebrows. "If you could turn that rust bucket into this incredible car, why didn't you fix that dent? You fixed everything else."

"I wanted to leave it," I say, a blush rising to my cheeks.

"Why?" She stands so close her pinkie finger brushes against mine.

"It's stupid."

"Good thing I like stupid, then."

I roll my eyes with a good-natured sigh. "Fine, I left it as a reminder of its rough times or whatever. You can buff them out and paint over them, but they're still there. Still a part of you, and that has to be okay, right? You have to live with it, but it's not the end of the world." I bite my lip. "Like I said, it's stupid."

"No," she says, looking at me so earnestly it hurts. "It's really not. It's . . ." She trails off.

"What?"

"It's just, you do the whole pageant thing and then all of this. I don't know a lot of girls who could pull off both at the same time."

I'd be marginally offended if she didn't sound so sincerely in awe. "Well, some girls do."

"Yeah," she says, bumping her shoulder against mine. "I guess they do."

And I swear to god I might explode if I don't kiss her right this second, but I know I can't. Not in public, not in places that aren't just hers and mine, that aren't safe. Not yet. I look at her, and she smiles. I hope she gets it. I hope she can feel how much I want to.

Even when I can't.

28

MORGAN

I don't know what Monday is going to bring.

I half expect Ruby to be waiting to drive me to school when I get out of the shower, and I half expect her to just never talk to me again. Neither is quite accurate, it turns out—the truth is somewhere in the middle.

She smiles at me in the halls instead of scowling and even says hi as she passes me on her way to gym. I catch her friend Everly staring at me more than once during the day. Did Ruby tell her about us? *Is* there an "us"? But when I smile at Everly, she doesn't react, so I decide it's all in my head.

When it's finally, finally time for Government, I'm practically bursting from nerves and anticipation. I get to sit next to her, with a totally discreet and socially acceptable cover . . . or I would have, if Allie and Lydia hadn't grabbed me as soon as I walked in.

"Oh, I was going to . . ." I say, gesturing to the other side of the room, but their exaggerated sad faces have me taking my old seat.

Ruby walks in a few minutes later, and I swear she looks a little hurt, or at least as disappointed as I am, when she sees where I'm sitting. I gesture toward my friends like, *What can you do?* and hope she understands. At least this way, we're directly across from each other, which should make it easier to watch her in class without getting busted. Which I pretty much do the entire period.

There are a lot of things I never noticed about her. Like the way she chews her pen, which usually I find super annoying but suddenly find kind of endearing. Or the way she scrunches up her forehead when she's taking notes. Or the way she bites her lip and looks up at me through her eyelashes every time she catches me watch—

"You're staring," Lydia whispers into my ear, startling me enough to send my pen spiraling out into the middle of the floor. Ruby smirks and puts the tip of her pen cap between her teeth, one eyebrow raised, both her eyes on the paper in front of her. I drop my head down so fast it thuds against the desk.

"Is something wrong, Ms. Matthews?" Mrs. Morrison asks.

"No," I mumble, rubbing my forehead.

"In that case, is there anything you'd like to share with the class?" I vigorously shake my head. Ruby laughs, and Lydia hands me another pen with a confused glance.

I bolt the second the bell rings, lost somewhere in the confusing middle ground between turned on and mortified. I sprint to my next class, slipping into my seat and taking a minute to regroup before the rest of the class gets there. My phone vibrates, and I pull it out. It's from Ruby . . . a single smirk emoji and nothing else.

I drop my head and stifle a groan before pulling out my precalc book.

The rest of the day slips back into normalcy, for which I am at least temporarily grateful. Besides an occasional head nod or smile in the hallway, nothing is noticeably different.

It's only when I'm in the locker room before track, pulling on my rainbow glitter CLOSETS ARE FOR CLOTHES tank top, that I start to worry yet again that this last weekend was just a one-off. What if we've peaked at smirking-across-the-classroom friends who occasionally kiss?

"Hurry," Allie whines, tapping her foot by the door. "I don't want to be late again and get stuck doing push-ups."

I open my mouth to say I'm coming, but then I see it—or her, actually. Ruby, peeking out at me from the showers in the back of the locker room. No one uses them here. I don't even know if they work. She holds her finger to her lips with a smile and then disappears.

I look at Allie. "Go ahead. I gotta screw in my spikes still."

"Oh my god." She sighs. "You're a disaster."

I flash her an exaggerated wince as she disappears out the door. I listen for a second to make sure we're alone and then tiptoe toward the showers. I creep up behind the edge of the stall wall and then jump around it, growling with my hands up . . . but she's not there. "Ru—"

My voice is cut off as hands snake around my mouth and waist. I kick and bite and try to scream, my instincts crowding out all rational thought as I'm dragged backward into the darkest corner of the locker room.

The hands let go, and Ruby lets out a "Jesus" along with a tiny pained laugh. I spin around to see her doubled over.

"Ruby!"

"Holy shit, you kick hard." She huffs, her hands on her knees.

"Are you okay?" My hands go flying, fussing over every inch of her until she stands up, somehow smiling. "What were you thinking?"

"You were trying to scare me first! I was just returning the favor. Or so I thought. Except then you went all Ronda Rousey on my ass."

"Sorry, oh god, sorry," I say. She pulls me closer and tips my chin up so we're face-to-face.

"Don't be," she says, and then leans in to kiss me. And there it is, that kind of euphoric, kind of terrifying, tingly upside-down feeling I get whenever I'm around this girl. Even a boring day of high school couldn't dull it. "I've been dying to do that all day."

"Same," I say, grinning because Ruby Thompson is kissing me in the gym locker room, and that's somehow absurd and perfect all at once.

She gently touches the scrape on my cheek, studying my face intently. "Are you sure you're okay to run?"

"Yes, Mom," I snark.

"You were limping yesterday."

"Yeah, but I distinctly remember someone making me put it up and ice it after dropping me off. So now it's better."

Ruby looks at me suspiciously. "Then why's it all covered in tape?"

"Preventative measure."

She frowns but then leans in for another quick kiss.

"What's that for?"

"Preventative measure." She smirks and then walks out.

After track, I run home for a quick shower and a FaceTime with my dad—who decidedly does not want to talk about the lawsuit at all and quickly puts Mom on instead—and then I bike over to the center. I have another meeting with Danny later today, and I'm really hoping that this will be the time when he really opens up to me. I've loved getting to know him; I'm just not sure if I've actually been *helping* him.

"Everything okay?" Izzie asks me when I walk in. She's standing in the common room, fussing with the furniture. She and Aaron have been working on setting up a space for the bags we're putting together with the donations from Pride Club. Anika and I just put the bins out and hung the posters the other day, but we're already getting some cool stuff. I can't wait to see it all here, where it can actually help people.

"Yeah," I say finally, because it is. I think. Mostly.

She studies my face. "You know, Morgan, you can always talk to me if something's bothering you. You've been doing great work as a peer counselor, but that doesn't mean we aren't a resource for you as well."

I sigh. "Am I that obvious?"

Izzie smiles. "No, but I've been doing this long enough to be able to tell when someone has something on their mind."

"It's . . ." I say, not sure exactly where to start. I glance over at the empty space she just made, and it hits me what's really wrong. "It's just that I'm not sure if I'm doing enough."

"Morgan," she says, "you have become an incredible asset to our center! I'm sorry if I haven't made clear how happy we are with you."

"Thank you, that means a lot. But I'm not just talking about here." I look up at her. "Here, I feel like I'm making a difference, but then I go home and the lawsuit is moving *so slowly*. Sometimes it feels like moving here was the equivalent of running away. Like yeah, my waiver's up in the air and all of that stuff is a mess, but I can't stop thinking about the kids at my old school or even Danny. What am I really doing to change things for people like me? Shouldn't I be out there, loud, like those Parkland kids or Nupol Kiazolu or Greta Thunberg or something?"

"I can understand that feeling." Izzie leans her shoulder against one of the shelves and gives me another soft smile. "But you are doing a lot—you're very involved in Pride Club, you volunteer here, you're in the middle of a legal battle even if it doesn't feel like it day to day, and you're an incredible role model. You risked everything to take a stand, and you're just getting started. I have no doubt that you are going to do big things for our community, but I need you to do me one favor."

"Anything," I say.

"Don't sell short the work that you're already doing and the things that you've already accomplished. You're not Greta, but you *are* Morgan Matthews, and that means something too. I promise that I'll help you find more opportunities, but activism isn't something that happens in just one way or in just one place. There will always be more battles, and beating yourself up about not being able to do it all, all at once, doesn't do anyone any good. Please take the time to honor what you're already doing, because that's important too."

The door opens behind us then, and Danny walks in, giving me the patented bro nod as he pulls off his hat.

"And I'm sure Danny would be the first to agree," Izzie says.

"About what?" he asks.

"Basically? That Morgan is awesome," she says. "Tell her. She doesn't believe me."

"Oh my god," I groan, my cheeks heating. This is almost mom-level embarrassment. "You do not have to tell me that."

He flashes me a confused look as we head toward the counseling room.

"It's true!" Izzie calls after us.

"Sorry about that," I say as I shut the door behind us.

"It's fine. I don't know if I'd say 'awesome' ..." He trails off as I drop into the chair next to him. "But I can agree that you don't totally suck."

I laugh. "Fair enough."

And that feels like a win.

29
RUBY

Today, Morgan Matthews is getting a proper date. She doesn't know it yet, but I do, and I'm practically bouncing off the walls.

It's almost the one-week anniversary of, well, whatever we are, and I want to mark the occasion. There's a lot to be grateful for: It's been a week of stolen kisses in hidden doorways, of making out in empty classrooms and locker rooms, of FaceTiming all night every night after Chuck falls asleep, of holding hands under desks.

It has also been a week of dodging Everly's questions: "What are you two exactly?" I still don't really know yet. But whatever this is and whatever it's becoming, we're one week closer to it.

Which means tonight is going to be a big step. Tonight is a real date, at an actual restaurant. We're going to hold hands. Flirt. Kiss. Do all the things that other couples do. Things that make my stomach flip in good and bad ways, but I know how much it's going to mean to Morgan, so it's worth it.

I've been counting down the seconds all day while I've been stuck at the studio working for Charlene. By the time classes are done and it's time for my private lesson, I'm too distracted to really focus on the practice interview questions.

"What is one moment in your life you'd like to relive and why?" Charlene asks.

It takes all my willpower not to answer, *When Morgan finally kissed me back.* Instead, I mumble something about past pageant duties, and she frowns and tells me to speak up.

Eventually, she takes pity on me and offers to check my walks and talent routine instead. Tap isn't technically her jurisdiction—I have a whole other instructor for that—but she says she wants to make sure it all "flows." I think we both know I'm useless until I burn off some of this jittery energy.

I practically run to my car afterward and barely even get it started before I'm texting Morgan. I remind her I'm picking her up and tell her to wear something casual but nice-ish. She jokes: **I guess that means no graphic tees then?** And I don't know what to say, because graphic tees are totally fine for where we're going. I worry that maybe I set her expectations too high.

I debate calling the whole thing off. Then I rush home to stress-dress instead.

"Where do you think you're off to?" my mom asks when I'm elbows deep in my closet looking for clothes that say I'm trying but not too hard.

"Out with friends," I say, settling on a cute top and jeans so tight I can barely breathe. I hope Morgan appreciates the way they show off my . . . assets.

"You have a pageant tomorrow," Mom says, leaning against the door frame. And god, I hate when she finds some stupid Sunday pageant to enter me in. They're almost always the mall modeling ones that aren't even worth the cost of entering. Mom watches me, waiting for me to say something negative, daring me, maybe. She's holding a coffee mug, but I smell the sharp tang of alcohol coming from it.

"Jesus, Mom, don't you have to work?" I pull the mug out of her hand, setting it on my dresser as I turn back to my clothes.

"What the hell, Ruby!"

"Don't let Chuck . . ." I trail off, because it doesn't matter. Chuck's going to drag Mom down if she lets him, and for whatever reason, she's too lovestruck to do anything about it.

"Mind your own business," she snaps.

"Kind of hard to mind my own business when yours is living in our house, getting you drunk before your shift."

"Watch it." And there's enough fire in Mom's eyes to tell me to leave it alone.

"Sorry," I say, softening my tone. "I just worry."

Some of the hardness slips from her face as she pats my

arm. "You don't have to worry about me, baby. You just focus on getting us the win tomorrow." She smiles when she says it, like it's a pep talk and not a leash around my neck.

"I will," I say. "But right now, I gotta go."

"Wait." She stops me as I walk by, my date outfit balled in my arms.

"What?"

"You tell that boy no hickeys this time."

I'm sitting outside Morgan's apartment, trying not to freak out, twenty minutes before the time I said I'd be here.

I found a gas station halfway between her house and mine and finished getting ready there, under the dingy lights of its old bathroom. The scent of cheap toilet cleaner and chemical air freshener still clings to my skin. Worth it, though, to get out of my house without answering any more questions.

Then I stopped at the grocery store and bought Morgan a flower—a single purple carnation—to kill time. I would've driven around longer, but I was worried about wasting gas. I tried to calculate if I could put more in and still cover dinner, but it seemed safer to park here and wait it out.

But the curtain keeps moving in Morgan's living room, and I'm almost positive someone keeps checking to make sure I'm still here.

I debate waiting for her to come out. I'm sure she will when she's ready. But I don't want to be the type of person who waits in the car, or worse, beeps. I want to be . . . respectable, if that's even possible. Because I've never done this before, but I bet she has. And I bet it was classy and with someone who could afford more than one stupid grocery-store carnation.

The curtain moves again, forcing my hand. I pop open my car door with a reluctant sigh and drag myself up the steps to her apartment way too early. The door swings open before I can even knock, and Dylan stands there, waiting.

"Uh, hi," I say, awkwardly ducking under his arm and into the living room. I realize too late I was supposed to wait to be invited in, but oh well. Here we are.

"You must be Ruby." He shuts the door. "I'm Dylan. Have a seat." I stay standing until he crosses his arms and arches one big hairy eyebrow at me, and then my butt hits the couch fast. "Thank you. I hear you want to take my baby sister out on a date."

I shake my head no on instinct because I don't know what's safe to share or what he knows.

Dylan tilts his head. "You *don't* want to take her on a date? Because she's in her room getting ready under the impression that this is, in fact, a date. If it isn't—"

"I wasn't saying it's not a date," I cut him off, worried she might hear.

He puffs out his chest. "You shook your head no when I asked if you were taking her out."

I wince. "I didn't mean *no* no. I meant no . . . I don't . . . *not* want to take your sister on a date."

"You shook your head no because you don't *not* want to date her?" Dylan asks, and I swear he's trying to hold in a smile when he rubs his forehead. "Let's try this again: Do you want to take my sister on a date?"

I nod slowly, realizing with relief that it doesn't feel weird to say that—or at least imply it with a nod—to another person. It feels kind of good—in fact, really good. Too good to be relegated to a nod only.

"Yeah, I want to take her on a date," I say, and then I suck my lips over my teeth because saying it out loud feels bigger than I expected.

"Good. And what exactly are your intentions with her?"

"My what?"

"Your intentions. What do you want to get out of this?"

"Um." I swallow hard. "Some food?"

I've never been grilled like this before. But then again, first date ever. First almost-one-week anniversary ever. Maybe that's just how it works.

Dylan shifts a little and clears his throat. "I meant more like, where do you see this relationship going?"

"Oh," I say, "uh . . ."

Is he asking me if we're going to have sex? I don't—

"What are you doing?" Morgan asks, bolting into the room. She looks incredible in black leggings and a silky pink halter top that matches her hair and shows off her shoulders. And shit, those are some perfect shoulders. I try—and fail—not to stare.

Morgan smiles at me and then turns her attention to her brother, her eyes going cold. "Seriously, Dyl, what are you doing?"

"I don't know! I'm winging it!" he says. "Keisha's father did this to me before our first official date, and I was just trying to pick up the slack since Dad's not here."

She groans. "Why are you so annoying, and how can I make it stop?"

"It's okay, seriously," I say, worried she's really mad.

"Annoying you is part of my job as your brother." Dylan musses up her hair and earns himself another scowl. "And pissing you off is part of my job as your temporary guardian." He points at me over Morgan's shoulder. "You seem cool, Ruby. Don't mess this up, and don't break my sister's heart, or I'll break your—"

"Dylan!" Morgan shouts.

"Too far?"

"Too far."

He shrugs. "Fine. Have fun on your date, be good, and Ruby, have her home by eight fifteen."

"Eight fifteen?" Morgan shrieks. "First of all, I don't even have a curfew, and second of all, if I did it wouldn't be eight fifteen! That's in like two hours!"

"All right, I give up," he says. "Parenting is too hard. Just come home safe before tomorrow morning, okay?"

"Thank you." Morgan sighs before stepping forward to give him a hug. "I promise to be safe and to be home before midnight."

"Great," he says cheerfully. "Oh, and I'm taking Keisha out again tonight, so I won't be here when you get home regardless."

She punches his arm. "You suck so much."

"Love you too, Morgie," he says in a baby voice as she yanks me out the door.

. . .

Morgan doesn't uncross her arms until we're on the highway, and even then, it's only to adjust the air-conditioning vents. She's had a death grip on the carnation since we left. "I'm sorry about that." She looks at me nervously. "I hope it didn't freak you out."

"I thought it was cute, actually," I lie, well, half lie. It was *a little* cute, aside from the whole utterly traumatic thing. I smile at her anyway, as hard as I can. I know what she's really asking is *Are you going to ditch me because of this?* and I'm not.

"Nothing about Dylan is cute," she huffs, going to recross her arms, but I grab her hand, pulling it into my lap and lacing our fingers. I zip into the fast lane, accelerating just hard enough for her head to hit the back of her seat. I feel like an absolute rock star, zooming down the highway in the best car with the perfect girl.

I could get used to this.

Morgan raises an eyebrow at the dingy restaurant when we pull in forty-five minutes later, and I can't help but think of her brother making the same face as he asked about my intentions. I hope she's not wondering about that too. I hope she's not pissed or disappointed that our first real date is three towns over, where I know for sure we won't run into anybody from school.

"This looks . . . nice?" Morgan says, her voice lilting up.

Yeah, so maybe asking her to dress nice-ish was mostly for my benefit, but still.

"I have it on good authority the food here is amazing."

"Whose good authority?"

"That hyper chef guy on TV. He came here once to film a couple years ago. See, they even have a sign about it right there." I point to a plaque next to the wheelchair ramp boasting the restaurant's status as a "Dedicated Divine Diner," just like the name of the show.

"Well, if there's a sign," she says with an amused glint in her eye.

"Come on, let's go check it out. Actually, wait. Don't move." Morgan watches me run around the front of the car. I nearly trip when a rock wedges into my flip-flop, but I pull it together at the last second. I fling her door open with an exaggerated bow and hold out my hand.

"Oh my god, what are you doing?" She laughs, putting her hand into mine.

"I literally have no idea." I smile. "But this is what they do in the movies."

"Do you get all your dating ideas from TV and movies?"

"Pretty much." I blush. "I've never done this before."

"Never done what?" Morgan asks, following me inside.

"Gone on a real date with anyone."

Our server shows up before she can respond, grabbing two menus and leading us to a little table at the back of the restaurant. I take the seat facing the door, just to be safe. I hate that I can't turn it off, the constant worry of being seen.

Morgan glances at the menu and sets it down. "Do you want to order for me?" she asks. "They do that in the movies a lot too."

"Uh, I can?" I say, feeling the pressure. The only things I've ever seen her eat are pizza and salad.

"Oh my god, you should see your face right now." She nudges my foot under the table.

"That bad?"

"Pure panic."

"Wow, I suck at this."

"You don't," Morgan says, tapping my menu to make me look up. "But is this really your first date?"

I nod, still staring at the menu, determined to get this right.

"Ruby," she says, and waits for me to look up. "I don't need movie dates. I just want to be with you."

If my cheeks weren't red before, they are now, because that is, like, the nicest. Why is she the nicest? And how?

The server comes to take our order before I have a chance to spin too far out. Morgan orders chicken tenders with fries, and I get a burger that winds up being the size of my head.

We both laugh when I bite into it and half the condiments squirt out.

Morgan makes laughing feel easy, like happiness is the default instead of something always just out of reach. For the first time in my life, my cheeks hurt not from forcing a smile onstage, but because I legit can't stop smiling at the person across from me. It's kind of nice.

Halfway through dessert, a brownie sundae we decide to split, I ask Morgan about her commitment letter for college and running Division I next year. She seems surprised, and I admit I've been googling a lot about running and college and how it all works—and maybe more about her too. I can't help it.

She gets quiet and messes with her napkin.

"What's wrong?"

"Nothing," she says.

"Something." Nerves well up inside me as I try to figure out what I did to veer us off the fast track to happy town.

Morgan shrugs, digging her spoon into the rapidly melting ice cream. "It's just everything is kind of up in the air with that."

"But you signed a letter of intent. The picture came up when I—"

"Yeah, I did."

"I'm lost."

"So a letter of intent is like me promising to go to their school and them promising me money, right?"

I nod.

"Well, apparently, they put loopholes in the pile of tiny little letters at the end, which, in my excitement, I didn't bother to read. So it went from a sure thing to 'pending based on the outcome of my waiver.' Basically, I'm screwed until further notice, everything's on hold, and I'm so sick of it. I just want to run." She shakes her head. "Sorry, I'm dumping my problems all over our nice date."

"Don't be sorry," I say, reaching over to hold her hand. "I get how that feels."

"You do?"

"With the pageants and stuff. I love makeup and dresses

and all that crap, don't get me wrong, but I hate the pageants themselves. And I hate how much money my mom spends on them."

"Couldn't you just stop doing them, then?"

"Not if I want a place to live." I laugh until I see her horrified face. "I'm kidding. Probably. It's complicated, and yeah, my mom and I have a lot of issues. But she could've been Miss Teen USA if I hadn't come along. Her whole life would have been different. She made a lot of sacrifices to have me, you know? I'm working on a way to get off the circuit, but I don't know if I could ever completely take pageants away from her. I owe her that much."

"You don't owe your mom your future just because you think she gave up hers for you."

I pull my hand back. "It's not what I think. It's the truth."

Morgan frowns. "I know, but this is your life! And the way you talk about this versus how you absolutely lit up at the garage? It's like you're two different people. You don't have to live like that. You have options."

"Why do you care so much about my 'options'?" I ask, making air quotes. Like an asshole.

"I want you to be happy."

"Are *you* happy?" Because it doesn't sound like it, and she has plenty of options.

"Right now, at this moment?" She tips her head.

"Sure," I say, even though I meant in general. But now I really want to hear her answer.

"Yeah, actually. I'm having a really great time with you."

"Good, me too," I say, battling against her spoon for the last bite of ice cream until she grins and lets me win. "Let's be happy, then. We can worry about the rest another day."

Morgan's quiet for a second and then reaches for my hand. "Tell me more about fixing up cars?"

So I do. And she listens the whole time, adding little comments here and there to let me know she's paying attention.

And this time, I don't let go of her hand once.

30
MORGAN

That date.

I don't even know.

That date will go down in history as one of the best dates in the history of all dates ever, even if I do wish she took my whole *it's okay to not do pageants* thing more seriously.

But then Monday comes, and we're in school, back to occasional secret stolen kisses in darkened doorways, and no matter how much I try to shove it down, it starts to feel like the absolute best and worst all rolled into one. Because we're not even two weeks in and Ruby's all I think about. She seems just as obsessed with me . . . but already I'm dying to hold her hand in the hallways and not just her car. I want to call her my girlfriend. I want people to *know*.

I make it a whole other week before I muster up the

nerve to ask her if she's in the same place. We're both walking toward the track after school, her pretending like she's there to watch lacrosse with her friends, me to actually work out. Lydia and Allie have gotten used to her just being around, but I say it low so no one can hear anyway: "What are we doing? What are we?" And the way she freezes up is not exactly reassuring.

"Do we need a label?"

I look her right in the eyes and say probably the most honest thing I've ever said to anyone ever. "We don't *need* a label, but I'd really like one."

She frowns. "I like you. You know that, right?"

I shrug.

"We like each other, right?" she asks, this time confusion lacing through her voice.

"Yeah, but—"

She takes my hand and leads me behind the bleachers, away from anybody's prying eyes. "What's going on? I thought we were good."

"We were," I say. "We are. I just…" I shake my head. Maybe I'm being selfish. Maybe I'm being unreasonable for wanting more. Should sneaking around school and having sleepovers after Dylan goes to bed be enough?

Ruby leans forward, kissing the words away, and then rests her forehead against mine. "As long as we're good, let's not worry about the rest, yeah?"

"Yeah," I say, slipping under her arm and darting off to track.

And I wish I meant it.

. . .

Ruby stays for practice and even gives me a ride to the center after. We both valiantly try to pretend I never said anything. Ruby's probably hoping to avoid the conversation altogether, and I'm wishing I never started it in the first place.

I should be happy with what I have. At least that's what I tell myself over and over and over again. We both smile when we kiss goodbye, but it feels empty somehow.

My brother picks me up on his way home after my shift and tells me there's something waiting for me at home. When I try to pry, he just smiles and says, "It's a surprise." I hope it's Ruby, but I know she has to teach a couple classes tonight and then has another practice session with her coach. I'm sure she'll be fried by the time she gets done.

Whatever I thought it could be, I did not expect the surprise to be my parents standing in the kitchen, four days early for their next visit. They're unpacking bags of takeout food like this is business as usual, but the suitcases in the living room suggest this isn't just one of our usual dinners.

"Surprise!" my mom shouts, rushing over to pull me into a hug. She squeezes me tight, and when the scent of her perfume drifts into my nose, it hits me how much I've really missed her. She smells like safety and home and *Mom*, and even daily FaceTimes just aren't enough.

We both wipe at our eyes with watery laughs as she leans back to look at me. "Oh, I needed that," she says.

My dad lets out a cheery "Hey, sport" as he sets some plates on the table, politely ignoring that fact that I'm a blubbering mess. I've been so focused on everything going on with Ruby and the center and the lawsuit that I forgot what it was like to just be a family for a minute.

The sound of nails on the hardwood floor alerts me to someone else's presence, and I turn just in time to see my dog, Dusty, barreling out of the bathroom, water dripping off his face. He probably just drank half the toilet bowl, but I'm so happy to see him I don't even care. He tackles me with his giant retriever paws, and we both go sprawling backward onto the couch.

"Down, boy," Mom says. Dad grabs Dusty's collar, trying and failing to pull him off me as his sniffs and snorts all over my neck and face, his tail wagging a mile a minute.

"No, he's fine. He's a good boy." I laugh, scratching my fingers through his fur and making his back leg thump wildly as I push us both up. And, okay, my arms and legs are a little scratched up, but it's worth it for such an epic dog hug from Dusty, the very best boy.

"He misses you," Dad says.

"We all do," Mom adds.

"Take her, then." Dylan snorts. "She leaves her damn hair everywhere, finishes the milk without saying anything, and thinks every peanut butter cup in the house belongs to her."

I stick out my tongue at his grumbling, and my dad pretends to be annoyed.

"Damn kids, always fighting," he says, which earns him a whap on the back of his head from my mom.

"What's with the suitcases?" I ask once Dusty ditches me

for a Kong toy my brother has helpfully filled with peanut butter.

"Do we need an excuse to visit our kids for a few days?" Mom asks, and I look stricken because that wasn't what I was implying.

"No, that actually sounds incredible. Netflix dropped like three new rom-coms just since I've been here, so we have major TV time to catch up on." I pull out the chair across from her and start shoveling food onto my plate. "You just didn't mention it on the group text."

"Must have been on the other group text." She winks.

"What other group text?" I ask, sounding utterly scandalized.

"The one that's just us and your brother," Dad says. "Where he warns us he dyed your hair pink and we make secret plans to come visit for a week, no doubt thwarting tonight's attempt to sneak your girlfriend in—which you think Dylan doesn't know about, but he does, and so do we."

"Oh my god, Dyl!" I shout.

He just shrugs and grabs a plate. "I've never raised a kid! I don't know if you're allowed to have secret girlfriend sleepovers! What was I supposed to do? Guess?"

"You're weren't supposed to ask Mom and Dad!"

"Well, I couldn't ask you!"

I groan. "How long have you known?"

"It's an eight-hundred-square-foot apartment, Morgan, and you're about as subtle as an elephant when you open the front door in the middle of the night."

"What the—"

"Kids," Dad says in his stern *no more fighting* voice.

"Now eat," Mom says, picking up her fork. We both shut up and do as we're told, but I make it a point to elbow Dylan twice as I reach for a napkin.

"Are you here to ground me or something?" I ask once everyone has had a chance to dig in.

"No," Dad says. "Not really any point to that, since you'll be leaving for college soon anyway. But we do want to meet this girl, and we'll all be having a serious talk about boundaries and appropriate behavior when you're living in someone else's house."

"You don't want Ruby to come over?" I ask Dylan. "I thought you liked her."

"No, she's fine," he says, rubbing his forehead. "I don't care if you come here to bang or whatever, but I don't want to hear it, and I don't want to wake up to the front door slamming when she sneaks out at five every morning. That's all."

My dad chokes on some of his rice, and my mom pats his back. "Arms above your head, honey," she says, and then turns toward me. "I may have put it a little more eloquently than Dylan did, but yes, your father and I recognize that you're almost eighteen, and we trust you to make good decisions. If you want your girlfriend to spend the night, you need to ask Dylan first and be respectful about it. And your father and I both hope you're practicing safe sex. If you have any questions . . ."

And, oh my god. Oh my god. Please let me disappear into

this pile of beef lo mein. Please, god. Please. It's all I ask. "Just to be clear, we're not," I mumble.

"You're not practicing safe sex?" Mom says. "Just because you're both women—"

And, oh my god. Oh my god. Make it stop.

"No, I mean we're not . . ." I say slightly louder. "We're not . . . We don't do that when she sleeps over. We just hang out." Three sets of eyebrows raise in unison. "Fine, okay, we make out! Is that what you want me to say? But we haven't gone further than that. Her mom works nights, and her mom's live-in boyfriend is a creep, and that's why she sleeps here all the time. We're not, like, constantly . . . you know?" I stab my fork into my food, my cheeks going bright red as the rest of the table erupts into laughter.

"Wow, TMI," my brother says.

"Shut up, Dylan!" He howls when I kick him under the table.

"Look, if Ruby needs a place to crash, I don't care if she comes over," he says. "But I want to know she's here so I'm not walking around in my ratty-ass boxers when there's a random girl lurking around the apartment, okay?"

I snort. "I'd personally like it if you never walked around in your boxers."

"And I'd like it if I didn't know what it sounded like when my little sister—"

"Okay!" Dad pipes up. "Moving on before I have to shove these chopsticks into my ears so I don't have to hear whatever the end of that sentence is."

Mom and Dad exchange a look. He gives her a little nod,

and she sighs. "There are other reasons we're here, Morgan," she says.

"Besides traumatizing me for life?"

"Yes," she says, and her somber look wipes the smile right off my face.

"Okay? What's up?" I glance at my brother, but he's staring down at his plate. He doesn't even look up when I nudge his ankle.

"Well, for one, the reason we have suitcases is because we're staying straight through for your meet this weekend," she says.

"My meet?" I ask, and she smiles.

"Yes, your first one with the new team."

"Oh my god! The waiver went through?" I nearly knock over my glass in a rush to hug her. "I can really compete?"

"Yes," my mom says, both of our eyes tearing up.

"I can't believe it. We did it! St. Mary's caved!"

"Beth," my dad says, reaching over and squeezing my mom's hand. "Tell her the rest."

I shift my gaze between them, the mood of the table growing serious again as I sit back down.

"And also . . ." She takes a deep breath. "Your father and I have decided to drop the case against St. Mary's."

"What? Why?"

"Our lawyers are telling us it would be exceedingly difficult to win at this point. It's a private school, a religious school—they could take it all the way to the Supreme Court. And with the way this country is right now . . ." She trails off.

"It's costing us a lot of money to keep this going, sport," Dad says. "We picked up some steam for a little while after the news interviews, but people have moved on, and the sponsors we had before can't commit with everything stacked against us like this. It's money better spent on your future."

"And St. Mary's has a lot of very influential donors supporting them. We didn't really have a choice," Mom adds. "But the good news is that, in exchange for us dropping the lawsuit, they dropped their petition to have you banned for unsportsmanlike conduct and retracted their claim with the athletic board that you were involved in any sort of recruiting scheme. They're even sending a favorable report to your new coach, and she can send that on to the colleges so we can put this all behind us. I know you're disappointed, honey, but we accomplished the most important thing for you—"

"What about the kids that come after me?" I ask, and they look down. "What about the queer kids at that school right now? You know they're there. You even know who some of them are! How could you just give up?"

Dad takes a deep breath, like he's deciding how much to say.

"What?" I ask. "What else aren't you telling me?"

"We did think about the other kids," Dad says. "We even reached out to their parents to try to turn it into a class-action lawsuit when things started to get too expensive, but they didn't want to. The sad truth of it is that everyone just wants to keep their heads down until graduation. No one else wanted to put their necks on the line. I'm sorry. I know this isn't the outcome we were hoping for, but—"

"I'm not hungry anymore." I shove my plate away and storm off down the hall.

I slam my bedroom door and throw myself on the bed, shoving a pillow over my head and hoping the fluff will at least muffle my scream.

My door clicks open, and I drag the pillow down, ready to shout at my parents to get out. Except it's Dylan, and he's got Dusty with him.

"Hey," he says, shutting the door behind him as my dog jumps up onto my bed. "I'm sorry. I know how much this sucks."

I hug Dusty tight, burying my face in his fur. "No, you really don't."

Dylan drags his hand through his hair and then sits beside me on the bed. "Maybe you're right. I've had it comparatively easy—straight white guy and all." He sighs. "But I have to tell you something, and you have to swear not to tell Mom and Dad that I told you."

"What?" I ask, concern dulling the edges of my anger a little.

"I know they made it seem like this was a choice they made, but it really wasn't."

"But they—"

"They almost lost the house because of it. They remortgaged it to get more money out for the lawyer fees and stuff. Dad's practice too. I actually covered the house payment last month when it was really bad. I know it's ridiculously unfair that they had to do that, and that you had to go through it at all—but you got out of the situation relatively unscathed, while they were still sinking fast."

I shake my head. "But isn't there any other way? Anything at all?"

"They even tried to get the ACLU involved. Trust me, they've explored every avenue here."

I sigh. "Great, so even the ACLU wouldn't touch this?"

"Who knows?" Dylan runs his hands through his hair. "I doubt they're even aware of it yet. Apparently, it can take forever for applications to be reviewed because they get so many every day. Mom and Dad couldn't afford to wait any longer. Morgan, you have to let them off the hook. The guilt is killing them, but they were going to lose everything if they kept fighting. And you could have too. If you lose that scholarship, with the state of their finances right now . . ."

I swallow hard. I don't know what to do with this information. I always thought of my parents as invincible. The idea that they sank so much into this that they had to borrow money from my brother makes me feel a little sick.

"I guess . . ." I say, gently petting Dusty. "I guess I could keep pushing for change in other ways. I already talked to Izzie about wanting to do more. That way it's not really over. It's just sort of paused while I find a new angle."

"Yeah." He smiles, relieved. "That sounds like a great idea. And in the meantime, can we just be glad you have a safe new school and a girlfriend who seems way too cool for you?"

"Hey!"

He smiles. "But seriously, can that be enough, just for now?"

"I just feel like such a sellout."

"You're not."

"Dylan—" My phone buzzes, cutting off the moment, and Dusty hops off my bed and scratches at the door.

"Is that Ruby?" he asks, getting up and opening the door for Dusty.

"Yeah."

"Invite her over," he says. "And please talk to Mom and Dad."

"I will," I say, not sure which I'm agreeing to. Maybe both.

Ruby suddenly and mysteriously cannot make it over to my house the entire week that my parents are there. She begs off, blaming homework and late-night pageant coaching sessions, and I try not to let it bother me.

She does show up to my meet on Friday night, though. My first official home meet at the new school, one where I'm finally not a volunteer but an actual participant.

She snags me underneath the bleachers and gives me a perfectly amazing good-luck kiss before my race. If my parents wonder why my lips are suddenly the same shade of pink as the lipstick on the girl sitting in the row behind them, they don't ask. If they wonder why she shouts the loudest when I win the 800 and when we win the 4x4, they don't ask that either.

Ruby texts me afterward, sentimental and proud, from the quiet safety of her car in the parking lot. She tells me she loved seeing me race, and that I'm the "best secret" she's ever had. And I convince myself that being her "best secret" feels good, that the ache in my chest doesn't mean anything. That we're fine, great, even. That we're just resting up for the next battle.

31

RUBY

"Where have you been?" My mother's voice cuts through my happy haze before I've even made it all the way through the front door.

Watching Morgan run? Fucking awesome. Coming home after? Kill me now.

"Well?" she says, her hands on her hips.

"You scared me." The dogs yip and paw at me while I set my car keys on the counter. "What are you doing home? Don't you have work?"

"I asked you a question first. Where've you been, Ruby Gold?" I hate when she uses my middle name. Hate it with a passion. She claims she named me that because I was *so precious to her*. Right. "And don't say you were with that lacrosse boy, because I saw him down the road with Marcus tonight, and you weren't there."

"Nowhere," I answer, the hair on my neck prickling over the fact that she's been checking up on me. "Just around. But why are you still here?"

She perches herself on the edge of her recliner, where Chuck is asleep, the TV still blaring Fox News. There's a lit cigarette in his hand, and she grabs it and stubs it out all nonchalant. Like it's not a big deal he could've burned the whole place down.

"I'm taking a little time off," Mom says, jutting out her chin, daring me to question her. I don't bother. I've been on this earth long enough to know that "taking a little time off" means she got fired or laid off again.

I sigh and head for my room, trailed by the dogs. Their incessant barking adds to my frustration. Mom follows after, her foot catching my door when I try to shut it.

"Don't you walk away from me, girl."

"What was it this time? Skip work too much to hang out with your waste-case boyfriend?" I immediately regret saying it. It's rarely her fault when this happens. She'll work herself to the bone if she has to. It's just the nature of the business. There are only so many cleaning contracts to go around, which means she has to keep switching agencies for hours. And when things dry up, the last one in is the first one out. Mom is *always* the last one in these days.

"What is the matter with you?" she asks, raising her voice enough to tell me she means it.

"Where should I start?" I snap. "We have no money, and now you don't even have a job!" And I don't know why I can't stop. I'm poking the bear tonight, but something about sitting one row behind Morgan's perfectly perfect family today has me riled up.

I meet her eyes just in time for her palm to connect with my cheek. "Don't you dare talk to me like that."

I put my hand to my cheek, my nostrils flaring with anger. "That fucking hurt."

"So do words." She walks to my closet, flips through the dresses, and then flings one at me. It lands with a thump and a rustle on my bed. "Do you know what I go through just so you can have the kind of chances that I never did? How much I sacrifice?"

"I never asked you—"

"I'm your mother. It's my job." Her whole demeanor changes then, as she morphs back into my sweet, tired mom, her beauty-queen smile adorning her face. "Put that on, baby, I want to see you walk."

And I hate it. I hate that she slaps me one second and calls me "baby" the next. I hate how bad I wish I could make her happy, how every angry word feels like my fault.

"Okay," I say softly, even though I'm exhausted. This is the quickest way to end the argument, the only way really.

My mom helps me into my dress—the evening gown has always been her favorite part—and then pulls out my ponytail. She grabs one of my brushes off my dresser and slowly runs it through my hair. "What were you really up to tonight?" she asks me again, her grip tightening just slightly.

"I was fixing Mrs. Williams's car." Not a complete lie. I did stop there after the meet.

"I went down there at six looking for you after I saw the boys drive by. She said you hadn't been there yet because you were watching some running thing."

"Oh yeah, I stopped at the track meet on my way to her house. I forgot."

"Everly doesn't run, does she? I know Tyler plays lacrosse."

I swallow hard. "No, they weren't there." I turn to look at her. "I just thought it would be cool to check it out. I've never been to one. Have you? We could both go sometime. It might be fun."

Mom looks me straight in the eye, a slight frown pulling at her lips. "I heard a rumor about you today, baby girl, and it better not be true."

This is bad. This is so bad.

"What did you hear?"

She sets down the brush, taking her time before answering. "I think you know, and I think it has something to do with why you were at that track meet today." She searches my eyes like she's looking for an answer or waiting for me to break. Miraculously, I do neither. "I will not have another situation like we did with your little pageant friend. Do you understand?" I nod. "Now put your shoes on and come out," she says, and storms down the hall.

Shit.

Shit! If someone knows about me and Morgan, if someone said something and it got back to my mom . . . But I can't worry about that right now. There's no time. Not when she's like this.

My shoes wait for me in the closet, two perfect, shiny reminders of how I'm not living up to my mom's expectations. I strap my feet into them, the memory of Morgan's wins today turning to ash in my mouth. It was a risk. A stupid risk. Why did I go?

I allow myself one quick minute to wallow, then I stand tall, poised and pageant ready. The sting of my mother's hand still fresh on my cheek.

32

MORGAN

Ruby and Everly are arguing when I walk into school. I make a
mental note to ask her about it later, giving them a wide berth
as I head to my locker. Ruby has hinted that Everly knows
about us, but since we've still never been formally intro-
duced, it doesn't feel like it's my place to go calm things down
between them.

Ruby was weird all weekend, distant. She still didn't come
over, not even after my parents left. I've been sort of freaking
out that it was something I did. But seeing Ruby and Everly
fighting . . . Maybe this has nothing to do with me, or us, at
all. Maybe anxiety from the rest of her life is temporarily
bleeding into our . . . well, whatever we have. I put on a
happy face and pretend it doesn't bother me how much she
compartmentalizes all of her relationships.

Ruby ignores me in fourth period. But then she drags me into the janitor's closet when I'm walking by during sixth. Sixth is my free period, but she has English, and I know she can't afford to be skipping it.

"What are you doing?" I half laugh, expecting her to kiss me or say something along the lines of *I couldn't wait to see you*. But her face is sad, pinched somehow, like she has a bad taste in her mouth she can't quite shake.

"We need to talk," she says, and my stomach drops. I know from experience that *we need to talk* often directly precedes *this was a mistake*, which is then swiftly followed by *I don't think I like girls after all*.

I wrap my arms around myself, bracing for the worst. "About?"

"There are rumors. About *us*," she says, looking absolutely panicked now.

"What kind of rumors?"

"You know what kind of rumors," Ruby says, pulling out her ponytail just to put it back up again. "Have you told anyone? You didn't, right?"

"Huh?" My brain is still trying to process the fact that I might not be getting dumped after all, but this doesn't sound good either.

"Have you told anyone about us? Anyone? Because Everly is the only person who knew from me, and she swears on her life that she didn't tell anyone." Ruby takes a shaky breath. Is she going to cry? "But Everly said she heard stuff on her own and did her best to shoot it down so I wouldn't freak out. If it wasn't her, was it you? You wouldn't do that, right? I *know* that you know how important this is. I'm an asshole for even asking, but I need to hear it. You didn't tell anyone, right? No one besides your brother knows?"

I shift under the weight of her pleading look. "I mean, not really."

Ruby looks so shocked, so hurt, my head spins. "Not . . . really? Not really?!"

"A couple of my friends, but they wouldn't—"

"Jesus Christ," she says, turning away from me. "Jesus Christ. Who?"

"A couple friends from Pride Club. That's it. And they would never say anything. I promise."

"Why would you do that? You knew! You knew I . . ." She's practically vibrating. With anger? Anxiety? I take a step toward her, intending to wrap her in a hug, but she darts away. "Who did you tell, Morgan? Specifically. I need to know."

"Nobody, really. Just, like, Aaron—"

"Aaron? My neighbor Aaron? Fuck. Who else?"

I look away. "I don't know. Anika, Drew, and Brennan were there too, but they would *never* tell a soul about us."

"What did you tell them about me? What right did you have?"

"I didn't tell them about *you*; I told them about *us*. It's not the same thing! It's not like I outed you or something!"

"Yes, you did!" she says, tears welling up in her eyes.

"I didn't. I swear. I just told them how happy you made me,

and . . . You have to understand. They're my friends. Am I just supposed to pretend that the best thing in my life isn't happening? That's not fair."

"I am not your best thing!" Ruby shouts, putting her hands on her head with a groan.

"I don't understand what the problem—"

"The problem is that people are starting to talk about us like we're dating or something!"

"Oh." I exhale hard, her words punching the air right out of me. I thought we *were* dating.

"Yeah, 'oh,'" she says, misunderstanding. "You knew this was a secret. This was for us and not for anyone else!"

"No, right. I got it," I say, blinking back tears. "Crystal clear. Message received."

Ruby reaches for me, and now it's my turn to move away. "Don't be like that."

I gulp down an angry breath. "I don't want you touch me right now, okay?"

"Fine." She drops her hand. "I thought we were on the same page with all of this."

I paw at my cheeks, wishing they weren't wet. "Yeah, I guess I just misunderstood."

"What do you think 'secret' means, Morgan? Because it's not telling our business to anyone who will listen."

"My life is not a secret," I say, a little louder, not even caring who hears on the other side of the door. "And sorry I got the wrong idea about us dating from the flowers and the constant kissing and, you know, the *date*. And speaking of kissing, did you ever think that maybe I don't just want to do that when we're alone anymore? That maybe I want to kiss my girlfriend after winning a race like everyone else kisses whoever they're dating, you know, without hiding under the bleachers like we're committing a crime?"

"You know we can't—"

"Yeah, now I do. We can't do any of that. Ever." I push past her to the door. "Because it turns out, I don't have a girlfriend. I just have a secret."

Aaron pops in while I'm sitting in the peer counseling room, my head on the table and my heart on the floor. Because Ruby hasn't texted or tried to reach out to me at all since our fight, and honestly, I don't even know if she will.

It hurts way more than I was expecting.

"Hey," he says, knocking on the door frame. "You okay?"

"Yeah, I'm fine," I lie. But when he just stands there, I add, "I don't want to talk about it."

"Okay," he says. "I just wanted to make sure you were still up for your appointment."

"Danny's here already?" I glance at the clock. All of this wallowing made me lose track of time.

"If it's a bad night, I'll do it. We just need the room."

"No, I'm good. Send him in." I sit up a little straighter and fix my T-shirt. Maybe helping him with his stuff will make me feel better, or at least help me pass the time between now and, I don't know, eternity?

Danny appears in the doorway a few seconds later. He's in an oversized hoodie, with the hood pulled all the way up.

There are sunglasses in his hand. It'd be comical how incognito he was trying to be, if he didn't look so miserable.

"Hey," I say, and shove the tray of cookies Izzie always leaves out toward him. He grabs a sugar cookie and eyes me warily.

"You look like crap."

"Thanks, you too."

Wow, I'm really nailing this peer counselor thing today.

I give him a minute to finish his cookie, but when he doesn't say anything else, I prod him a little. "Did you want to talk about anything in particular? Or is this just a social call?"

"I don't know," he says, wiping his lips, his knee already bouncing. We've been locked in this dance for a while now, talking about surface-level fears when I can tell there's something much bigger churning underneath it all.

"What position do you play again?"

"Why?" He snaps his eyes to mine. "You suddenly like football?"

"Some. I like the Patriots and all that."

"The Patriots suck," he says.

"They hate us 'cause they ain't us, right?"

"No, we hate them because they're evil and horrible."

"And I guess the other teams are all angels?"

Danny shrugs and takes another cookie. I wait for him to say more, shifting in my seat.

"I'm a wide receiver," he finally says.

"Let me guess. You're in love with who? The quarterback?"

"No." He looks offended.

"Another wide receiver?"

He looks down, grumbling to himself, and snatches another cookie.

"Another wide receiver it is." I offer him a sympathetic smile.

"How did you know?"

"Because you look as miserable as I do today, and I think only love can do that to you."

"Holy crap, that's dark."

"Are you going to tell me the deal or make me keep guessing?"

He sighs. "You're very annoying."

"I pride myself on it," I say. "Intra-team dating can be a nightmare."

"Yeah, I guess you speak from experience. You know, I really thought you were a gay urban legend until I saw you on the news."

"Nope." I laugh. "But, you *are* two-thirds right."

He raises his eyebrows.

"The 'gay' and 'legend' parts, obviously," I say, fanning myself.

He scoffs and tries to hide a small smile. "Yikes."

"Enough about me, though. What's your damage? Are you two together? Or is this, like, crushing from afar?"

"You're pushy too," he says. "Annoying and pushy."

"That's why they pay me the big bucks."

"They pay you for this?" He looks skeptical.

"I mean, no, I'm a volunteer." I grab a cookie of my own. "Are you going to answer the question now, though?"

Danny leans back in his chair. "Keep guessing. It's amusing."

"You're together?"

He nods.

"And someone found you two out and is causing problems?"

He shakes his head.

"You're both out, and you live in the gay-friendliest town on earth, and everything is roses since our last talk?"

He shakes his head again.

"You're the only one who's out?"

Another head shake.

"He's a shitty boyfriend?"

He laughs and shakes his head hard at that one.

"You're the shitty boyfriend?"

"No." He smiles. "We're both good for each other."

"I give up. I'm stumped. What's got you driving ninety minutes to this center to see a peer counselor?"

He taps his fingers on the table and lets out a long sigh. "I didn't come out yet. But I did tell him that I want to be out, and he said he doesn't. And ever since, it's been like . . ." He pauses. "It's felt like I'm suffocating or something. I'm in it with him, really in it, but nobody can know. It's messed up."

And, oh, those words drop into my lap like a pile of bricks. All the hurt and frustration I feel from Ruby and our argument flares up fresh inside me. "It's beyond messed up. It's complete and utter garbage."

"Excuse me?"

"If you're both in love with each other and you have a good relationship, then why shouldn't you shout it from the rooftops? In my opinion, she's not really taking your feelings into account at all. She's manipulating you. It's not fair."

"*He*," he says.

"What?"

"You said 'she.'"

I wave it off. "You knew what I meant. Your boyfriend should want people to know that you're in love. It's part of being in love."

"He says it's not that simple."

"Then screw him. Don't let someone trap in you in a closet, literally or figuratively. Because it sucks, and it doesn't get any better the longer it goes on. Trust me, I know all about that too."

He blows out a breath, his cheeks puffing out as he considers what I said. "It *is* complicated, though. We both have another year of high school; we're only juniors. I don't care what happens to me; I'm not some football superstar. But he could be. He's being scouted by colleges already. He could get a scholarship, go pro, even."

"And what, then you'll be his secret in college too? If you two even make it that far with all the sneaking around and lying."

"Hey!"

"Your perfect boyfriend needs to earn that label. And you need to have some tough conversations with him. If you make each other happy, why does what anyone else thinks matter? They won't kick him off the team for being gay."

"Didn't that literally happen to you? We *would* be risking everything if we came out. I'm ready, but—"

"Then we'll sue them. And we'll sue the colleges. And we'll sue the entire friggin' NFL if we have to. But you're coming out. And your relationship is *not* going to be a secret for one more second!"

A knock on the door frame snaps my attention, and I see Izzie standing there with a tight smile. "Morgan, can I see you for a moment?"

"I'm in the middle of—"

"No, I know," she says. "I'm going to have Aaron come in to finish up. I just need to borrow you for a minute."

"Okay." I stand up slowly and look at Danny. "I'll be back as soon as I can."

"Maybe don't bother." He looks pissed.

I open my mouth and then shut it before following Izzie to her office.

"Have a seat," she says once she's behind her desk.

"What's happening right now?" I sit down slowly. "I've never seen you interrupt a peer counseling session before."

"Is everything okay, Morgan?"

"Yes."

"It seems like you're a little on edge today."

"I'm fine."

She takes a deep breath. "Morgan, you suggested suing the NFL as a viable option to help Danny with his relationship."

That's a fair point. "Okay, maybe I'm not completely fine."

"Do you want to talk about it?"

"Not really," I say. "Can I just get back to work?"

"Unfortunately, I have some real concerns about your ability to peer counsel right now. It's fine if you don't want to confide in me. That's why we have a peer counseling program here in the first place. But I would love it if you would—"

"You think I need therapy? You think I'm screwed up?"

"Peer counseling is about talking things out and finding solutions that work. Everyone could benefit from that. It's not any sort of judgment about your mental health. I just want to make sure that you have the support you need."

"I *am* the peer counselor. Peer counselors don't get counseling."

"Actually, most of them do. It's never meant to be a one-way street, and with everything you've had on your plate recently, I think it could really do you some good."

"Thank you for your concern, but I've got things under control. Really. Can I get back in there? Danny and I have made a lot of headway, so—"

"I'm afraid not," she says, giving me a sad smile. "Your behavior today crossed some lines that I'm really not comfortable with."

"Oh my god, are you firing me?" I ask, jumping out of my seat. "Am I getting fired from a *volunteer* position?"

"No, Morgan. Of course not. I still think you're an asset to this center. But for the time being, I'm going to take you out of the peer counselor program."

"Seriously?" I feel like I'm going to snap. First I lost the lawsuit. Then I lost Ruby. And now I'm losing the only thing that actually lets me still feel like I'm making a difference at all.

"I know how much you enjoy your role here, and I have other things for you to do, but right now I'm not convinced you have the emotional space to be giving to other people."

"I do. I have all the space. Too much space. Please. I need this."

"Aaron told me about the outcome of your lawsuit and how much you've been struggling with that. You have a lot going on outside of the center, and I care about you too much to risk you burning out. It would be irresponsible of me to let you take on more."

"I'm not—"

"We can reevaluate this in a few weeks, but for now my decision stands. I'd love for you to stay on in another capacity, if you're open to it. If you'd like to leave early today, or take some time to think about it, I understand."

I sit there for a second, mouth open, forehead scrunched, letting her words sink deep into my skin, where they can mingle with all my other failures.

And then I snap my mouth shut because this day, this day is not going to break me. "I can stay for a little while. Anika is dropping off some of the donations with a few of the Honor Society kids tonight. I'll help get them organized."

Izzie smiles. "That sounds like an excellent idea."

Ruby is waiting in the parking lot after my shift, leaning against her car under the streetlight and looking totally and unfairly kissable.

"Can we talk?" she asks.

"I don't know. Can we?"

"I'm sorry about earlier." She sighs. "Let's go for a drive. Figure this out."

"Aaron's my ride today. He's just finishing up inside, and then we're heading home. I just came out to get some air."

"At least let me bring you home, then," Ruby pleads. "I'll make it quick. I just don't want to leave things like they are."

"Are you sure you want to?" I ask. "I don't know if it's smart to be seen in public with your secret."

"You know that's not what I meant!" she says, raising her voice right as Aaron steps outside. Except I'm pretty sure that it is *exactly* what she meant, but okay.

"Is everything good here?" Aaron asks.

"No," I say, at the same time that she says, "Yes."

Aaron walks toward his car, which happens to be on the exact opposite side of the lot from Ruby's. "You still want a ride home?"

I nod and follow him.

"Please," Ruby says. "I'm begging here."

Aaron opens his car door, and I walk a little faster. I can do this. I can hold my ground. But why does it feel like I'm being ripped in two?

"Morgan," she says, and she sounds so pitiful I stop.

Aaron watches me from his car as I hang my head. "Actually, I think I'm going to catch a ride with Ruby."

"You sure?" he asks. But I know what he's really asking: Do I feel safe? Do I need his help? Is this a good idea? And the answer to all of those questions is probably some horrible combination of yes and no, but I'm not ready to confront any of that right now.

"I'm good." I sigh. "I'll see you in school tomorrow."

He flashes a warning look at Ruby. "All right, I'll see you."

I lurch forward and hug him goodbye as he starts to get inside, feeling weirdly emotional after this nightmare day from hell. He squeezes me tight and jokingly whispers, "Say the word and we'll run."

I force out a smile and then turn to face Ruby.

33

RUBY

"Do you really want me to take you right home?" I ask when we've been driving for a bit. Aaron waited to leave until after we did, and now he's following us, making sure I get her home okay. I know there's nothing romantic between them, but it still makes me jealous. I want to be the one looking out for her, not the one catching glares from her friends.

"I don't know," she says. "Yes, I guess. What else is there to say? You made your point at school."

I rub my forehead and turn into her apartment complex. Aaron flashes his lights once but keeps going, and I relax a little.

"I'm sorry. I know I handled it like shit earlier." I pass her apartment as we drive through the complex.

"Um ... I live over there." Morgan gestures behind us.

"I thought we could go to the pond at the edge of the complex to talk a little. Is that cool? I'll turn around if you want."

"It's fine, I guess," she says, settling in against the seat.

I pull into a parking space near the pond. Morgan's out the door and heading down to the little bench before I even shut the car off. She sits near one of the sleeping ducks, who barely even stirs. My mom used to bring me here to feed them back before things went off the rails. Back when I was still her little princess.

The moonlight glints off the green water as Morgan picks up a rock and tosses it into the pond, sending ripples shivering across it. I take a deep breath and get out of my car. I don't know how to fix this, or if I even can. But I really want to.

"Can I sit?" I ask.

"It's a free country," she says. "Sort of. For some."

I stand there, fidgeting. "I don't know if that means yes or ..."

Morgan huffs and scoots over, fixing her eyes on the fountain spraying in the center.

"I understand why you're pissed," I start. "You have every right to be—"

She cuts me off. "What am I to you?"

"What do you mean?"

"Do you love me?"

"Jesus, Morgan," I say, digging my fingers into my knee.

"Well?" she asks.

"Do you always have to push so hard? I'm trying to tell you I don't want to break up, and you—"

"How can we possibly break up when we're not even dating?"

I sigh. "You know I don't do labels."

"Do. You. Love. Me?" Morgan asks, and I feel like I'm going to be sick.

Because love is . . . well, love is a trap. Love is getting knocked up and abandoned. Love is a handprint on a cheek and your entire childhood wrapped in tulle. Love is letting someone have the power to hurt you in ways you haven't even thought of yet.

"It's a simple question," she says.

"No, it's not."

"How?" she asks, and I don't look up. I can't. Not when the only possible answer I can give her is something I'll never say. I *can't.*

"Morgan . . ."

"If I matter to you, then answer me!"

"I can't," I say, squeezing my eyes shut at her sharp inhale. It all goes quiet then. Even the sound of the fountain dims in my head, stuck in that tiny void of silence right before everything explodes.

"Because you don't, or because you're so stuck on not 'doing labels.'" I hear it, the hurt under the anger, tingeing her voice with pain. I'd do anything to make it stop. I lean in for a kiss—if she'd just let me show her, I've been desperately trying to show her from the start—but she jerks back. "Stop it. You can't fix this with your body."

"Not that you even let me get that far," I snap, my temper flaring from yet another one of her rejections.

"Why would I?" Morgan asks, and it feels like I just got sucker punched in the mouth. I don't know what she sees in my face, but her sneer slips and she grabs for my hand. "I didn't mean it like—"

"It's okay," I say, pulling away. I'm used to people making me feel like I'm less than, making me feel unwanted. Just not her. Never her.

I get up and walk to the edge of the pond, but it's still not enough. I need space. An escape. I think about walking straight through the middle of it and out the other side, not stopping till I hit the ocean two states away. I wonder if even that would be enough space, if enough space could ever exist between me and the moment Morgan Matthews ripped my heart out.

She steps up next to me and reaches for my hand, but I shove it into my jacket pocket before she gets the chance.

"I didn't mean I wouldn't have sex with you someday, or that I don't want to," she says softly. "Whatever you're thinking right now, that's not it, I promise."

I flick my eyes to hers and then to the pond.

"But I've never done that with anyone, and I'm not going to do it just to make you feel better or to end a hard conversation."

I face her, narrowing my eyes. "I would never do that to you."

"You've already tried," Morgan says. "More than once."

And I go back to staring at the pond because we both know she's right, even if I wish she weren't.

"It's just sex." I shrug, not even sure why I'm arguing the point. I may be an asshole, but I'm not that much of an asshole. At least I didn't think I was.

"Not to me," she says, and I snap my eyes to hers. "I'm not going to lose my virginity to someone who . . ." She trails off.

"Someone who what?" I ask, running through the ten thousand possibilities in my mind: someone who's slept around, someone who doesn't have her shit together, someone who's trash.

"Someone who's not sure if they love me."

And, oof, that hurts more than anything else. Because I may not be able to say the words, but why can't Morgan feel it? How does she still not know?

I shake my head. "How do you not understand how much you mean to me? After everything! I don't get it."

"I need the words," Morgan says, like it's that simple.

"Why do they even matter? It's all bullshit! People say them one second and take them back the next."

"You don't!" Morgan snaps. "You don't say them. You don't even say you love your car, even though I know you do. It might not mean much from most people, but it would mean a lot coming from *you*."

"But you know how much I care."

"Then maybe knowing's not enough if I'm the only one who does!"

"Which is it, Morgan? Are you mad I won't say the *L*-word to you, or are you mad that I won't take out a billboard to let everyone else know?"

"Both!" she shouts.

I rub my temples. "You knew who I was when we started this. If you wanted PDA and labels, you should have asked someone from your precious Pride Club," I say, jealousy lacing through those last few words.

Morgan glares at me for a second and then storms up the path.

"Where are you going?" I ask, chasing after her.

"Home."

"I'll give you a ride."

"It's right around the corner. I can handle the walk."

"But I want to." I reach for her hand to slow her down. "Please."

"No, thank you."

"I don't want to fight with you. The whole reason I'm here tonight is because I want us to go back to the way things were before I acted like an asshole. Please!"

"They can't," Morgan says, shaking me off.

I don't want to believe that. I won't.

I follow her as she cuts across the courtyard and around the corner, everything quiet except for the sound of our footsteps and the stray croak of a tree frog. Morgan slides her key in and unlocks the front door, hesitating as she steps inside. Dylan must not be home yet, judging by the lack of lights.

"Will you let me in at least?" I ask.

"Are you sure you want to? What if someone sees?"

"My car's down by the pond. It's not like anyone will . . ." I trail off, realizing too late that she was being sarcastic. "Obviously, I want to come in. Please."

"Suit yourself," Morgan says, pulling open the door.

34

MORGAN

I kick off my shoes and flick on a lamp.

Usually, Dylan is home by now, but I'm glad he's not this time. I don't need an audience while getting dumped for the second time today, which is what I'm pretty sure has happened—or is still in the middle of happening now—especially after essentially getting fired too.

A bunch of mail was shoved through our mail slot, so I scoop it off the floor, carry it to the table, and flip through it as Ruby unlaces her sneakers and leaves them by the door. It's mostly junk mail, but then I see a letter from the dean of admissions at my college. Or, well, my potential college.

"Oh my god," I say, dropping the envelope.

"What?" Ruby grabs it off the floor and reads the label. "Is this your school?"

"Yeah," I say, our arguing put on hold as 100 percent of my focus is shifted to the envelope in her hands.

"It's light." She bounces it up and down a little. "Is it good that it's light?"

"How should I know? Everything else from them has been an email!"

Ruby holds it out to me with a small smile on her face. "Only one way to find out."

"I can't." I shake my head. "You do it."

"Are you sure? This is kind of a big moment."

"Open it," I say. "Please, I'm dying."

Ruby takes a deep breath, carefully tears open the top, and then slowly pulls out a single page.

"Read it faster! Come on!"

"Okay, okay," she says. A grin spreads across her face as her eyes scan the page.

"It's good?"

Ruby nods. "It's really good."

"Let me see." I snatch the letter out of her hand, nearly tearing the paper in the process. My eyes scan it quickly. It's a very kind letter about the official reinstatement of their offer and how excited they are to formally invite me to join their team.

For a second everything clicks into place, and all happiness is restored. I get to go to my dream school; I get to *run* for my dream school.

And then I notice the date on the letter—the day after it was announced that my lawsuit was formally dropped.

Of course.

I scrunch the paper up in my hand.

It was all for nothing. The lawsuit didn't help anyone; *I* didn't help anyone. I'm right back where I started, like nothing ever happened. I took a stand to change the world, and all I did was make life infinitely harder for the people on my side.

"Morgan? What's wrong?" Ruby asks, and I just . . . I can't with her anymore. I can't with this time loop I seem to be stuck in. Same situations, different faces. *I'll love you, but I won't tell you. I'll kiss you, but it has to be a secret.* I feel like I'm going to scream.

"I need to be alone right now." I rush to my bedroom and bury my face in the pillows, trying not to cry. The bed dips a moment later as Ruby sits beside me, rubbing my back. I sniffle a little and sit up. "What are you doing?"

"Trying to help. I don't know what's wrong, but—"

"You don't know *anything*, Ruby."

"I know you just found out you're definitely in at your top-choice school, and those do not look like tears of joy." She wipes at my cheek. "I don't understand. I thought this was what you wanted."

"If there's one thing I've been shown today, it's that what I want doesn't matter."

Ruby looks away, and I know my jab landed.

"I'm gonna ignore that," she says, like it's big of her or something. "But this is good. This is a good thing, right? You're in. You have a scholarship."

"Yeah," I say. "This is a good thing."

"Then what?"

"Look at the date," I say, gesturing to the now-smoothed-out letter in her hand. "They sent it right after the lawsuit was dropped. Right after we caved to St. Mary's. I'm being rewarded for giving up my principles. I thought I could . . ." I shake my head. "Whatever."

"Not whatever. Talk to me. I'm here. I want to be here."

I look up at her. "I thought I could change the world. Isn't that stupid? I really thought that standing up for myself would make an impact. But it was all for nothing."

Ruby gives me the softest smile and tucks a stray piece of hair behind my ear. "Not for nothing. You inspired a lot of people. And you're helping people at the center. Even today, I bet you—"

"I got fired today."

"You got fired? How? Why?"

"Because I went off on somebody about coming out and suing their school. Like actual full-on, stressed-out yelling."

Ruby rubs my back again. "That sounds like a lot."

"Yeah." I huff out a bitter laugh. "Apparently, I'm only qualified to destroy my parents' finances and stuff backpacks."

"Okay, well, you have time to figure that all out. It's not—"

"Wow, even my girlfriend doesn't believe in me." I roll my eyes. "Oh, wait, no, I forgot. I don't have a girlfriend."

"I do believe in you! And I also believe that you deserve only good things. You deserve everything you want. But sometimes in the real world what you deserve doesn't really matter. I'm sorry you're just finding that out now."

My mouth falls open in disbelief. "You think I don't know

what the real world is like? I gave up my school, my friends, my whole life, just to take a stand!"

"And no one can ever take that away from you. But not everyone is brave like you."

"They should be," I say, gritting my teeth. "If everybody would just stand up for what was right, then—"

"It's not always safe to do that! And the ignorant people you're fighting against think they're right too."

"So what? I should just give up until the world reaches a consensus on whether or not it's okay for me to like girls?"

"I didn't say that, and I definitely don't think that," Ruby says, running her hands up and down my arms. "I'm saying it doesn't matter if you didn't win the lawsuit. You *are* helping people. You've helped *me*."

I snort. "How? A little while ago you were basically telling me that we can't see each other because people are starting to talk."

"I didn't say we couldn't see each other. We just have to find a way to keep it quiet. Maybe if I hang out with Tyler a little more, it'll balance out the gossip."

My jaw literally drops. "Are you serious?"

Ruby smiles, apparently oblivious. "Yeah, people will probably assume that—"

"That you're fucking him," I say, surprising even myself with my harshness. But I'm mad and I'm hurt and I'm in no condition to fight fair right now.

She winces. "Don't say it like that."

"It's true, isn't it?" I shoot out of bed, standing over her.

"Why would you even suggest that? And does Tyler get to be in on this plan? Or are you going to hurt him too?"

She hangs her head. "I don't want to hurt anyone! I just want to find a way we can be together without people knowing."

"I want people to know." I groan. "I want labels and PDA and someone who doesn't call love 'the *L*-word.' And I definitely don't want the entire school thinking you're screwing Tyler Portman if we're together!"

She looks away, biting her lip. "I really, really don't know what you want me to say here."

"I literally just told you!"

Ruby sighs and looks at me. "But you know I can't give you any of that."

"If you admire how 'brave' I am," I say, whipping out air quotes for good measure, "why can't you be brave too?"

"You knew the deal! You knew. You can't change the rules now."

"Sometimes change is good," I plead. "I . . . I need this."

"You *need* this? Morgan, my coming out is mine. It's not something to slap in your win column so you can feel better about yourself."

I cross my arms and look away.

"Do you even hear yourself right now? This is my life we're talking about. You don't get to turn it inside out just so you can have the shake-up you're looking for."

"That's not what I'm doing."

"Maybe not intentionally, but . . . Look, for a lot of reasons,

I need people not in my business. Okay? It could mess a lot of things up for me."

I look her straight in the eyes. "If you don't want anyone knowing your business, then why is it okay to make them think you're hooking up with Tyler?"

"You know why," Ruby says, setting her jaw.

"No, I don't. I need you to tell me," I say, even though I do know, and hearing her say it might break me.

She shakes her head. "Because Tyler is a boy," she says softly. Resigned. "And girls aren't supposed to like other girls."

"Well, some girls do," I say, echoing her words from the shop.

Our words hang heavy between us, neither of us sure where to go from here.

"You don't understand," Ruby says after what feels like an eternity. "If my mom . . ."

"No, I do." I drop my head. "I do. And I'm not going to be the person who forces their partner to come out or issues an ultimatum."

"Thank you," she says with a tiny smile. "I knew if we talked we could figure—"

"But I don't think I can keep pretending either." I look away. "I promised myself I would never let anyone shove me back in the closet, but I really, really thought I could make an exception for you. Or, honestly, I really, really thought you'd come around to the idea of being out. I know that's not fair."

The silence stretches on so loud it makes my ears ring.

"So we're just over, then?" Ruby finally asks. And I don't answer, because we both already know, and once I say it out loud . . . Ruby drops her head against my shoulder, her tears hot and wet against my skin.

"I love you," I say. And she looks up at me. "I've been in love with you since you handed me that bag of peas."

The saddest smile I've ever seen snakes across her face as she wipes her eyes. "Yeah?"

"Yeah. I wish there were some way . . ."

Car headlights dance across my wall, probably Dylan coming home just in time to witness the absolute catastrophe of us.

"Me too." Ruby sniffs. She presses her forehead against mine—just for a second, just long enough for me to feel that her heart's cracking too. "See you around, Matthews."

And then she's gone.

35

RUBY

"Dammit." I groan, sliding out from under the car and slamming my wrench on the ground.

Billy glances at me and then goes back to tinkering with a motorcycle engine on the other side of the shop.

I sit up, hanging my elbows off my knees as the sweat drips down my face. We were hit with an early heat wave, which means it's about a billion and a half degrees in here. And I'm stuck in gloves because I can't risk messing up my manicure this close to the pageant. Perfect.

A water bottle appears in front of my face, Billy's grease-covered hands gripping it tightly. "Are you gonna tell me what's going on?"

The bottle crinkles when I grab it. He tosses me a clean

rag, and I pour some water on it and wipe it over my face and neck. "The brake caliper piston seized."

He takes a sip from his own bottle, seeming to consider his words carefully before moving on with a simple "You know that's not what I'm talking about, kid."

And I know it's not. He wants to know why I've been here at the shop every spare second that I'm not at school or doing pageant prep, but I can't tell him. He wouldn't understand, and if I told him everything, he might even get freaked out. I couldn't bear that on top of . . . well, on top of everything else.

"Come on, what's eatin' you?"

"Nothing," I say, walking over to the radio. Billy has it set to some terrible classic rock song about painting things black, which is perfect for my mood. I crank it up loud and grab a fresh rag and a carburetor that needs to be cleaned from my workbench, pointedly sitting with my back to him.

I assume he's gone back to working on the bike—Billy's never been one to push—until I hear him turn the radio down. I spin around in my seat slowly and find him watching me, completely amused.

"What?" I pout.

"I was just thinking that people have probably been throwing fits and blasting that song since 1960, but this is the first time I've ever seen it happen in real life."

"You weren't even alive in the sixties." I snort.

"Doesn't mean I'm wrong." He squirts some GOJO into his hands, scrubbing off the grease in the industrial sink beside me. "Come wash up."

"I'm still working," I say right as a delivery guy pulls up to the door.

"Not when dinner's here, you're not," he says, going to pay the guy and grab the bags of food. They're from Mama's Restaurant—I can already tell—which means it's probably Mama's roast beef sandwich special. My mouth waters at the thought of it. At $8.99 a sandwich, it's a rare splurge.

I pull the gloves off my hands as quick as I can and then duck into the bathroom to clean up a little extra before joining him at the picnic table behind the shop. He's already halfway through scarfing his down by the time I'm out.

Billy slides my box over to me as I drop into my seat.

"Thanks." I take the biggest bite I possibly can, my cheeks puffing out like a chipmunk's, but I don't even care. Billy doesn't give a shit about me being presentable, pageant-ready, or lady-like. He doesn't care if I inhale roast beef and love grease and loud, fast cars. He doesn't give a shit about anything at all as long as I keep my workspace clean and do a good job.

Or so I thought, but then he sighs and gives me a look I've never seen before. It seems almost . . . worried?

"All right, I've let this go on long enough," he says, like it's actually killing him to say this. "You gotta tell me what's wrong before I get an ulcer."

"Nothing's wrong."

"Ruby, you're talking to a guy with two ex-wives, okay? I know what it looks like when a woman's upset. And I also know . . ." He hesitates. "I know your mom can be . . . a little difficult about things. If you want to talk, I'm—"

"I don't."

"Well, if you do," he says, picking a stray bit of lettuce off his wrapper and chewing it thoughtfully, "I'm not saying I'm the best at advice, but you could do worse. That's all. I'm here for you, whenever you need me."

I stare down at my sandwich, blinking hard, because that's probably the nicest thing any adult has ever said to me, and I am not equipped for this. I don't know what to do with it. I don't even know how to begin to feel about it.

Because the truth is, I want to tell him. I want to tell someone. Because this has been hell for me, and nobody knows it. I've even been putting on a brave face for Everly, even though helping her with her Heart Eyes project is killing me. But seeing Morgan in school, sharing a class with her, acting like everything's okay? It's too much.

Last week, I even had to move my seat in Government because I couldn't take sitting across from her anymore. The kid whose seat I stole was pissed until I told him I'd make sure his car passed inspection next month. See, I get that. I understand the whole one-hand-washes-the-other thing.

But I don't understand caring about someone just for the hell of it, even if it hurts. I don't understand wanting to change the world for people you don't even know. And I sure as hell don't understand having enough faith to say *I love you* and mean it, even when the other person couldn't possibly say it back.

"I just need to keep busy right now."

Billy wipes his face with a napkin. "Mm-hmm."

He sounds like he doesn't believe me, but it's true. It helps. I've been working here nonstop, picking up extra classes at the studio, and practicing my pageant stuff 24/7. Charlene and I have been running interviews and walks and looks until I'm too exhausted to even move, but it still isn't enough to keep my mind off Morgan.

Everything reminds me of her now. I hate it. I can't even go to the grocery store for a Cup Noodles without walking by their stupid flower display and remembering our first date. I've been doing everything I can to ignore the absolute home-sickness I'm feeling for that girl. But every time I stop moving, it all catches up to me.

Billy crumples his wrapper up, throwing it into the giant barrel he uses as a trash can and raising his arms in the air. "And the crowd goes wild!" He imitates the roar of people cheering before heading inside. I know Billy didn't realize he was picking at a scab that's barely healed, but I wish he'd just left it alone.

I keep telling myself that this is for the best, that not being together has to be easier on both of us. And maybe it is for her. I don't know. Every time I see her, she's off with Allie and Lydia, training or laughing about something. I guess "living her truth" has been good for her. I know I should be relieved, but . . .

The state meet is this weekend, and I'm apparently a masochist, so I'm planning to go. I know she's going to win by a landslide. Just like I know there's a whole side of her life that I was never really a part of. A happy life. A Division I kind of life.

Maybe I was the thing messing it up all along.

I stare down at the grain in the picnic table, the gray wood that should have been stained long ago and is just out here rotting away because no one's taking care of it. People should take care of their things. Whether it's an old picnic table or . . . or your person.

And all of a sudden, it feels like I'm going to explode, words welling up in my chest, like I'm choking, like if I don't get them out immediately, I'll drown in them.

I walk over to where Billy is working on the motorcycle, an old Harley one of his buddies owns, which he's charging half price for even though I know he really needs the money. I clear my throat, and he stops, leaning back in his squat just enough to make eye contact and raise his eyebrows.

"I might be bi or something," I mumble, the words falling out of my mouth like glass and smashing on the floor below. I expect him to act all weird or tell me to get out, but he just looks at me like he's waiting for me to say more. But there isn't any more. "I'll go."

"I kind of figured that when you brought the girl here," he says, switching out his wrench. "She the one who's got you all twisted up?"

I freeze. "You knew?"

He glances up at me as he tightens a bolt. "She looked at you like you hung the moon, and you had the dopiest smile on your face the whole time. Plus, she's the first person you ever brought here to show your stuff to. I would have suspected even if you didn't suck at being subtle."

"Hey, I brought Everly here! And Tyler!"

"Yeah, once each, to use the lift and patch up their piece-of-shit cars." He laughs. "Not to give them an introduction and a grand tour. You didn't even let Tyler come in while you worked, remember? The lady across the street called the cops because he kept looking in the windows and she thought he was casing the place."

He's got me there.

"You tell your mother?"

I shake my head. "No, but she heard a rumor and wasn't happy about it."

"I bet." He looks up at me, studying every inch of my face. "You okay?"

I shrug and look away.

"Ruby." He stands up, and I can see a flicker of anger beneath his eyes. "Is your mom treating you right?"

I nod. Covering for her even now. Protecting the wrong person. Loving the wrong person. Always.

"Then what?"

"Morgan and I ended things. I couldn't risk Mom poking around anymore, plus the whole pageant thing. I'd be screwed if they ever found out."

He raises an eyebrow. "You hate the pageants."

"I do, but this next one has a scholarship to a place with a good automotive program. I'm thinking about maybe doing that, if I can pull it off."

"Automotive program, eh?" He smiles.

"Yep," I say, feeling oddly proud of myself.

He huffs and mumbles something I can't hear into the side of the bike.

"What?"

"I said"—he raises his voice—"I still think you're a dipshit."

I let out a startled laugh. "Me?"

"Yeah, you," he says. "If you're telling me the reason you were walking on air was because of that girl, then you're a dipshit for ending it, no matter how your mom acts or anyone else. Christ, I don't have much, but you know I have a couch with your name on it anytime for as long as you need it, and I won't ask shit about shit unless you force my hand."

"Really?"

"I divorced your mom, kid, not you. You'll always have a place to crash and food to eat while I'm on this earth. Now get your head out of your ass and start making some real plans for yourself, instead of just running scared, doing what your mom wants all the time."

I open my mouth, intending to say, I don't even know what, but all that comes out is a little gaspy inhale as I try not to cry.

"Now, don't do that," Billy says with an exaggerated stern face. "I can deal with a lot of things, but girls crying in my shop isn't one of them. Don't you have a car to fix?"

"Yeah." I nod, wiping my nose. "Yeah, I do."

36

MORGAN

I find my lane on the track among the pack of other girls running the 3200. We're the best of the best when it comes to distance running in the top division. I find my parents in the crowd of spectators and waste a few seconds scanning the rows around them, like Ruby will somehow just be there. But of course she's not.

The starter tells us to get ready, and I sink down into my stance, my whole body taut and electric. I'm the only one from the team that even qualified for this heat, and I'm not going to let a little heartbreak slow me down.

The gun goes off and so do I, shoving everything I have into every single footstep. All of this heartbreak, all that I've been through and am still going through—it fuels me. I feel the other girls nipping at my heels as I hit my stride. They think they can catch me? They can try.

Out here on the track, there is nothing but me and the sound of my breath and the burn in my legs.

Out here, I meet my expectations and surpass them.

Out here, I don't let anybody down with failed lawsuits or bad ideas.

Out here, I am free.

Out here.

Out.

When I cross the finish line, I collapse into Lydia's arms, sobbing, wishing they were Ruby's. My whole team rushes to hug me, patting me on the back and whooping that I took first place. And then my mother is there holding me up, holding me tight.

I let them all think the tears are from exertion. Boys puke, girls cry—that's what the coaches always say.

Nobody needs to know the truth.

"Are you just going to sit in your room and mope forever?" my brother asks, leaning in the doorway.

"No," I deadpan, "I have to go school in an hour."

"Nice. So your plan is to just drag down everybody around you trying to learn? Excellent decision," he says with a giant mocking smile and two big thumbs-up. I fight the urge to throw something at him.

It's not his fault I'm miserable. He didn't move his seat

in class just to avoid looking at me. He didn't blow off my state meet.

"I'm just tired," I say, which is not a lie. Spending all day at school smiling and acting like I'm fine is exhausting.

Aaron knows the deal; I've cried to him more than once. And Anika and Drew keep sandwiching me in the hallway, trying to block my view of her. Even Allie and Lydia keep asking me if I'm okay. The answer is always "Yes, of course," and then "I can't believe we won states," which inevitably distracts them.

But when I'm home, I curl into a little ball and watch stupid cartoons on my iPad and try not to breathe too much, because sometimes breathing hurts when you can't be with the person you love.

"You sleep pretty much all the time," Dylan says.

"Yes, because I'm tired," I say through gritted teeth.

"Is this about the center? Because I'll call and see if I can get you reinstated as a peer counselor. If it's upsetting you this much, then maybe you shouldn't still be spending so much time there."

Dylan doesn't know the reason I spend so much time there is because it's the one place I can let myself well and truly fall apart. I've even started going to counseling. Izzie has been a godsend.

"Can we talk about something else?" I ask.

"Fine, how about the fact that I haven't seen Ruby in like a week when she used to practically live here?"

"Seventeen days," I say, "not a week." I realize too late that knowing the exact last time she was in my apartment probably doesn't help make my case for how well I'm doing.

"How has it been that long? The state meet was barely a week ago. If you stayed awake more, maybe you'd actually know what day it is."

"What does Ruby have to do with states?"

"Uh, 'cause she was there," Dylan says. "Oh, sorry, are we still not acknowledging she exists when we're in public?"

I bolt up in bed. "Ruby was there?"

He suddenly looks very uncomfortable. "I thought you knew."

"Why didn't you say anything?!"

"I assumed you guys snuck off to make out under the bleachers whenever we weren't looking."

I stare at him, my head spinning out. Why was Ruby there? Why didn't she say something to me? She's been so cold, so good at keeping her distance. I thought she was happy. If she went all the way to—

"Morgan?" Dylan asks, but the buzz of my phone alarm saves me from any more conversation.

"I have to get ready," I say, rushing to the bathroom.

I don't know what I expected would happen when I got to school, or why I thought the sudden revelation that Ruby had gone to my competition a week ago would change anything. It doesn't.

I watch her move through the building, searching hard for

cracks in her calm exterior or evidence that she still cares. She sits with Marcus and Everly at lunch, smiling just the right amount and pointedly not looking in my direction. I sit with Anika under the guise of helping her inventory the last of the donations—she's sorting clothing, I'm doing canned and dry goods—but the truth is, I'm just too tired to keep up the charade around Allie and Lydia anymore. Though, judging by their worried faces, I'm not sure I'm fooling anyone anyway.

"Maybe you should talk to her again," Anika says after the tenth time I check to see if Ruby is looking. She is not.

"And say what? Nothing has changed."

"I don't know, but you seem way more miserable now than you did before."

I pull out three cans of green beans and log them on the sheet in front of me. "What do you think? There's probably enough for, what, six or seven more bags with all this?"

"I'm hoping for eight so we'll have donated an even twenty . . . And don't think I didn't notice your little subject change."

"Sorry." I pull out the final item, a giant case of mac and cheese, and then drop into my chair. "I didn't think being away from her would suck this bad. I mean, we weren't even official!"

Anika shrugs. "It took me over a year to get over the first person I ever really loved."

I log the mac and cheese on the form and sigh. "You're telling me I have eleven-plus months left of this?"

"No, I'm telling you not to be like me," Anika says. "Breaking up with them was the biggest mistake I ever made."

"So why did you?"

"Because I thought they were cheating on me, but it turns out the person I saw them with was their cousin. I didn't even give them a chance to explain, and when I finally found out the truth, they decided that *they* didn't want to be with *me* anymore. I broke their trust by overreacting and not believing in them."

"But that's different."

"Yeah," Anika says, folding a pair of pajama pants. "But I think the regret part is going to be exactly the same."

I peek again at Ruby, who is now engaged in what appears to be a lively conversation with Tyler. I wonder if they're hooking up again. I wonder if that's how she's moving on so quickly. "Well, Ruby seems to be doing just fine."

Anika looks over at her. "I don't know. Maybe she's just better at pretending than you are. She *does* have all that pageant experience. No one can possibly be that happy to be standing on a stage in a bikini."

"Hey, I'm good at pretending too."

"Clearly," Anika says with a little laugh.

"What's that supposed to mean?"

Anika lifts up my inventory sheet and holds it in front of me. "Look at the last thing you wrote."

"Mac and cheese?" I say, scrunching up my shoulders.

Anika taps the sheet. "Try again."

I wince when I read what's really there. "Mac and Ruby. One case."

"Yeah," she says.

"It could be like an experimental flavor! I'm an innovator."

"Mm-hmm, sure."

"I'm hopeless." I pull the log out of her hand and correct it.

"Kinda," she says just as the bell rings.

Ruby gets up from her table, with Tyler following close behind. Our eyes meet when she walks by, and she gives me the tiniest smile. It only lasts a second, and I'm not even sure it was intentional, but I'll take it.

37

RUBY

"Hey," I say, walking into my house. I left early this morning to run an errand before my pageant today. Chuck is still asleep, but Mom is already at the kitchen table with her coffee. She looks sleepy and warm, happy in a way she only gets on pageant mornings . . . which makes this so much harder.

"Morning," she says. "Where were you off to so early?"

"I had to drop off notes for a friend."

"This a school thing?"

"Just someone from my Government class." I pull out my chair and sit down in front of her. "But I need to talk to you about something. And don't get mad, okay? Please?"

Mom sets her mug down. "How do I know if I'm going to get mad until you say it?"

"Well, it probably will make you mad." I run my tongue over my teeth, biding my time, working up the courage to say it. "But I hope you hear me out anyway."

"Ruby, what are you talking about? Did that Tyler boy get you—"

"No, no, I'm not pregnant."

"Oh, thank god," she says, picking her coffee back up. "Don't go scaring me like—"

"But I need you to know that no matter what happens today, I'm not . . . I'm not doing pageants anymore."

"Nonsense," she says, raising her voice. "I am not letting you throw away your life! I want better for you. I—"

I reach across the table and grab her hand. "I'm not throwing away my life. I've got a plan. There's this great automotive program, and I . . . Pageants are *your* thing, Mom. They always have been. Please try to understand."

"You're good, baby. You're really good. I refuse."

"Refuse what? I'm eighteen! It's time to let me start figuring out what *I* want, instead of just—"

"Just what?" She pulls her hand back, her eyes going cold.

I look away. "Just trying to make you happy. I know you gave up a lot for me, and I'm grateful, but you have to actually let me live my life now."

"And what exactly do you think you've been doing?"

"Living *your* life, the one you lost when you had me. I'm sorry that happened to you, but I need to be done paying you back for being born. I just . . . I want to make my own decisions, even if you think they're wrong."

"Ruby, quitting pageantry isn't just wrong. It's throwing

away everything we've been working toward since you were a little girl."

"But I'm not. You know I'm not on track to actually even *go* to Miss America, let alone win it. I haven't had a major title in years, and I'm not even winning the little ones anymore."

"We'll work harder. You still have a few more years of eligibility, and you'll have a lot more time for it once you graduate."

"No. This is the last one." I meet her eyes and take a deep breath. "But . . . I'm also not just talking about pageants."

Her eyes narrow and then go wide. "What, then?"

"You know what I'm talking about, Mom. You even know *who* I'm talking about."

"Get out of my kitchen." She stands up so fast her chair tips over.

"Mom—"

"Get out of my sight right now, Ruby," she says, her hands shaking. "Go."

So I do. I run to my room and grab my stuff as fast as I can, but she follows me anyway.

"I raised you better than this! I tried my hardest to do right by you!" she shouts, grabbing a trophy off my shelf and throwing it to the ground. "I gave up everything— *everything!*—so you could live, and this is what I get?" She grabs another trophy. "This is my payback for working shit jobs and putting every penny I could toward these competitions?"

"I didn't ask you to do that!" I say, ducking as she throws the next one right at me. "I didn't ask to be born!"

"Maybe that was my first mistake," she says, and then room goes silent. Even the dogs stop yipping as her words land like missiles all around us.

"Wow," I whisper.

"Ruby, honey," she says as the realization of what she just said seems to wash over her.

I run out the front door.

"Baby, wait," she calls from the porch. "I didn't mean it. We'll figure it out. Just like we did with Katie. You don't have to—"

I slam my car door shut and peel out, choking back sobs until I get to Everly's. I've barely got my car in park before I'm banging on her front door.

A very sleepy-looking Everly pulls it open, her eyes going wide as soon as she sees me.

"Ruby?"

"Can I come in? I just need a place to—"

But I don't get any more out before she wraps me up in a hug so tight that I can't breathe.

"You never have to ask," she says as I bury my face against her. She runs a hand over my hair and tells me everything is going to be okay.

And even though it feels like my entire life just got bounced up on a trampoline, somehow, I believe her.

38

MORGAN

There is a single purple carnation stuck in the spokes of my bike wheel, a piece of paper wrapped around the stem. I sit down on my porch steps, staring at it like it's going to bite me, not sure what else to do.

Dylan comes out a few minutes later, his coffee mug still steaming, ready for the long workday ahead. "I thought you left. Don't you have a shift at the center?"

"There's a flower in my bike," I say, like that explains it.

"Do you . . . do you need me to get it out for you?" he asks, clearly confused.

"I think it's from Ruby," I say, still staring at it.

"Ah, okay." He sits down beside me on the steps, and then we both just look at it for a minute, saying nothing.

I glance at him. "Aren't you going to be late for work?"

"It can wait." He takes a sip of his coffee while staring at my bike. "This feels more important."

I let out a sigh. "What do you think the note says?"

"Probably something good."

"Really?"

"You don't hide flowers and notes for people unless it's something good."

"Okay." I nod but don't move from my spot.

"Okay," he agrees, taking another sip of his coffee so calmly, like we both aren't being ridiculous, like we both aren't already late for things and getting later by the second.

I rub my hands together quickly, trying to psych myself up. "I'm going to grab it."

"Good plan."

"Totally going to grab it," I say again, still not moving.

"Smart move."

"I'm doing it." I stand up. "For real."

"Go get 'em, tiger," Dylan says, and I raise my eyebrows. "Too far?"

"Too far."

"How about 'Godspeed'? Does 'Godspeed' work?"

"That works," I say.

"Godspeed, then."

I jut my chin and march over. My hands tremble as I pull out the flower, nearly dropping the note in the process. Then I run back to the steps.

"Good work, soldier," Dylan says as I unfold the paper. "What's it say?"

I take a shaky breath, and my eyes scan the words in front

of me. "She says I've inspired her, and she wants to talk. She says she understands if I don't want to, but she really hopes I will."

"How do you feel about that?" Dylan asks.

I rub my thumb over her swoopy handwriting. I can't bear to look away. "I don't know. I miss her so much."

"Then what's the problem?"

"Is there even a point?"

Dylan nudges me. "There's always a point when you love someone."

"But it doesn't say that. It just says I inspire her, like, me standing by my principles."

"Morgan, it's a note, not your wedding vows."

I look at him. "But I don't want to inspire her. I want her to be in love with me."

"I can't decide if it's endearing or annoying how obtuse you are." I fold up the note and slip it in my hoodie pocket as Dylan stands to leave. "You want me to drop you off at the center on my way to the shop?"

"No," I say, trying to put all this together in my head, trying to figure out what it all means. "I think the bike ride will do me good."

The ride to the center is too short, mostly because I pedal as hard as I can, the confusion mixing with adrenaline to make me feel one step short of a superhero. A very unsure, cautiously optimistic superhero, because that note . . . Maybe Dylan is right about it. Maybe it could be about love, if you squint.

Aaron catches me when I walk in, pulling me into the break room to hand me a bottle of water.

"You okay?" he asks. "You look a little off."

"I feel a little off," I answer honestly. "But possibly in a good way. Ruby left me a note."

"Hmm," Aaron hums, looking thoughtful. "She also had a screaming match with her mom this morning. I could hear them all the way in my house. Why do I have a feeling it's related?"

"Is she okay?" I blurt out.

"I don't know. She peeled out of the driveway, and that was that."

"Aaron," Izzie cuts in, leaning her head into the break room. "Your next visit is here."

Aaron looks like he wants to say more, but he dutifully heads out, leaving me alone in this too-small room with a bottle of water and a brain full of questions.

I pull out my phone, not even hesitating before shooting Ruby a text: **I got your note. It was really nice.**

And then I add: **I miss you.**

Three dots appear, but then they go away. I stare at my phone, my heart in my throat, and wait for them to reappear.

They don't.

Frowning, I head into the common room. After school yesterday, a bunch of us came here to drop off the last of the backpacks and celebrate completing our end-of-year project. The new display table looks awesome with the donation bags on it.

Now that that's done, my plan for today is reorganizing the

bookshelf. Normally, they're alphabetical by author, but Izzie gave me the green light to reorganize them by color for Pride Month. Sure, making a rainbow out of books is a mindless job, but I like it.

I'm an hour into my shift when a familiar voice pulls me out of my work. "Hey."

"Hey." I turn around, giving Danny a small smile. Guess I know who Aaron's appointment was with. I look at him, not sure if I should apologize or if apologizing will only make it worse. For all I know, he's coming to tell me how glad he is he never has to see me again.

"You hungry?" he asks, holding out a napkin with a couple cookies on it. I haven't had one since the day I lost it on him.

"Thanks," I say, taking one. He bites into the other, a thoughtful look on his face.

"What's all this?"

"I'm redoing the bookshelf," I say. "I'm not doing peer counseling here anymore, obviously. So I'm just trying to be useful somehow."

"Cool," he says.

"Look, I'm really sorry about what happened. I shouldn't have flipped like that. It wasn't really about you, and I shouldn't have let my own drama cloud my judgment."

"It's okay," he says. "I know what it's like to get super overwhelmed. For what it's worth, I'm sorry you're not a counselor anymore."

I shrug. "I sucked at it anyway."

"No, you didn't."

"We both know I'm way too much of a mess to be counseling anyone right now, but thanks."

"Sometimes those make the best counselors, I think," he says. "Besides, when you weren't yelling at me to sue the NFL, you did give pretty good advice."

"Does that mean you told your boyfriend how important it was for you to be out?"

Danny nods. "I was scared, but I told him exactly how I felt, just like you said. I told him I didn't care if it meant the end of my football career, but that I really hoped it didn't. And I told him I wanted the whole world to know how grossly in love we are with each other."

I grin. "That's awesome. Now you guys don't have to hide anymore."

"Thanks. But we're actually not out."

"But you just said—"

"I said I told him everything that I felt."

"But wasn't the whole point that you weren't happy being a secret anymore?"

He shrugs. "Kind of?"

"You lost me."

"After I told him all that, I let him talk. It got really heavy. There was a lot of shouting at first, and it was harder than I thought it would be. But *someone* once told me not to shy away from tough conversations, so I didn't."

"You guys broke up, then?" I ask, because this sounds so, so much like me and Ruby.

He shakes his head, and my eyes widen. "I realized that my 'truth' or whatever wasn't more important than his reality. He's not comfortable being out, and his home life isn't the most supportive. I decided that I love him enough that I can wait."

"So you guys are going to keep lying?" I ask, and he flinches at my words.

"I'm not lying. I'm protecting the person I love the best way I can. And it might not work out; the pressure could get to both of us. But we agreed if that started to happen again, we would be honest and go from there. Right now, we're good. We both get where the other one's coming from. If my choice is having him some of the time or none of the time, I pick some."

"And you're okay with that? For real?"

"I have to be. I'm not going to break up with the person I love just to prove a point."

And it feels like someone just dropped an anvil on my head because . . . That's not what I did, is it?

"Oh my god," I whisper.

"What?"

I snap my eyes to his. "I made a huge mistake."

"No, your advice was great. I probably never would have had the courage to be honest with him without it. I went in there all fired up, ready to tear the hinges off the closet because of you." Danny laughs. "And even though that can't happen right now for a bunch of reasons, the conversation made us closer. If you hadn't pushed me, I wouldn't have said anything until I was so fed up that we would have been beyond saving. I should be thanking you."

I swallow hard, staring at the table. "I didn't listen."

"Well, I'm not going to repeat it." He smirks. "Now it just feels like you're fishing for compliments."

"No, I heard *you*. But not the girl I cared about. The girl I *care* about. I did exactly what you did, but then I didn't listen. I made her feel like there was no option." I shake my head. "I thought there wasn't. And now I think maybe she's trying fix things. She left me a flower, and she wrote this note. But I think I should be the one trying to make it up to her."

"Oh," he says, "shit."

"Yeah." I look up at him. "What do I do now?"

"You really still care about her?"

"I love her," I say firmly, no hesitation.

He scratches his eyebrow. "Then it sounds like you have a tough conversation you can't shy away from."

"She's at a pageant . . . I can't . . . Should I go? I should go, right?"

"You should always go."

I narrow my eyes. "Wait a second. Does this mean *you* just become *my* counselor?"

"Probably." He grins. "So . . . you need a ride or what?"

39

RUBY

If it wasn't the way the door slammed when she rushed in during the final round of the pageant that got my attention, it was definitely the way she snagged the microphone wire on her foot as she found a seat in the front row, pulling it from the announcer's hand, which made him kind of awkwardly shuffle down to pick it up without exposing that the back of his suit was actually "tailored" with fabric tape.

And so now I'm standing onstage beside the other semifinalists—fifteen down from forty—perfect posture, neck arched as long as it can go, leg angled to accentuate the slit of my gown, chin tipped down, smile wide—staring into Morgan's eyes with my heart thrumming in my chest like a hummingbird on meth.

I'm next up for the interview question, which is possibly going to decide my entire future, and having Morgan here has me distracted. Consumed. In absolutely zero scenarios did I think the result of my note would be her charging in here. I wasn't even she sure would read it. Did the lights just get a million times hotter?

"Next we have Ruby Gold Thompson," the announcer says, reading off my bio and all my past wins and placements as I glide across the stage. The train of my gown flutters elegantly behind me, its beads glinting under the lights. Mom spent two whole paychecks on this dress, and now she's not even here to see it. I swallow that thought down, bitter like bile.

I come to a stop beside the announcer as he finishes introducing me—perfect timing as always—and flash my best smile out into the audience. Morgan is sitting right behind the judges. Somehow, she looks just as nervous as I am.

The announcer lifts a glass fishbowl off the stand beside him and holds it out to me. Inside are dozens of folded-up questions, one of which I'll have to spontaneously answer with some semblance of grace. Historically, I suck at it, but Charlene and I have been practicing this part the most.

"Now, dear," he says, "please select your question."

I slide my hand inside, shutting my eyes quick and saying a little prayer that I get something easy. Something where I can flash my smile and say just the right thing. My fingers catch on one, and I pull it out and hand it to the announcer.

He unfolds the paper and reads: "Tell us about the person you most look up to and how they will be your guiding light during your reign as Miss Teen Portwood County."

He tilts the mic toward me. I take a step closer to him and fight the urge to clear my throat—that would be an unforgiveable number of points deducted.

I pray my score isn't already dropping from my moment of silence, that I seem thoughtful and contemplative rather than totally freaked out. Because I know what I want to say. And I know what the judges want to hear. But I'm just not sure they're the same.

"Thank you," I say, buying myself a few precious seconds to steel my nerves.

He smiles at me reassuringly.

"This year, this spring, actually," I say, looking at the judges with an expression that I hope conveys an open earnestness, "I had the opportunity to meet someone very special. Someone who really changed my perspective on a lot of things. Someone who is braver than anyone I've ever met and lives by her principles to a level I never thought possible. She has an unwavering faith in her ideals, no matter how much the world tries to tear them out of her. Most of us, we see bad things and we look away, but not her. Not Morgan Matthews. She's different."

I look at her just long enough to see her eyes go wide. So okay, maybe this answer is a little more intense than I'd hoped for, but it's all I've got.

"I met Morgan when she transferred to my school, and every day since then, I've watched her work to make the world a better place, not just for herself and the people directly around her, but also on a greater scale.

"Morgan and I got off to a rough start when I almost hit

her with my car. And then not too long after that, I actually *did* hit her, even though she'll tell you she fell."

A few people laugh. Someone coughs. Morgan sits stone still. Watching.

"Somehow, despite everything, we grew closer. She taught me that love and inclusivity are what make us human, that it's okay to be . . . to be whoever you are." I swallow hard, trying to stay poised, to stay perfect, but I can feel everyone's eyes burning into me. "Morgan sees through me, to the person I really am, and because of that, I've learned to accept myself, to embrace it. To be proud." I look at Morgan, her eyes welling up, and I take a deep breath. "And I love that about her. That's why I'm picking . . . That's why I'm *asking* Morgan to be my guiding light, whether I'm lucky enough to be crowned Miss Teen Portwood County or not. Because even in the short time that I've known her, I've seen what a force for good she is in this world. I want to be that too. Thank you."

There is a smattering of awkward applause as I walk back to my spot in the row of contestants, nothing like Lilah or Hannah got after responding to similar questions with "my mother" and "Meghan McCain" respectively.

The announcer moves on, thanking everyone and reading off the official sponsors while the judges tally up their scores. I paste on my best Vaseline smile and stare at a spot on the wall, doing everything I can to not look at Morgan, terrified of what I'll see if I do.

The names of the ten finalists are passed up. Somehow, I make the cut. I take my final lap around the stage, smiling and waving and praying that I make the top six, before returning to my spot in line.

It takes far too long for the judges to join our host up onstage, their arms full of sashes and bouquets, and I'm a trembling mess of nerves. The announcer exchanges his list of finalists for three bright red envelopes, opening the first one with a practiced smile.

"The second runner-up of the Miss Teen Portwood County Competition is . . . Pia Roth!" the announcer says, calling her up like a game show host. Everyone claps and cheers while she accepts her sash and flowers.

The rest of us wait nervously in our row. We grab one another's hands and hold on tight. Later, we'll go back to being fierce competitors, but right now, we're just scared children wondering which of us the world loves the most.

"The first runner-up is . . ." he says, and I squeeze the hand of girl next to me. "Hannah Bronsky!"

Hannah walks out for her sash and roses and takes her place beside Pia. I take a deep breath. Only one spot left in the court. But there are still eight of us in the line.

"Now I would like you all to give a very warm welcome to our new Miss Teen Portwood County . . . Amber Valejo!"

The crowd goes wild, cheering and clapping as Amber is crowned. She does her victory lap to "There She Is, Miss America" while people throw roses on the stage.

It's all very dramatic—and slow—and I fight the urge to grab the final score sheets off the judges' table.

The curtains finally shut, and the winners clear off, hugging and crying, while the rest of us wait for placement. There are only three chances left for the scholarship, but there are seven of us still onstage. One of the judges comes over, checking our scores on the clipboard and pointing at various girls. "Four," he says. "Five."

"And six." This time, he's pointing at me.

Oh my god, I did it. I rush forward and hug him as he points to another girl and says, "Seven."

"Thank you, thank you, thank you," I say, before bundling up my skirt as best as I can and running offstage. I dip down the steps and peek out at the audience, searching for Morgan, but she's nowhere to be seen. The high of winning the scholarship gives way to disappointment, and my eyes burn from the whiplash.

Maybe her coming here was like me going to states. What if she was just planning to ghost in and out? But her text . . .

A hand wraps around my wrist and drags me to a little hidden alcove. Suddenly, we're face-to-face for the first time in what feels like forever. I want to kiss her so bad, but I don't know if she wants that. I don't know if this changes anything at all. I don't know if I took too long to catch up.

"Hi," Morgan says with a smile, and I melt.

40

MORGAN

Ruby doesn't say anything for a long time, and I shift from foot to foot, not entirely sure if she's happy to see me or not. But her speech, her speech said "love." I slide my grip from her wrist to her hand, rubbing small circles into her skin with my thumb.

"Hi, yourself," she finally says softly. Her face is a mixture of joy and apprehension. "What are you doing here?"

"I was trying to pull off a grand gesture, but nothing can top what you just did."

"In fairness, I didn't plan it," Ruby says, her voice filled with nerves. "So I don't know if it counts."

I let out a little laugh. "It definitely counts."

"Yeah?"

"Yeah," I say, and a hesitant smile breaks across her face. "But—"

Ruby's smile disappears. "But?"

"But I've been doing a lot of thinking, and I want you to know I was wrong. I was wrong about a lot of things. And I don't want you to feel like you have to—"

"Can I kiss you?" Ruby asks, and that shuts me right up. "Because I really want to kiss you." I nod so hard she laughs.

"I'd like that." I barely have a chance to get the words out before her mouth is on mine, soft and reverent, the beads of her bodice scraping against my tank top, and please, please, please let this moment last forever.

"I missed you too," she says, leaning her forehead against mine, both of us breathing a little harder in the quiet of this secret space I found. "I tried to text back, but I got called onstage before I could finish."

"Thanks for the note," I say, tucking a stray hair behind her ear. "And the speech. It was—"

"Too much?"

"No, it was—"

"Over the top?"

I gently put my hand over her mouth. "I was going to say 'amazing.'"

"Thanks," Ruby says.

"I'm sorry you didn't win. You deserved it. You worked so hard."

Ruby grins. "I still got the scholarship, though."

My eyebrows shoot up. "Really? Oh my god! That's huge."

"Uh-huh," she says, absolutely radiating with happiness. "I'll have you know that you are looking at the sixth-place finisher for Miss Teen Portwood County. That's a big deal, you know. If the five girls in front of me suddenly drop dead, then I assume the duties of the crown."

"Wow."

"I know. I might have to, like, cut the ribbon on an ice-skating rink one day or something."

"Oh, shut up," I say. "You did it! You're going to the automotive program!" I throw my arms around her without thinking but then quickly step back.

Ruby frowns. "Why'd you stop?"

"Am I allowed to hug you? I don't . . . What are the rules here? Like, you kissed me, so I thought . . . But then . . ."

"Depends," she says with a little smirk.

"On?"

"On what *your* grand gesture was going to be."

"Um," I say, waving my hand around us, "kind of this?"

"Hiding backstage with me?" she asks, scrunching up her eyebrows.

"Sort of." I wince. "I was hoping to, like, stealthily lure you into a private place and—"

"Holy shit. Was your whole 'grand gesture' to make out with me in some dark corner?"

"When you say it like that . . ." I say, blushing furiously.

Ruby straight-up cackles. "That's the best thing I've ever heard."

"Shut up."

"No, really, I respect it. Total power move."

I push her shoulder, trying not to laugh along with her. "It wasn't just the making out, although I had hoped. I also wanted to let you know that I know I was wrong. I get that our circumstances are different, and if I have to wait, if we need to keep things quiet . . ." I look at her, wanting her to see how much I mean this. "You are absolutely worth it. I've been more miserable these past few weeks without you than I could ever be with you. I don't want to lose you. I love—"

Ruby kisses me then, cutting off my words. "You are perfect."

I smile again—I can't help it—because this feels a lot like making it work. "I'm really not, but I'm here for you, and I want to be with you."

"Good." She kisses my forehead. "I think I'm gonna be crashing with Billy until I find my own place or I can get into student housing." She takes a deep breath, looking nervous. "He knows how I feel about you, and so does Everly. But for everybody else, I don't know how fast I want to . . . I don't even know what to call myself yet. Bi? Pan? The label thing still freaks me out. I need time to catch all the way up to you."

"You have it." I kiss her face all over, not even caring that I can taste the foundation and setting spray. "We can go as fast or slow as you want," I say between kisses. "Whatever we are, I trust you to set the pace."

"Yeah?"

"Yeah." I nod, a sense of hope making my brain tingle until it feels like a full-body grin. "And if it's getting tough, I'll come to you before—"

"Hey, is your brother home?" Ruby interrupts.

I shake my head. "No, he's at work. Why?"

"Come on, then." Ruby grabs my hand. "I can think of some other ways we need to catch up."

41

RUBY

I'm lying on Morgan's pillows, watching her sleep, soaking in every last detail. Like the way her eyelashes tangle together, just a little, when her eyes are shut like this. And the way her lips curve slightly into a smile—even in her dreams, she's happy. And the way the hickeys, which I swear to god I didn't mean to give her, have bloomed into tiny red dots on her collarbone.

It's been three weeks since the pageant, and a lot has already changed. Like I've officially retired from pageant life, which feels great but a little weird at the same time. I'm still very occasionally helping Charlene with her makeup classes, but only because it's fun now that I'm not being forced. Mostly, I work part-time—on the books, even—for Billy, with plans to go full-time for the summer.

I'm still not really talking to my mom, but I know I'll have to soon. She's left me a couple apologetic voicemails, but I'm just . . . not ready yet. Meanwhile, Billy cleaned out an entire room for me, even though I told him I was fine on the couch, and last week Morgan's parents came up, not in their own car, but in a giant rented U-Haul. They asked me to open it, and when I did, I found it stuffed with a bedroom set they claimed to have had "lying around," even though there was an invoice stuck on the mattress dated from that morning.

Talk about grand gestures.

And Morgan, well, she's already back to work changing the world. She and this football player are trying to start this student athlete rainbow coalition thing. They're in the really early stages, but I've never seen her this fired up before. She's been going to rallies and even guest-speaking at random schools' GSAs and stuff. Her boss, Izzie, has been helping her. Sometimes, I even go with her.

But today, this morning, I have something special planned just for us.

"Wake up, sleeping beauty," I say, kissing her on her nose, her forehead, her neck, the spot behind her ear that makes her squirm. Her sleepy smirk turns into a full-on smile as she opens her eyes.

"You're here," she says, her usual morning greeting. I try not to let it bother me that she still worries about that. Given our track record, I suppose it's fair.

"Can't get rid of me that easily, Matthews," I say, which

is *my* usual response. She tries to pull me down under the covers. "Nope." I push them away. "You have to get up."

"Why?" she whines, grabbing her phone to check the time. "It's like nine a.m."

"We promised your family we'd go out for brunch, remember?"

"That's not till ten!" Morgan rolls over, yanking the blanket over her head.

"Nuh-uh," I say, poking her in the side where she's the most ticklish. She shrieks and jerks across the bed.

"You are evil."

"You like it." I stand and walk to her closet.

"Yeah," she grumbles, finally sitting up in bed, and it's kind of cute how much of a morning person she *isn't*.

I flip through a few shirts, deciding on the KISS MORE GIRLS shirt, which earns me an eyebrow raise when I fling it at her along with a pair of leggings. "Get. Dressed," I say, grabbing her by the ankles and pulling her down the bed until she giggles. "I'm gonna go freshen up in the bathroom, and you better be ready when I'm done. I want to stop somewhere first."

"Yes, sir." She fake salutes me just as I pull the door open and see her brother in the hallway.

"I don't want to know," he says.

"Good morning to you too, Dyl," I call after him, but he just flips me off with a smile. Rude.

It's not long before I'm back, my teeth brushed with my finger—not the best, but it works in a pinch—my hair up in a bun on top of my head. She's dressed when I walk in, flipping through pictures on her phone of me at the pageant. She's kind of obsessed with reliving our "epic double grand gesture," as she calls it. It's become a running joke now, where I pretend I'm taking notes whenever we see one in a movie—and we've seen a lot lately thanks to her Netflix rom-com addiction. Morgan says nothing will ever be able to top my pageant interview, but we'll see. I'm hoping today might.

"This dress is so beautiful," she says, running her hand over the screen like it's not hanging in my closet at Billy's for her to touch whenever she wants.

"You can have it," I say. I don't even know why.

"We should donate it," Morgan says, always thinking of others. "The center gives out prom dresses to people who can't afford them. Imagine going there and finding *this*."

"Okay." I take the phone from her hands and set it down on the dresser. "We'll donate it. Now go get ready and meet me in the car."

She groans, but I can tell she's curious, so off she goes. And less than ten minutes later, we're pulling out of her parking lot.

"Are you going to tell me where we're headed?" Morgan asks.

"Nope," I say, squeezing her hand.

We drive mostly in contented silence, her fiddling with the radio, turning it up when a Harry Styles song comes on. It doesn't take long before we're parking at the library.

"Okayyyy." Morgan looks at me curiously.

"Come on," I say.

Morgan follows me inside to the little community room. She scrunches up her forehead as we walk past the sign announcing the school art show. "What's this?"

But I don't say anything. I just lead her past the ceramics and paintings to a wall of photographs. Everly's senior project, Heart Eyes. Her art teacher was so impressed with it, she chose it as one of the few projects to display for the whole town.

"Are these Everly's? She's so friggin' talented," Morgan says softly, taking them all in. She's seen a few of Everly's photos before—we've all been hanging out a lot lately—but I've never shown her the one of me.

"Yeah," I say, waiting.

"Oh," Morgan whispers, and I know she's found me among all the other shots. She steps forward, studying the picture before turning back to me.

"Who are you looking at?" she asks, and she looks a little worried, like it could possibly be anyone else but her.

I swallow hard. "Um, you."

Morgan's face breaks out into a smile. "Really?"

I nod.

"When was this?"

I bite my lip and take a deep breath. "That day you hit my car and stole my seat."

"No way," Morgan says. "That was my first day."

"Yep," I say, watching Morgan read the little tag beside it.

RUBY THOMPSON
"First Crush"

"Oh my god." Her eyes look a little glassy. "I thought you hated me!"

"I know. That's why I wanted to show you this. How I really felt back then."

"Ruby—"

"The label's wrong, though," I interrupt, and Morgan tilts her head. "It's not a crush."

"Ruby." Her voice goes quiet.

"I love you," I say, the words rushing out before I lose my nerve. "And I know this is cheesy as hell, but I'd like to be your girlfriend. Officially. If that's cool."

"What happened to 'no labels'? You don't have to—"

"I know. I want to." I lace my fingers with hers. "It feels right."

She smiles, tearing up. "Well, this definitely tops the speech."

"Is that a yes?" I ask. Because, for once, it's me who needs the words.

"Yes," she says, moving closer until we're completely face-to-face. "I'd love for you to be my girlfriend, Ruby. And I love you too."

I tip forward till I feel her lips against mine, and then I pour every ounce of myself into our kiss. My whole life might be a never-ending series of question marks right now, but this I'm sure of. This I want.

"Come on, then," I say when we finally pull apart. "I want to take my *girlfriend* to brunch."

Morgan smiles, looking at the picture once more, then reaches for me as we walk out. I take her hand and squeeze like I have a hundred times before. But this time feels different.

This time, I don't ever want to let go.

ACKNOWLEDGMENTS

So many incredible people played a part in getting this book into your hands.

A huge thank-you to:

My editor, Stephanie Pitts, for really understanding the heart of this story and helping me bring it to life. Jen Klonsky for your ongoing support and enthusiasm; Matt Phipps for all of your help; my publicist, Lizzie Goodell, along with Felicity Vallance, James Akinaka, and everyone at Putnam and Penguin Teen for all of your support.

Jeff Östberg for another gorgeous illustration, and Kelley Brady for pulling it all together into a stunning cover design.

My writer coven, Karen Strong and Isabel Sterling, whom I would be absolutely lost without. Also, Kelsey Rodkey for continually reminding me books need plots and not just kissing and angst, and Rory Power for keeping me sane and supplying me with constant cat pics (and Scally for being a willing and sometimes unwilling model).

Becky A. for always being a shoulder to cry on/amazing cheerleader/all-around fantastic friend—love you! Sophie for keeping my DMs interesting and my skin glowing, and Rachel Lynn Solomon for raising the bar and making me want to be a better writer (that yearbook, though).

Claribel, who inspires me to no end, even if her opinions on Pennywise leave a lot to be desired; Sarah for always being there; Rosey for constant cat pics and love; and everyone in kidlit who holds space for queer authors, out and otherwise.

Shannon and Jeff, who simultaneously manage to pump me up and make sure my head doesn't get too big all at once. Dennis, who is truly the best big brother I could ever ask for, and to all my family for your love and enthusiastic support. Joe, Brody, and Liv for constantly inspiring me and making me laugh.

And last but certainly not least, to all of my readers, thank you for showing up time and again. This book is for you.

ABOUT THE AUTHOR

Amber Hooper

JENNIFER DUGAN is a writer, a geek, and a romantic who writes the kinds of stories she wishes she'd had growing up. She's the author of the young adult novels *Verona Comics* and *Hot Dog Girl*, which *Entertainment Weekly* called "a great, fizzy rom-com" and *Paste* magazine declared "one of the best reads of the year, hands down." The writer/creator of two indie comics, she lives in upstate New York with her family, her dogs, her beloved bearded dragon, and an evil cat that is no doubt planning to take over the world.

You can visit Jennifer at
JLDugan.com

or follow her on Twitter and Instagram
@JL_Dugan